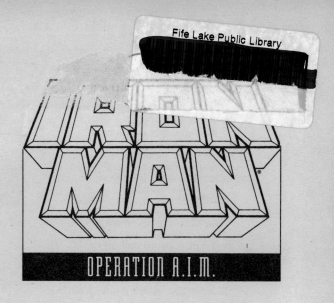

OPERATION A.I.M.

IRON MAN

OPERATION A.I.M.

GREG COX

ILLUSTRATIONS BY TOM MORGAN

BYRON PREISS MULTIMEDIA COMPANY, INC.
NEW YORK

BOULEVARD BOOKS, NEW YORK

Special thanks to Ginjer Buchanan, Steve Roman, Lara Stein, Stacy
Gittelman, and the gang at Marvel Creative Services.

IRON MAN: OPERATION A.I.M.

A Boulevard Book
A Byron Preiss Multimedia Company, Inc. Book

The Putnam Berkley World Wide Web site address is
http://www.berkley.com/berkley

Check out the Byron Preiss Multimedia Company
World Wide Web site at http://www.byronpreiss.com

Make sure to check out *PB Plug*, the science fiction / fantasy
newsletter, at http://www.pbplug.com

PRINTING HISTORY
Boulevard edition / December 1996

All rights reserved.
Copyright © 1996 Marvel Characters, Inc.
Edited by Keith R.A. DeCandido.
Cover design by Claude Goodwin.
Cover art by Tom Morgan.
Interior design by Todd Sutherland.
This book may not be reproduced in whole or in part,
by mimeograph or any other means, without permission.
For information address: Byron Preiss Multimedia Company, Inc.,
24 West 25th Street, New York, New York 10010

ISBN 1-57297-195-9

BOULEVARD
Boulevard Books are published by The Berkley Publishing Group,
200 Madison Avenue, New York, New York 10016.
BOULEVARD and its logo
are trademarks belonging to Berkley Publishing Corporation.

PRINTED IN THE UNITED STATES OF AMERICA

10 9 8 7 6 5 4 3 2 1

To the Malibu Diner on 23rd Street,
and the Wednesday Lunch Group

ACKNOWLEDGMENTS

Writing my second Iron Man novel was even more fun than the first time around. Once again, I am indebted to all the Marvel Comics writers, artists, and editors who have labored on *Iron Man* and related series over the years for giving me such a wealth of material to work with. My thanks in particular to Marvel Creative Services for help in developing the outline for this book, as well as to Keith R.A. DeCandido, my editor at Byron Preiss Multimedia Company, and to John Ordover for waiting patiently for the two *Star Trek* novels I owe him. Thanks also to my friends and colleagues at Tor Books for all their support and encouragement, and to Sumi Lee for helping me catalog the native flora of Wakanda.

And, most of all, thanks again to Karen Palinko for all manner of assistance, including letting me fill up our kitchen table with *Iron Man* comics and paraphernalia. The twelve-inch *War Machine* figure with attachable laser cannon adds a particularly cozy touch to the apartment. . . .

"O what fine times, this age of iron!"
—Voltaire (1736)

"Tighten your transistors, frantic ones—
you're in for a blast!"
—Stan Lee (1992)

MONDAY. 3:30 PM. PACIFIC COAST TIME.

"Welcome to Stark Enterprises," Iron Man said. He looked more like a robot than a human being. His entire body was covered by gleaming, metallic armor, and his golden faceplate betrayed no sign of emotion. He looked out at the world through two narrow eyeslits. Otherwise, the gilded mask was flat and featureless. His voice, electronically amplified, had the slightly artificial ring of a recorded message. The armored figure stood over six feet tall, with gold and crimson plating covering the exaggerated musculature of his metal suit. *Pretty impressive*, Percy McQueen thought, *especially for a hologram.*

Percy knew that this wasn't the real Iron Man standing before him and the rest of the senior citizen's tour group, but just an illusion created by lasers or some such. Percy shook his head in amazement; he was old enough that he still considered color television an astonishing new invention. How in the world had he ended up in this strange new world of faxes, computers, and holography? Leaning forward, letting his cane support most of his weight, he considered the apparition a few feet ahead of him: the recorded image of a man disguised as a machine. *Is it live or is it Memorex,* he thought, *and how is a person supposed to tell the difference these days?*

About a dozen elderly men and women, all visitors from the Silicon Valley Senior Center, stared with Percy at the holographic "Iron Man." They huddled together on what appeared to be a spacious green lawn in front of the entire Stark Enterprises complex. Futuristic buildings constructed of shining steel and glass rose before them, stretching toward an impossibly blue sky. Aerial walkways and monorails connected the various domes and towers. Everything, from the buildings to the lawn, was clean and well maintained, looking as though they were brand new. Peering through his bifocals, Percy searched in vain for any trace of graffiti or disrepair. The whole thing reminded him of a World's Fair he'd attended decades ago; this was exactly the "World of the Future" that he'd been promised for pretty much his whole life. Buck Rogers would have felt at home here, and so would have Flash Gordon.

Then, smoothly and without a jolt, the grass seemed to shift beneath his feet and he felt himself being carried forward on an invisible conveyor belt. He looked around. George and Vivian and the rest of the tour group were moving as well, as was their illusory tour guide. "Founded only a few short years ago," the hologram said, "Stark Enterprises has grown to become the world's largest privately owned research and development firm."

Abruptly, the scene around him changed. Grass and sky disappeared, replaced by a shining tile floor and walls covered by sophisticated scientific equipment. Seemingly unaware of the aged sightseers' presence, a team of industrious, efficient workers sat at computer consoles and monitored a wide variety of screens and gauges. Percy had no idea what any of the apparatus was for—he'd been a high school principal before he retired—but it certainly looked impressive. The researchers talked among themselves as they worked, producing a soft murmur made up of many intense conversations. "Oh my goodness!" he heard Margerie Whitman exclaim nearby. He had to agree. When he'd first signed up for this "Virtual Reality Tour" of Stark Enterprises, he'd had no idea what to expect. The instant switch from outside to inside had caught him totally off guard.

The image of Iron Man, however, was not taken aback by the sudden change in their surroundings. "The Silicon Valley main complex, seen here, is equipped with an extraordinary range of state-of-the-art facilities and staffed by teams of dedicated personnel, each the finest their respective fields have to offer." A hand gloved in crimson metal gestured toward the concentrated activity going on about them. He snapped his fingers and the scene changed again.

An automated factory materialized on both sides of the unseen conveyor belt. Beneath a high ceiling almost a hundred feet above Percy's head, mechanical arms manipulated a wide assortment of intricate electrical components. Sparks flew from tiny welders and soldering irons. Modular pieces were melded together by waldoes of every size and shape, examined by telescoping lenses, then sprayed with fixatives and/or lubricants. The entire assembly process was faster than Percy's eyes could follow, and appeared unsupervised by any human controller. "Here you see Stark's most unique employee at work," the hologram announced. "HOMER, short for Heuristically Operative Matrix Emulation Rostrum, is a revolutionary computer system jointly designed by Anthony Stark, founder and chief executive of Stark Enterprises, and Dr. Abraham Zimmer, director of our engineering division. The most advanced development in the field of artificial intelligence, HOMER runs most of this complex, including several high-tech manufacturing systems directly under his control. HOMER, say hello to our guests."

"Good afternoon, ladies and gentlemen." The voice came from nowhere in particular. Curiously, it sounded more alive and human than the hologram's preprogrammed spiel. "I hope you are enjoying the tour."

"Goodness!" Margerie exclaimed again. Along with Percy and the other tourists, she tilted her head back to look for the source of the bodiless voice. "Where is he?"

"Here and about," HOMER answered. "At present, portions of my programming are performing several simultaneous operations at various locations throughout the complex. One of the advantages of being primarily software is that I can be in several places at once, and visit with nice people like you even as I keep up with the rest of my work."

I don't believe this, Percy thought. *We're talking with a living computer.* "More than a mere machine," the armored guide continued, "HOMER is a vital, irreplaceable part of the Stark Enterprises family. Thanks for chatting with us, HOMER.''

"My pleasure," the disembodied voice replied, as the computer's mechanical limbs whirred and buzzed in ceaseless motion. Lasers scanned microchips smaller than a baby's fingernails. Components that did not meet HOMER's exacting standards were discarded and carried away, while approved bits of circuitry jumped into place as though magnetized. Percy wondered what new scientific marvel was being created before his eyes and how it would change his grandchildren's lives. *The shape of things to come,* he thought, remembering a movie he'd seen as a child. *We called them "talking pictures" back then, and here I am now, walking and talking inside a full color, 3-D picture so real it feels like I could reach out and touch it.*

"From the microscopic architecture of the silicon chip—" their guide declared, as Percy and the others found themselves standing atop a gigantic crystal wafer veined with intersecting strands of silver and copper "—to the endless reaches of the final frontier—" space shuttles and satellites orbited above their heads, while comets soared and nebulae swirled where HOMER's factory had existed only heartbeats before "—Stark Enterprises is there, creating a new and better future and—"

"EEEEEEEE!" An ear-piercing siren blared from somewhere overhead, interrupting the virtual Iron Man's lecture. Percy covered his ears with his hands, almost dropping his cane in the process, but his thin, arthritic hands did little to keep out the high-pitched siren. *What's going on?* he wondered. *Is this part of the tour?*

The holographic guide froze momentarily. The red-and-gold figure flickered once before speaking again. "Do not be alarmed," he said. "Please remain calm and stay where you are." He raised the volume of his voice to be heard over the alarm. "Do not be alarmed. Please remain calm and stay where you are...."

"Percy! What's happening?" Margerie grabbed onto his arm. "I don't understand. Is something wrong?"

"I think so," he told her. The lights dimmed briefly, and he heard familiar voices crying out in alarm. The magnified computer chip they were standing on vanished in a blink, as did the spacecraft and astronomical wonders above them. Blank white walls, looking rather like empty movie screens, appeared to the left and the right of the tour group. Looking down, he finally saw the segmented rubber conveyor belt that had been carrying them through the tour. *Was this reality,* he thought, *or just another illusion?*

"Iron Man, can you tell me what's happening? Are we in any danger?" He felt like a fool talking to a hologram, but there didn't seem to be any other option. The siren kept on shrieking, and he had to shout his questions at the armored figure. "Please, tell us what we should do."

"Do not be alarmed," the guide repeated. "Please remain calm and stay where you are." Percy swore under his breath. Obviously, the hologram wasn't going to be any help for the time being. A "fully interactive guided tour" indeed! Should they holler for a real person, or would that only be a waste of breath?

Beside him, Margerie let out a scream of utter terror. She tugged on his arm, her nails digging into his flesh even through his jacket and sweater. "What the—?" he began, then saw what was frightening her. His heart began to beat at a dangerously fast rate.

The blade of a knife protruded through the wall-sized screen to his left. The knife sliced easily through the slick, reflective wall, which looked at least two inches thick. A faint red aura outlined the blade. *It is more than merely sharp*, Percy realized. The knife was super-hot and charged with energy. The smell of burning plastic offended his nostrils.

There was a man behind the knife, tearing his way through the wall. He pushed aside a flap of white plastic screen and stepped quickly into the same room as the elderly tourists. Percy's eyes widened behind his spectacles. He raised his cane defensively.

The man was young and athletic looking. A colorful skintight costume covered his muscular body from head to toe. The suit was dark blue, mostly, except for his boots, gloves, belt, and mask which were a bright, canary yellow. Pouches stuffed with god-knows-what ran along his belt and down the sides of his legs. His gloves and mask were held on by blue metal studs. Percy's eyes were drawn to the sinister symbol emblazoned on the man's chest: a dagger superimposed upon a sphere. *We're really in trouble*, Percy thought. He had never met a super-villain before, but he knew one when he saw one.

Which one is this? he wondered. *The Grim Reaper? Count Nefaria?* Percy didn't recognize the costume. *Not that it matters*, he realized. *We're as good as dead.*

The masked criminal ignored the seniors at first. "Iron Man!" he snarled, spotting the holographic guide. "I'm ready for you this time!" He aimed the point of his glowing knife at the glistening metallic figure, then depressed a button upon the weapon's hilt. A beam of scarlet fire shot out of the knife's tip, crossing the room at the speed of light only to pass harmlessly through the hologram. The beam burned a hole through the wall behind "Iron Man" but produced only a momentary blur in the hero's projected image. Despite his lemon-colored mask, the crook was visibly startled. "What sort of trick is this?" He turned on the terrified senior citizens. "Nobody move!" he ordered, waving his knife.

Margerie held onto Percy tightly. He could feel her trembling. *A few more moments like this*, he thought, *and this monster won't need to kill us. We'll have all died of fright.* Keeping the knifetip pointed in the tour group's direction, the unknown super-villain looked up and down the corridor, apparently contemplating his next move. His head jerked back suddenly, as if he had heard something from above. He stared at the ceiling, his fingers wrapped tightly around the hilt of his dagger.

A few seconds later, Percy heard something as well: a powerful rushing noise like a jet engine flying low overhead. The noise grew louder by the moment, drowning out the alarm and the nervous whispering of his friends, until he spotted something in the corridor ahead of them, flying just below the ceiling and zooming toward their captor faster than a missile. Gold and scarlet metal, polished to a brilliant sheen, glinted in the light. A booming voice preceded the missile. Strong, deep tones rung out over the deadly scene. "Give it up, Spymaster. You should have known better than to come skulking around here again."

This was no hologram, Percy knew at once. This was the *real* Iron Man, the world-famous hero and Tony Stark's own personal bodyguard. Percy had seen pictures of Iron Man on TV, not to mention the holographic duplicate that had been droning on minutes earlier, but none of them captured the awesome power of the genuine article. His armored fists extended before him, the Golden Avenger (as the papers tended to call him) seemed as unstoppable as an oncoming bullet. The pentagon-shaped spotlight embedded in the center of his massive iron chest emitted a blinding light, catching the villain—Spymaster—in its glare. Percy had to blink against the light, even as hope unexpectedly blossomed within his weary bones. "Hang on, Marge," he whispered to his companion, patting her arm reassuringly. "We just might have a chance after all."

Spymaster seemed to take Iron Man's arrival in stride, however. His voice actually sounded smug as he shouted, "Not so fast, Avenger. I'm afraid you have a hostage situation on your hands." Another crimson beam burst from the tip of his knife, this one searing the air just above the tour group's heads. "Who are these geezers anyway? The senior division of your fan club?"

Iron Man slowed his approach, then came to a halt in front of Spymaster. Rockets flared from the soles of his boots as he levitated about seven feet above the floor. The knife-wielding villain stood defiantly between the tour group and the hero. "Don't even think of hurting them, Spymaster," Iron Man said.

"That's up to you, old pal," the crook replied. "Maybe I should off one of these coots just to demonstrate how serious I am." He stepped closer to the huddled senior citizens. Percy saw a gloved hand reach for Marge. Without considering the consequences, Percy pulled Marge away from Spymaster and stepped in front of her. The villain laughed derisively. "A bit old to be playing hero, aren't you, Pops?" He brandished his knife at Percy.

"Get away from him, Spymaster," Iron Man warned. He hovered a couple yards away.

"Oh yeah?" the criminal replied. "How you going to stop me, tin man?"

"Like this." As if in response to an invisible signal, the conveyor belt beneath their feet surged back to life, throwing both the seniors and Spymaster off balance. Then the holographic display came back online. "Welcome to Stark Enterprises," the Iron Man hologram said as the tour program started again from the beginning. Laser-generated "grass" concealed the floor of the chamber while pristine laboratories and office buildings blinked into existence around

11

them. Momentarily disoriented, Spymaster staggered upon the trim green lawn. Iron Man—the real Iron Man—took immediate advantage of his foe's confusion. An incandescent purple beam leaped from the palm of his armored glove to strike Spymaster's glowing red knife. The impact of the purple ray knocked the blade from Spymaster's hand. It went tumbling through the air to land on a section of holographic sidewalk not far from Percy.

"So much for that little toy," Iron Man declared. Below him, his illusory double continued to extol the virtues of Stark Enterprises even as the simulated outdoors was replaced by the interior of a Stark laboratory. Percy spotted a slight ripple in the otherwise-convincing illusion. *Must be where Spymaster's knife tore the screen,* he deduced.

Spymaster ignored both the hologram's lecture and the change of scenery. Despite the loss of his knife, he regained his bearings. His hands swiftly retrieved another weapon from one of the pouches on his belt. As Percy and the other tour members backed away, Spymaster revealed a pair of metal rods linked together by about ten inches of chain. Holding on to one of the rods, he sent the other end spinning at the end of the chain, executing tight circles so quickly that all Percy saw was a blur of motion. Coruscating yellow electricity crackled along the length of the steel rods, so that the twirling end produced circles of golden fire in the air. *Like a pinwheel on the Fourth of July*, Percy thought. He guessed that Spymaster's gloves were insulated against the charge of his weapon. "Remember these, hero?" Spymaster taunted Iron Man.

Fists first, Iron Man swooped toward the super-criminal. "Your electrified nunchakus didn't save you that time on Long Island," he said.

"I've upgraded," Spymaster said. His nunchakus met Iron Man's attack. Sparks flew and Percy heard the sound of metal crashing against metal. He imagined the glowing nunchakus slicing off Iron Man's hands like the blade of a spinning propeller, but as the ringing died away, he saw Iron Man standing on the lab floor, a length of chain wrapped around one armored fist. The gleaming red metal looked completely unscratched.

"So have I," Iron Man said. He yanked on the chain and sent Spymaster flying. The costumed villain soared into one of the lab walls, passing through a deceptively solid-looking bank of computers to smash into the real wall about a yard beyond. Letting go of his end of the nunchakus, he threw out his hands to soften his fall, then scrambled hastily to his feet. Percy scowled. A crash landing like that would have knocked the fight out of a lot of men, but Spymaster didn't look about to give up.

Still, the villain's headlong flight had put even more distance between Spymaster and his hostages. Marge tugged on Percy's arm as his friends retreated across the simulated lab scene. Percy hesitated. The holographic environment made it hard to identify the real exit. Besides, as frightened as he was, he was even more curious to see how this battle turned out. If nothing else, watching Iron Man combat a diabolical archfoe was a darn sight more exciting than playing bingo and cribbage back at the Senior Center. "You go on," he told Marge. "I'll be right with you." He glanced to his right. Scuffless white tiles covered the floor where grass had grown in the previous holographic scene, but Spymaster's laser knife still lay where it came to rest a few minutes before. Looking around to see if anyone was watching, he took his cane and walked as quickly as he could toward the knife.

Meanwhile, Iron Man disposed of Spymaster's second weapon. Heat radiated from his gloves as the steel nunchaku melted in his grip. He threw the now-harmless mass of molten slag onto the ground and stepped closer to Spymaster. His holographic twin was superimposed on top of him, producing a slight double image. "I'd hoped I'd seen the last of you," he said to his enemy. "What sort of slime are you working for this time?"

"Sorry," Spymaster said. "I have to protect the confidentiality of my employers. Professional ethics, you know."

"Your kind wouldn't recognize ethics if they were stamped on your forehead." Iron Man stepped out of the image of his double, leaving the automated tour guide behind. HOMER's automated factory materialized in place of the laboratory setting. Motors hummed and mechanical arms went about their work, assembling and analyzing bits and pieces of intricate circuitry whose functions Percy could not begin to imagine. He reached for the knife on the tile floor only to find it suddenly immersed in a maze of complicated equipment. A miniature welding torch produced a blue-white flame only inches away from where the knife now rested. Percy drew back his hand instinctively, then chastised himself. *You old fool*, he thought. *It's just an illusion.* Still, he found it hard to stick his fingers in front of that brilliant blue flame. *Okay*, he conceded, *it's a very good illusion.* He reached out tentatively.

Across the room, Iron Man advanced on Spymaster. The criminal backed up against an automated assembly line. Tiny transistors zipped by while HOMER's lasers etched their surface. Iron Man's heavy metal boots pounded upon the tiled floor. "Hope you like the decor," he said. "You're going to be pressing a lot of license plates where you're going."

"I wouldn't be so sure." Spymaster's mask covered his entire face, but Percy could hear the smirk in his voice. Looking up from the knife beneath the welding torch, he saw Spymaster tap one of the metal studs on his canary-colored gloves.

The factory disappeared. Without warning, the holographic tour switched off, taking the extra Iron Man with it. The illusory welding torch vanished and so did the red-hot glow surrounding Spymaster's knife. Percy snatched up the knife, then turned to see Spymaster casually stepping out of Iron Man's path. The Golden Avenger's heavy tread had given way to silence. The formidable robotic figure appeared frozen in midstride. Spymaster circled Stark's paralyzed protector, rapping his knuckles against Iron Man's armor. "Nothing like a little electromagnetic pulse to screw up anything computerized, from holographs to heroes," he gloated. "I wish I had time to carve my initials in your armor, but, as I recall, you only need about six minutes to reboot your operating systems. Of course, by then I'll be long gone."

"Not long enough," Iron Man said. His voice sounded less amplified and more human. "I don't care what rock you crawl under, I'll track you down eventually."

"Maybe, maybe not. You're forgetting I'm also a master of disguise." He gave Iron Man a playful kick. "See you later, tin man. Let's do this again sometime." Spymaster laughed and had just begun to turn away from Iron Man when Percy's cane came down hard on the back of his head. "What the hell?"

Percy struck Spymaster again, hoping to hear the reassuring crack of wood against bone. Instead Spymaster's cowl seemed to absorb the brunt of his cane's impact. He certainly got the crook's attention, though. Spymaster spun around and yanked the cane savagely out of the old man's hands. He threw the cane away while clutching his head with his free hand. *I guess I did some damage*, Percy thought. *Good.*

"I remember you," Spymaster snarled. "The would-be hero." He took his hand away from his head. "Too bad you didn't know about the absorption mesh lining in my uniform. Tough luck, Pops, you should have gotten away while you could."

Percy raised Spymaster's knife and pointed its tip

at the younger man's chest. "Don't move," he said. "I don't want to use this."

Spymaster laughed again. "Hate to break this to you, old-timer, but that EMP took out my gadgets as well. There's no more juice in that thing."

True enough, Percy thought. The blade no longer glowed. "A knife is still a knife," he said. Could it cut through the protective lining in Spymaster's costume? Percy sure hoped so.

"You, me, hand-to-hand combat?" Spymaster sounded amused by the very thought. "You must be joking, right?"

Probably, Percy admitted silently, but he'd had enough of this young punk's attitude. Throwing all his remaining strength into one desperate attack, he lunged at the smug super-villain, thrusting his knife at the symbolic dagger outlined on Spymaster's chest. *I'll show you*, he thought. *Take that!*

It was a good try, but a futile one. Spymaster deftly evaded the stab, then brought down the heel of his hand on Percy's wrists. The karate chop shattered the aged bones in his hand. Percy cried out in pain and dropped the knife. Spymaster plucked the knife from the air before it could even hit the ground. "Not bad," the criminal commented. "You've got spunk for an old guy." He raised the dagger above Percy. "You know what they say, though: he who lives by the sword, etcetera, etcetera." Clutching his broken wrist, Percy stared at the knife that was only heartbeats away from killing him. He thought he could see his entire life reflected in its polished steel. *Good-bye.*

Iron fingers descended on Spymaster's shoulders. They dug deep into his padded costume, then lifted the surprised criminal off his feet. As Percy looked on, astonished, Iron Man shook Spymaster until the knife vibrated loose from his fingers. Iron Man tossed Spymaster straight up into the ceiling. An iron fist met the crook's chin on the way down. Absorption padding or no absorption padding, Spymaster was out cold even before he landed at Percy's feet. "Like I said, I've upgraded," Iron Man said to the unconscious super-villain. Retrieving the discarded cane, he handed it to Percy. "Thanks for buying me some time, sir. Are you okay?"

Percy nodded. "Except for my wrist . . . I think so." Now that the threat of immediate death was over, he couldn't believe that he was actually talking to Iron Man. He could see his own face reflected in the hero's shiny golden faceplate. *Wait until I tell George and Marge back at the Center.*

"Let me take care of that," Iron Man said. He gently placed Percy's injured wrist in the palm of his metal glove. A cool green foam spurted from concealed nozzles in the glove, enveloping his wrist in numbness. The foam quickly solidified, leaving his wrist encased in a cold, frozen sheath. "There's an anaesthetic in the foam that, along with the cold, should help deaden the pain until the paramedics arrive. The cast will also immobilize the fracture until it can be looked after properly. I've already called for emergency services via the radio transmitter in my helmet."

"Thank you," Percy said. He lifted his hand experimentally. "I think it does feel better now." He contemplated the blue-and-yellow-clad figure sprawled upon the floor a few feet away. "Who was that creep anyway?"

Iron Man shrugged his metal shoulders. "A mercenary, specializing in industrial espionage. He's been after Stark's secrets for years. Like you said, a creep." He walked over and knelt beside the fallen criminal. "I'm not sure I've ever seen his real face." His fingers tugged at the edge of Spymaster's mask. "Let's see what he looks like this time."

Iron Man did not bother with the metal studs holding the mask in place. He simply tore the thick, insulated padding away from the studs and over Spymaster's head. "Good Lord!" he exclaimed, and Percy could hear his surprise even through the electronic distortion in his voice. He hobbled over for a better look, then nearly dropped his cane in shock.

Beneath the mask was . . . nothing. There were no eyes, no nose, no mouth, no face, only a blank expanse of pinkish flesh stretching from the thing's brow to its chin. He touched the nonface with a trembling finger. It felt warm, like real human skin. "I don't understand."

"It wasn't Spymaster at all," Iron Man explained, "only an adaptoid."

"Adaptoid?" Percy didn't recognize the term.

"An android duplicate of the real Spymaster, complete with all his characteristics and abilities." Iron Man stepped away from the creature's body. "I've run into these things before."

It was all too much for Percy. He shook his

head wearily. "Androids, holograms—how is a person supposed to know what's real these days? I can't begin to figure out where technology ends and humanity begins."

Iron Man paused for several moments before replying. "Tell me about it," he said grimly.

CHAPTER 2

WEDNESDAY. 10:30 AM. PACIFIC COAST TIME.

"Steve. Jim. Good to see you. Please come in."

Tony Stark, head of Stark Enterprises, welcomed his two visitors into his office. Tony cut a dapper figure, as befitted one of the richest bachelors in the world. He wore a custom-made Armani suit and smelled faintly of expensive cologne. His dark black hair was neatly groomed, as was the pencil-thin mustache above his smile. Looking at this urbane executive and notorious ladies' man, few would guess that he also spent much of his time as the armored hero known as Iron Man. That was just the way Tony liked it, although he kept few secrets from the men who now entered his office.

He stood up behind his large mahogany desk. The tall picture window behind him revealed a breathtaking view of Silicon Valley. He pressed a concealed stud on the underside of his desk and the door to his office locked with an audible click. "There," he said. "That will guarantee us a little privacy."

Tony contemplated his guests. Jim Rhodes, a tall black man casually dressed in a turtleneck sweater and slacks, was probably his oldest friend in the world. They had fought beside each other for years, ever since Jim assisted a very new Iron Man in Southeast Asia years ago. Then Jim had flown a U.S. Army helicopter; now he often zoomed across the sky in his own Stark-designed suit of armor, fighting for human rights in the guise of War Machine. Jim walked across the carpeted floor of Tony's office and found a stylish metal chair. "This about something hush-hush?" he asked in a deep baritone voice.

"You can never be too careful," Stark said, "especially in our line of work."

"Loose lips sink ships," his other visitor said. "At least that's what we used to say in my day."

Steve Rogers looked about the same age as Tony and Jim, but Tony knew his friend was much older than he appeared. A handsome blond man with a square jaw, blue eyes, and astonishingly perfect posture, currently clad in a conservative grey suit, Steve had been battling evil as Captain America since before the other two men were born. Tony still remembered the day he and the other Avengers, all members of the world's greatest super hero team, had found Cap frozen in that iceberg, preserved in suspended animation for many years. Even after associating with Steve for all this time, the idea still took Tony's breath away. He and Jim were just heroes. Captain America was a walking, breathing piece of history. *How do you get used to hanging out with a legend?* he wondered.

"Thank you for coming," Tony said, getting down to business. "Because of recent events, I thought we should get together and compare notes on one of our mutual adversaries, namely A.I.M."

Scowls and stern expressions appeared on his friends' faces as they heard that name. They had all come up against the persistent malevolence of Advanced Idea Mechanics, a secret society of criminal scientists out to control as much of the world as they could snare with their diabolical discoveries and inventions. If not for Iron Man and his fellow heroes, A.I.M. would have conquered the entire planet years ago, or else destroyed it.

"A.I.M.?" Steve echoed. "What are they up to now?"

"Nothing good, I'll bet," Jim said. "A bunch of megalomaniacal eggheads if you ask me." He grinned at Tony. "Present company excluded, of course."

"I know what you mean," Tony agreed. "A.I.M. gives us mad scientists a bad name. Unfortunately, they seem to be extremely active at the present." He told his guests about the bogus Spymaster's infiltration of Stark Enterprises and what exactly the imposter had turned out to be.

"An adaptoid." Steve Rogers nodded thoughtfully. "That sounds like A.I.M. all right. Next to Modok and the Cosmic Cube, the adaptoids are probably one of A.I.M.'s most deadly—and distinctive—inventions."

You should know, Tony thought. *You've been fighting A.I.M. longer than anyone else.* "Right now the adaptoid I captured appears to be out of commission, but I'm having it kept under constant guard just in case."

"Good idea. You ought to turn it over to S.H.I.E.L.D. eventually," Steve said, referring to the Strategic Hazard Intervention Espionage and Logistics Directorate. Stark had helped create S.H.I.E.L.D.

years ago to deal specifically with dangerous terrorist organizations like A.I.M.

"I don't get it," Jim protested. "Why didn't the EMP take out the android as well as your armor?"

"That just goes to show how well an adaptoid mimics its original," Tony explained. "There was nothing mechanical or electronic about the duplicate Spymaster. Adaptoids are constructed from unstable molecules which, in this case, transformed themselves into a near perfect replica of organic tissue. The electromagnetic pulse scrambled his weapons and equipment, but not the adaptoid himself because he was imitating flesh and blood. *Artificial* flesh and blood, granted, but pretty much indistinguishable from the real thing."

Reed Richards of the Fantastic Four had first discovered unstable molecules, but neither he nor Tony had ever cracked the secret of exactly how the adaptoids were able to duplicate their originals so completely. As nearly as he could tell, an adaptoid had merely to subject its original to some manner of psionic scan in order to reconfigure itself into a precise copy, complete with all the original's special powers and attributes. Indeed, as Tony knew from harsh experience, an adaptoid could even form clothing, armament, and weaponry from its own substance to imitate those wielded by its foes; over the years, he had seen adaptoids create fully functional duplicates of such unique items as Captain America's shield, Hawkeye's bow and arrows, and even his own Iron Man armor. Tony knew there was no way that A.I.M. could have gotten their hands on

detailed specs of his armor. Only psionically triggered, self-programming molecules capable of vast
reorganization could account for the adaptoids' phe-
nomenal talent for producing exact reproductions of
individuals and equipment. "Don't forget," he said,
"the imitation also managed to duplicate the real
Spymaster's high-tech weapons."

"That's a creepy idea," Jim said. He scratched
his dense black beard. "How can you tell one of
these things from a real human being?"

"I wish I knew," Tony said. He had personally
built Life Model Decoys that could impersonate real
people, including himself, for long periods of time.
LMDs, in fact, had saved his secret identity on more
than one occasion. Compared to A.I.M.'s adaptoids,
though, his LMDs were little better than department
store mannequins. "Under ideal laboratory conditions, there are advanced tests that can discriminate
between a human and an adaptoid on the molecular
level, but in the field? Well, that's a lot trickier."

Steve Rogers rose from his chair and began pac-
ing. He looked concerned. "What do you think the
adaptoid was after, Tony?"

"I don't know," Tony said. "That's where you
two come in. We've all had close encounters with
A.I.M. in the last few months. Maybe if we put our
heads together we can figure out what their overall
objective is." Tony turned toward Jim. "Jim, why
don't you tell Steve about that business in Florida a
few weeks back?"

"Don't remind me," Jim joked. "Seriously,

though, you may have heard about some of this on the news. . . .''

It had begun with Tony Stark's abduction. A mysterious kidnapper, who was later revealed to be Baron Wolfgang Von Strucker, an old foe of both Iron Man and Captain America, had demanded as ransom an incredibly powerful new energy chip developed by A.I.M. To secure the chip, Jim Rhodes had donned his War Machine armor and invaded A.I.M.'s undersea laboratory. After a heated battle with A.I.M's high-tech defenses, War Machine had captured the chip. Later, after War Machine helped Tony escape from captivity, he and Iron Man had confronted Baron Strucker in the courtyard of an abandoned English castle. In the course of the struggle, the energy chip had been activated—with catastrophic results. The unleashed energy of the chip had reduced the entire castle to a smoking crater in the middle of the English countryside. Iron Man barely survived, unlike Baron Strucker who apparently perished in the disaster.

''We should be so lucky,'' Steve Rogers said after Jim finished his story. ''Strucker couldn't die that easily. His kind never do.''

''I know what you mean,'' Tony said. He sighed and leaned back against his chair. ''If I had a dime for everytime that madman escaped certain death, I could buy myself another corporation or two.''

''Do you think Strucker has something to do with the adaptoid you caught spying around here?'' Jim asked.

Steve shook his head. ''I doubt it. A.I.M. started

out as a division of Hydra, Strucker's own organization, but they broke off from Hydra a long time ago. Remember, Strucker needed you and Tony to steal the chip from A.I.M., so I can't see him having easy access to any adaptoids. I think we ought to assume that A.I.M. is in this operation on its own.'' Steve paced back and forth across the carpet. A man of action, he was always ready to fight for liberty at a moment's notice. Tony couldn't help envying Steve's casual grace and easy command of his body. Despite a long history of health problems, from heart attacks to a hard-won victory over alcoholism, Tony considered himself to be in fairly good shape these days. *Still*, he thought, *everytime I see Steve I feel like an invalid.*

"What you say about this chip worries me," Steve continued. "For a while now I've had reason to suspect that A.I.M. is trying to construct a new Cosmic Cube. It could be that this chip is a vital component for a new Cube, which is an absolutely terrifying prospect."

Tony knew that Steve was not indulging in hyperbole. The original Cosmic Cube was, in the wrong hands, the ultimate weapon: a palm-sized crystal cube that granted its holder total control over reality itself. It was the technological equivalent of Aladdin's lamp and, stolen from A.I.M. long ago, it had granted more than one villain god-like powers for as long as they held the Cube. Fortunately, Tony recalled, that original Cube had eventually achieved sentience on its own and left Earth to explore the cosmos. Could A.I.M. really be attempting to assemble a second Cube? He tried to imagine what A.I.M. could do with that sort of unlimited power and shuddered at the thought. Steve was right, as usual. The possibilities were terrifying.

"Damn," Jim swore. Tony could see that the full implications of Steve's suggestion had not escaped Jim. "So now what do we do?"

"I think the key is that undersea lab you raided, Jim," Tony said. "Do you think it's still there?"

"Off the coast of Florida? Maybe." Jim scratched his beard again. "I did a lot of damage there, but I left the place basically intact. Hell, I didn't want to drown all those scientists and lab workers even if they did work for A.I.M. Once I got my stainless steel mitts on that chip, I blasted out of there as fast as I could."

"Don't think I don't appreciate it," Tony said. He hadn't enjoyed being held hostage while War Machine took on A.I.M. to get the chip. *That blasted white room*, Tony thought, recalling the empty cell he had been confined to for many long hours. *God, how I came to hate that place.* "That underwater lab sounds like a real loose end to me. Perhaps I should check it out."

"Maybe we all should," Steve suggested.

"I'm not sure that's necessary," Tony said. "Now that Jim has compromised their security, they've probably relocated to another hidden lair. Still, they could have left a few clues behind that might give us a hint as to their future plans." He smiled reassuringly at his friends. "Besides, I'm sure you both have your own business to take care of."

"That's true," Jim admitted. "What with Bosnia and Latveria, WorldWatch has a pretty full agenda these days." In his civilian identity, Jim was in charge of one of the world's most respected—and effective—human rights watchdog organizations. Tony remained impressed with all Jim had accomplished since he left his job at Stark Enterprises a few months back. "On the other hand, if you really think you'll need me...."

"You'll be there, I know," Tony finished for him. "Trust me, if I dig up more than I can handle, you'll be the first to know." He looked at Steve. "What about you, Steve? Frankly, deep-sea diving sounds more like a job for a man in an iron suit than a red-white-and-blue hero."

"I won't argue with you there," Steve said. "And, to be honest, I need to look into reports of renewed Serpent Squad activity near Seattle. But that can wait if you need backup."

"Not yet," Tony insisted. He was touched by both men's willingness to drop everything and face danger by his side. *The life of a super hero is not always an easy one*, he thought, *but it has its rewards as well, like good friends and allies you could count on in a crisis*. "Thanks for the thought, though."

The three heroes chatted for few moments more, reminiscing about old battles and mutual friends, then Jim Rhodes and Steve Rogers went their own ways. Alone in his office, Tony checked his calendar for the next few days, then contacted Mrs. Arbogast, his executive assistant, and asked her to reschedule the rest of the day's meetings. A.I.M.'s undersea laboratory probably was not going anywhere soon, yet Tony felt a strange sense of urgency.

His memory took him back to that stormy night in England, when the unfettered power of the stolen energy chip had engulfed him. In a last, desperate ploy against Baron Strucker he had tapped into the chip in hopes of recharging his Iron Man armor. The experiment worked and then some. He'd felt the full power of the chip surging through his armor and weapon systems, obliterating Strucker (or so it seemed) and everything else in the vicinity. Once let loose, the energy had been impossible to control. In the end, the chip burned itself out, but not before it fused every circuit in Iron Man's armor and reduced a centuries-old castle to rubble. Looking back, it seemed a miracle that he had lived through that night at all.

Advance Idea Mechanics built the first chip in their lab beneath the Atlantic, Tony recalled. Could they have already constructed another? Even if Steve was wrong, and the chip wasn't intended to be part of a new Cosmic Cube, the technology involved in the chip itself was far too dangerous in its own right. He knew he wouldn't be able to sleep at night until he knew what A.I.M. was planning next.

He pressed a button on his office intercom. "Mrs. Arbogast, call the airport. I want my jet fueled and ready to go within the hour. Tell the pilot we're going to Miami."

Time to go fishing, he thought.

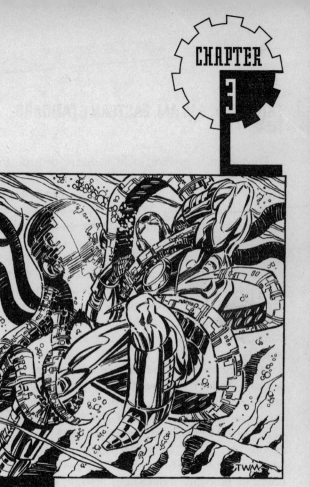

THURSDAY. 9:15 AM. EASTERN STANDARD TIME.

Tony Stark's private yacht, *Athena*, drifted atop the Atlantic Ocean, several miles from the coast of Miami. The shifting surface of the ocean reflected the cloudless blue sky. Waves rocked the yacht, and the air smelled of brine. Seagulls circled quietly overhead. Nothing about this peaceful scene suggested that a criminal lair lurked below the surface, but, according to War Machine, these were exactly the coordinates for A.I.M.'s underwater laboratory. Iron Man had no reason to doubt that the navigational computer in War Machine's armor had recorded the data accurately; after all, he'd built it himself.

Standing alone on the deck of *Athena*, Iron Man scanned the horizon. There was no land in sight, nor any other ships. Nothing but ocean surrounded him for as far as he could see. *Good,* he thought. He didn't want anyone snooping on him while he snooped on A.I.M., especially since he was going to be leaving his yacht unattended for awhile. He supposed he probably should have brought along Bethany Cabe, his Director of Corporate Security and occasional lover, or some other trusted confidant who was in the know about his dual identity, but that would have involved more scheduling and delays. As it was, it had taken him most of Wednesday to get to Miami and make all the necessary arrangements for today's expedition. Still driven by an intuitive sense of time running out, he had piloted *Athena* out of Miami at dawn, bringing with him only one vitally important piece of equipment: his specialized deep-sea armor.

Just as he had continuously modified and improved his basic Iron Man armor over the years, Tony had also devised a number of special purpose suits designed for specific tasks and conditions. The Deep Submergence Model (Mark II) had proven its worth on several previous adventures. Iron Man guessed it would also serve him well today. His regular suit, like the War Machine armor, could function underwater for short periods at a time, but it was not really equipped for a lengthy stay on the ocean floor. This suit, however, utilized the most recent innovations in undersea technology and was built expressly to withstand the unique conditions of a deep-sea environment.

The diving suit was a bulky affair that fitted over his ordinary, more streamlined armor. Reflective gold plating covered reinforced iron alloys built to endure pressures of roughly 8,000 pounds per square inch. A transparent fishbowl helmet, constructed of newly developed aligned crystal, made Iron Man look like an Apollo-era astronaut. Beneath the clear plastic dome, his inner helmet continued to hide Tony Stark's face from prying eyes.

Iron Man double-checked the connections on his outer suit. Everything appeared in order, so he stomped across the deck of the yacht to the very edge of boat. A yellow plastic rope strung at waist-level formed a guardrail to keep passengers from accidentally falling overboard. Iron Man unhooked the rope from its posts, then looked down at the beckoning blue water. Who knew what secrets waited beneath the waves? *Time to find out*, he thought. *Ready or not, here I come.*

The massive diving suit made a graceful dive impossible, so Iron Man simply hopped off *Athena* and hit the water boots first, producing an enormous splash that sprayed the yacht with brine. Weighed down by several hundred pounds of armor, he sank quickly. The morning sunlight filtering down through the ocean depths soon faded entirely, as the seawater grew darker and darker until Iron Man found himself falling through a world of liquid ebony. Silence engulfed him as well. He could hear only his own steady breathing and the gentle hum of his armor's electrical systems. At approximately one mile below sea level, he activated the halogen lamp embedded in the outer suit's chestplate. The lamp projected a brilliant beam of white light that swept through the murky blackness. Iron Man spotted a school of snappers darting away from him and decided to check out Miami's seafood after he wrapped up this mission. A good fish filet, along with a bowl of fresh bouillabaisse, sounded just right for lunch.

Careful, he reminded himself. *Don't let your mind wander too much.* As quiet and tranquil as this underwater world seemed, like the world's biggest sensory deprivation tank, there could still be plenty of danger lying in wait the nearer he came to the submerged A.I.M. base. War Machine had encountered heavy resistance during his raid on this very same laboratory, including submarines, torpedoes, and giant robotic crabs equipped with razor-sharp pincers. Although Jim had minimized his own bravery in the recounting, Iron Man could tell that War Machine had barely managed to reach the lab alive and intact. Had A.I.M. abandoned this base since that battle, or had they simply beefed up their defenses? *I had better be ready for anything*, he thought, continuing to sweep the inky depths with his halogen beam.

Down and down he sank, until his sonar alerted him to the presence of a large structure about five hundred feet below him. Activating a cybernetic control, he switched from visual reconnaissance to ultrasound imaging. An optical display appeared on the inside of his eye lenses, outlining shapes in glowing neon lines of holographic light. He saw a three-dimensional image floating in front of him, depicting a large, solid, hemisphere resting upon the sandy ocean floor. *That must be the lab, right where Jim said it was.* He dropped straight toward it like a sinker on a fishing line.

Let's get mobile, he thought, alert to the possibility of an underwater assault. Halting his underwater freefall, he activated the aquatic impeller jets in his armor. Streams of tiny bubbles spewed from the concealed jets in his heavy iron boots as he leveled out and began flying horizontally over the ocean floor. Switching off the ultrasound display, he checked the readouts running along the rim of his outer helmet before descending any further. The readouts reported no malfunctions. Everything seemed to be operating perfectly: oxygen flow, electrical relays, propulsion jets, as well as the internal pressure and temperature controls. Despite the icy cold of the ocean depths, Tony remained comfortably warm beneath two layers of armor. Nevertheless, a thin layer of sweat appeared on his brow as he approached A.I.M.'s deep-sea headquarters. If he was going meet any opposition, this was where it was going to happen. He hoped this specialty armor fought as well as it dived.

He could see the lab now: an immense concrete structure about the size and shape of the Seattle Kingdome, sitting like a gigantic grey blister atop a carpet of rock and silt. The dome was bordered on one side by a deep trench whose bottom was concealed by impenetrable darkness. Iron Man tried to estimate what the water pressure must be at the very base of the abyss and felt a chill despite the heating units in his armor. He wasn't sure even his reinforced outer suit could stand up to the forces at work that deep beneath the ocean floor. War Machine, he remembered, had almost been dragged down into that trench by one of the mechanical crab monsters. Iron Man searched the surrounding waters with his halogen light, determined not to be caught offguard.

The dome itself looked like it had seen better days. Jim had described it as smooth and featureless except for a blinking, blue signal light at the top of the dome. The light was broken now and the dome's grey exterior was pitted and cracked. Gold-plated fists extended in front of him, Iron Man zoomed toward the dome like a torpedo. His searchlight preceded him, exposing gaping fissures in the dense concrete domes, as well as what looked like craters and scorch marks. All in all, the structure looked like it had been through a war. Had War Machine underestimated how much damage he'd done to the complex, or had some other disaster befallen the dome? Either way it seemed as though A.I.M. was long gone. Looking at the gouged and wounded dome, Iron Man couldn't imagine that the submerged laboratory had remained watertight, let alone inhabited. His tense muscles relaxed slightly as he grew ever more convinced that the lab had been deserted for some time. He reduced the power to his boot jets as he circled above the dome, looking for the best way inside.

Without warning, something large and fleshy wrapped around Iron Man's torso, yanking him from his path. ''What the blazes?'' he exclaimed, his outer helmet trapping the sound inside with him.

The constricting whatever-it-was tightened, squeezing him. His readouts reported increasing pressure on his outer armor. Iron Man grabbed onto the thick lasso of flesh and struggled to pull it off him. Tony Stark's muscles, amplified and assisted by transistors in the inner suit, strained to overcome the thing's formidable grip. *What in the world is this anyway, and why didn't my sonar detect its approach?* In the dim light, his halogen lamp partially covered by the thing coiled around him, he could barely see what held him.

Maybe if I increase the heat from the searchlight. The light blazed brighter and Iron Man thought he felt the grip of the coil loosening. *Too hot to handle, eh?* Marshalling his strength once more, he managed to pull the coil away from his armor and into the glare of the spotlight. Beneath his golden mask, his eyes widened in horror as he saw dozens of pink, pulsating suction cups covering the underside of what he now realized was an enormous tentacle. *Shades of Jules Verne*, he thought, remembering the giant squid from *Twenty Thousand Leagues Beneath the Sea.* The suckers on this tentacle were as large as hubcaps.

He twisted convulsively in the clutch of the tentacle, turning his armored body so that he could see the source of the tentacle. Sure enough, his gaze fell upon the gargantuan form of an impossibly large octopus. Its ruddy, bulbous head was as big as Iron Man himself, with a huge, parrot-like beak that snapped spasmodically beneath two glowing, green eyes that seemed to project their own phosphorescent illumination. Two more tentacles wrapped around Iron Man while several more writhed like eels around the creature's head, churning the ebony water in which he and the monster grappled. Warning lights flashed inside his helmet, alerting him that the armor's structural integrity was in jeopardy.

Eels, Iron Man thought again as he watched the giant cephalopod's free tentacles whip about in the undersea currents. Because some of his usual weapons were of limited use underwater, he had equipped his deep-sea armor with defenses modeled on those of aquatic wildlife—including the unique assault capabilities of the electric eel. Cybernetic controls in his helmet transmitted instructions to subdural circuitry in his outer armor, which channeled emergency power to miniature electrodes just beneath the surface of his armor. *Here's hoping a little electroshock therapy improves your mood*, Iron Man thought before releasing a massive electrical charge into the octopus's constricting tentacles. Lightning flashed, momentarily brightening the darkness, and megavolts of electricity jolted the tentacles, which recoiled automatically from the Golden Avenger. To his surprise, he saw sparks ignite along the lengths of the thick, meaty tentacles, almost as though the gigantic sea monster was suffering from a multitude of short circuits. *How bizarre*, he thought, even as he used his boot jets to put some much-needed distance between the beast and himself. *Is this an animal or a machine?*

Bubbles streamed from his boots as he hovered in the water several yards above the octopus, inspecting the creature by the light of his chest beam. The creature was not entirely natural, he realized, as if its Brobdingnagian size and luminescent eyes were not already giveaways. Looking more carefully, he spotted the telltale glint of metal threaded through the monster's tentacles, plus what looked like circuitry implanted beneath the loose skin covering its head. Even the beast's beak, now that he examined it, appeared to be made of polished, serrated steel. He had no doubt that this beak was sharper and more dangerous than that of an ordinary octopus. The entire creature was a deliberate combination of mollusk and machinery. *A cyborg cephalopod*, he thought, aghast. Doubtless one of A.I.M.'s devilish experiments, and obviously built to be sonar invisible.

For a moment he entertained the hope that his electrical discharge had fried the cyber-ock's wiring for good. No such luck, though. Trailing its colossal tentacles behind it, the creature launched itself at Iron Man. He wasn't too surprised; A.I.M.'s engineers were second in ingenuity only to himself—or so he hoped. Reacting automatically, he raised the palm of his golden gauntlets and attempted to repel the monster with a violet beam of pure force. The beam struck the creature's head, but only slowed it down. The artificial kraken kept on coming.

Blast. His celebrated "repulsor ray" actually consisted of neutrons transmitted along a column of ionized air. Above the waves, in the open atmosphere, the beam retained its efficacy over several tens of meters. In an underwater environment, however, both the range and the impact of the ray was diminished substantially. He had adjusted the lasers in the Deep Submergence armor to provide for maximum oceanic penetration. Unfortunately, that didn't seem to be enough to stop the cyborg at a safe distance. Either the monster's head had been surgically reinforced or it was just the most stubborn bionic calamari he had ever encountered.

Better to rely on weapons specifically designed for this environment, he concluded while fifty-foot long tentacles reached greedily for him. Golden plates slid away above his shoulders, revealing concealed missile launchers. Automatic positioning systems transported ammunition from storage compartments attached to the back of his outer armor. Targeting computers calculated the distance and velocity of the approaching sea monster. The entire process took less than a heartbeat. Iron Man fired immediately.

More bubbles turned the water to froth as a pair of minitorpedoes rocketed toward the octopus, detonating upon contact with the attacking tentacles. Iron Man could feel the shock waves even through two suits of armor, but the cyborg creature looked merely wounded. Chunks of pinkish meat had been blown away by the twin explosions, exposing the gleaming metallic infrastructure underneath. One of the tentacles now drifted limply in the deep sea currents; Iron Man guessed that his torpedoes had damaged something vital on that limb. The creature seemed oblivious to its crippled tentacle, though. Its remaining tentacles swung toward Iron Man, who barely zipped out of their way in time.

One down, seven to go. He fired another volley of torpedoes. Thank heaven this particular suit of armor came complete with plenty of stored oxygen. Beating this monster was not going to be easy.

The torpedoes, shaped like miniature boomerangs, connected with their target. More explosions rocked the depths, but the shock waves only seemed to enrage the octopus further. Shaking off bits of blood and tissue, it charged at Iron Man. Trying another of his armor's subaqua defense mechanisms, he released a cloud of inky black fluid that quickly spread from nozzles in his gauntlets to form an impenetrable liquid cloud around the embattled Avenger.

Ironically enough, this trick was inspired by or-

dinary octopuses. With any luck, he could elude the cyborg monstrosity entirely and slip into the dome unnoticed by its bestial guardian. Granted, the swirling black oil obscured his vision as well. Fortunately, he still had his sonar to rely on.

Locating the shattered dome on his monitors, he dived at approximately a forty-five degree angle to the seabed. Chemical darkness continued to spread out around him, faster than the ocean currents could wash the blackness away. For a few seconds, Iron Man thought he was free and clear.

Then two glowing, emerald eyes penetrated the darkness directly in front of him. He saw the eyes emit their eerie, green radiance, watched the sharp, serrated teeth of the monster's beak crash together only a few yards away from his face. Iron Man tried to alter his course, take evasive action, but he was too late. Heavy tentacles wrapped around him, pinning his arms to his side. Hungry suckers clung to his armor, refusing to let go. Another tentacle draped itself over the plastic dome forming his outer helmet. He could see the suction cups flattening themselves against the transparent plastic. He almost fired two more torpedoes, then he realized that overlapping layers of tentacles now covered the mouths of the missile launchers. There was no way to explode the torpedoes without blowing himself up. *Blast.*

Iron Man felt himself accelerating downward. Craning his neck to peer past the tentacles blocking his view, he saw with alarm that the octopus was diving toward the seemingly bottomless trench. There was no way to tell how deep the underwater valley went, but Iron Man knew there were limits to the depth even his deep-sea armor could withstand. *Terrific*, he thought sarcastically. *If the ock doesn't kill me, the pressure will for sure.*

He had to break free from the tentacles before it was too late. He fought to tear his arms free from the monster's grip, but the bionic tendrils wouldn't budge. Iron Man's armor amplified his natural strength until he was practically as strong as the Hulk (well, *almost*), yet the crushing power of the tentacles was more than he could overcome through brute force alone. Tony Stark's muscles ached from exertion. More warning lights went off inside his helmet. His armor was in danger of springing a leak. He knew that would be the end. At this pressure, the ocean would burst its way through the slightest crack in his armor, destroying the suit and drowning him instantly.

He was reluctant to try the electric eel stunt again. The first time had drained most of his emergency power from his batteries. If he tried it again, he would be left with nothing but his reserves. Besides, the first jolt had only repelled the creature for a moment. It had inflicted no permanent damage. Still, there weren't that many other options. . . .

The shadowy mouth of the abyss grew larger in his sight until it swallowed him entirely. Locked together by the monster's unbreakable tentacles, the octopus and Iron Man dropped below the rim of the fissure. Was it just his imagination, or could he feel the water growing darker and colder every minute they descended?

The sound of metal scraping against metal seemed to vibrate along the length of his armor. Looking down he saw the octopus's jagged beak gnawing on one of his heavy golden boots. He tried to yank his foot free, but it was almost impossible to move with all these bionic tentacles holding on to him. He couldn't even use his repulsor rays without blasting his own legs off. Helpless, he watched the octopus dig its beak into his boot. *Just my luck. I would get attacked by the only sea monster equipped with its own can opener.*

What would shatter his armor first? The beak, the tentacles, or the awesome water pressure at the bottom of the trench? *Either way, I lose*, Iron Man realized. *Time for desperate measures.*

Explosive charges went off around the rim of his outer helmet. The clear polymer dome came unattached from Iron Man's armor, releasing a flurry of bubbles. A second later, he jettisoned his outer suit entirely. Wearing his ordinary, red-and-gold Iron Man armor, he shot free from the deep-sea armor like a greased sea lion slipping through a poacher's gloves. The hollow, golden armor crumpled beneath the squeezing of the cyber-ock's tentacles, but Iron Man was already jetting for the top of the trench. His regular armor could hold against the terrible pressures of the deep, but only for a few minutes at best. He had to make it to the level of A.I.M.'s dome laboratory, and preferably inside it, as soon as possible.

He spared a second, though, to look back over his shoulder at the octopus as it sunk further into the trench. Had it realized yet that its prey had escaped? It didn't matter, Iron Man knew, because he never wanted any discarded suit of armor to fall into the wrong hands. Consequently, his hasty departure from the deep-sea armor had automatically triggered its self-destruct mechanism.

Within seconds, thermite charges flared, igniting chemical compounds isolated within the armor itself, and a tremendous explosion shook the ocean floor, the shock wave propelling Iron Man even faster toward the top of the trench. He cleared the underwater cliffs just in time—the walls of the trench collapsed in on themselves, burying the remains of his armor, and whatever was left of the octopus, beneath hundreds of tons of rubble.

The explosion threw up vast quantities of silt, turning the surrounding waters into a cloudy, muddy mess. Iron Man did not wait for the slurry to settle. Using his sonar to navigate, he headed straight for the ruins of the underwater laboratory. An ultrasound analysis of the concrete dome revealed a sizable fissure near the top. Iron Man landed a few feet away from the gap. Clearing away some sand and debris, he found what he had hoped for: a human-sized entrance into the dome. He cautiously lowered himself into the gap.

Despite the attack of the cyborg creature, Iron Man still assumed that the lab was deserted. Indeed, it briefly occurred to him that maybe the giant octopus had itself trashed the dome, although that would hardly explain the scorch marks. Perhaps A.I.M. had attempted to use explosives against their berserk creation? *Well*, he thought, *I'll know soon enough.*

The crack was a tight fit. He barely managed to squeeze his armored frame through the opening in the dome. One of the advantages of slimming down to his inner armor; his bulky deep-sea suit would have never made it through the crack. At the bottom of the fissure tightly packed rubble blocked his way, so Iron Man unleashed his repulsor rays. At close range, the rays retained most of their devastating power. He easily blasted his way through the rocky barrier, finally making his way into the interior of the dome.

No alarms sounded at his intrusion: another sign that the lab was abandoned. He landed on a steel catwalk running along the inner wall of the dome and swept his searchlight over the scene below. "Oh my God," he gasped.

Just as Jim had described it, the area beneath the dome was taken up by a single lab of enormous proportions. Monitors and computer consoles ran all around the wall of the dome, stacked atop each other like the tiers of a hanging garden. When War Machine had invaded this complex, the vast chamber was filled with activity: busy A.I.M. technicians, wearing their distinctive yellow uniforms, sitting at the work stations or hurrying about on errands vital to the construction of the deadly energy chip. Iron Man imagined the laboratory buzzing like a beehive, hundreds of A.I.M. scientists going about their business with laudable industry and malevolent intent. A dark reflection of his own Stark Enterprises.

Nothing buzzed now. Seawater filled the dome from top to bottom, converting the entire structure into a gigantic aquarium/mausoleum. Advanced scientific equipment had been reduced to shattered ruins. Blind, bottom-dwelling fish swam amidst the broken computers. Tiny crabs scuttled over cracked plastic monitors, avoiding the hungry anemones rooted to the useless keyboards and control panels. Seaweed drifted through what was once a state-of-the-art scientific installation. An engineer and industrialist, Tony Stark was appalled by the sheer waste of it.

Worst of all were the bodies. The lifeless forms of hundreds of A.I.M. workers littered the floor of the lab. They lay where they must have fallen, sprawled on top of each other like stacks of kindling. The bright yellow fabric of their uniforms seemed inappropriately cheery under the circumstances. Thankfully, whatever blood had been spilled had long ago been absorbed and dissipated by the ocean, but Iron Man knew a massacre when he saw one. *"Full fathom five thy father lies,"* he thought, recalling his Shakespeare, *"Of his bones are coral made. . . ."*

He shook his head sadly, taking it in. Surely War Machine had not been responsible for this carnage; someone or something had attacked the lab after Jim's visit. The cyborg octopus, turning Frankenstein-like on its creators, or another enemy as yet unknown?

Jetting away from the catwalk, he descended reluctantly to the floor of the laboratory to take a closer look at the victims. His iron boots found one of the few sections of floor not covered by corpses. He walked grimly over to the nearest body. The figure was trapped under a futuristic metal chair; one gloved hand still sat on a control panel as though he or she had been reaching to activate some crucial program. Iron Man gently lifted the body out from under the chair and inspected the remains.

A.I.M.'s traditional uniform resembled a beekeeper's outfit. A padded yellow bodysuit made from synthetic fabric covered every inch of the body's flesh, while a cylindrical hood concealed the technician's features. Advanced Idea Mechanics did not value individuality. Every scientist in the lab wore an identical outfit. Numbers rather than names identified each worker. The numbers were printed in heavy block letters along the front of their hoods. For once, Iron Man was grateful for A.I.M.'s dehumanizing fashion sense; he was glad he didn't have to see all the dead technicians' faces.

Forcing himself to maintain an analytical perspective, he noted that the chest of this victim had been seared and shredded, probably by some form of energy weapon. That pretty much took the octopus off the hook. He grew more convinced than ever that someone else had attacked the lab and killed all these people. Hydra? D.A.N.T.E.? The Maggia? The Secret Empire? The Brotherhood of Evil Mutants? His brain ran through a list of rival organizations that might hold a grudge against A.I.M. Once more he swept his searchlight over the scattered bodies, noticing this time that there appeared to be no enemy forces among the dead. If a battle had been fought here between A.I.M. and some mysterious adversary, then the other side had either suffered no casualties or else taken away their own dead. *Curiouser and curiouser*, he thought.

He turned his attention back to the cadaver in his arms. Biting down on his lip to keep from gagging, he pulled the hood off the dead person's head. The victim turned out to be an adult male, Caucasian, in his early twenties, and presumably human. *Do adaptoids decompose?* He was no pathologist, but the body appeared to have been dead for at least a week.

The victim's obvious youth saddened Iron Man. *What a waste.* A.I.M. did not employ dummies, so this young man must have possessed considerable scientific expertise and talent. Bad enough that he ended up working for a crooked outfit like A.I.M. at such an early age; too bad he had to die before he had a chance to go straight. *All that potential*, Iron Man mused. *Destroyed for what, some secret war between rival terrorists?*

He gently lowered the body to the floor, making a mental note to arrange a full-scale salvage operation after he got back to his office. He'd been too late to prevent this massacre, but at least he could see that the human remains were properly disposed of and that some of the technicians' research was preserved.

Treading carefully through the strewn bodies, he approached a bank of computers running along the base of the dome. The equipment looked well and truly trashed, not to mention drowned. *No clues here,* he conceded. There seemed no point in even trying to retrieve any data from the wrecked and submerged computers, especially since he was running low on oxygen. Calling up a holographic visual display, he checked his air supply. Now that he'd discarded the deep-sea suit, with its generous reserves of oxygen, he had less than forty-five minutes worth left. *Better hit the road. There's nothing more I can do here.*

Before leaving, however, he decided to subject the installation to one last ultrasonic scan, just in case something had survived the devastation intact. Standing among the fallen bodies, he let his sonar map the laboratory, listening carefully for any anomaly that might suggest a working mechanism or subchamber. At first, his sensors detected nothing but shattered stone and twisted metal. He was about to leave the dome and head for the surface and *Athena* when he heard something unusual coming over his audio receptors: a regular, rhythmic thumping that he recognized immediately as the beating of a human heart.

"Good Lord!" he exclaimed. Someone was still alive in here! He couldn't believe it, but the sound of the heartbeat was unmistakable. His own heart pounding in his chest, he followed the thumping noise to a mass of rubble and debris on the other side of the spacious domed chamber. Iron Man focused his other sensors on the source of the heartbeat, confirming the astounding truth. Thermal scanners detected a single entity radiating body heat beyond the wreckage, while a sonic analysis of the surrounding structures suggested a working airlock buried somewhere beneath the heavy debris. Reluctant to use his repulsors for such delicate work, Iron Man dug into the pile with his gloves, hurling aside great chunks of concrete and metal in a desperate race to reach the trapped survivor before his air supply ran out. He had only a bit more than half an hour of breathable air left, but there was no way he was going to leave another human being stranded in this undersea morgue. "Hang on," he muttered under his breath. "I'm almost there."

Finally, he uncovered a large steel door built into the floor of the lab. Both the door and its handle were sealed shut, but, as miniaturized servomotors *whirred* within his armor, he tugged the door open. Inside the first chamber of the airlock, he was relieved to discover that the door had remained watertight; the airlock controls were not damaged at all. Pulling the outer door back into place, he operated the airlock by pressing a series of plastic buttons with one heavily armored finger. Automated pumps sucked seawater out of the chamber before a green light flashed over the inner door, signifying that it was now safe to open. "Hello?" Iron Man said, carefully entering the chamber beyond. "Don't be afraid, whoever you are. I'm not here to hurt you."

The room beneath the laboratory floor was completely dark. Iron Man guessed that the emergency lights must have given out sometime earlier. He heard frightened breathing a few yards in front of him. "Hang on," he said as reassuringly as he could. "Everything's going to be fine." He directed his chest beam at the sound of the breathing. The spotlight fell on a thirtyish black woman huddled in a corner at the opposite end of the chamber. Her eyes blinked against the spotlight's glare. She wore a torn and wrinkled yellow uniform without the cylindrical headpiece. Both hands were wrapped around the butt of a high-tech laser rifle aimed right at Iron Man's head.

"Don't move," the woman said. She had a slight Caribbean accent. "I know how to use this." Iron Man heard the fear in her voice, saw the hands gripping the rifle tremble even as they pointed the weapon at him. *Remember, she probably saw all her friends and colleagues butchered.* He realized that he could see her better than she could see him. He dimmed the light on his chest and took a few steps backward.

"My name is Iron Man," he said. "I'm one of the good guys. I don't know exactly what happened here, but I promise you I'm here to help you. Please put down the gun."

"Iron Man?" she echoed him. She seemed to recognize the name. The muzzle of the rifle dipped slightly, then jerked back into place. Iron Man stayed where he was and raised his hands in what he prayed was a nonthreatening manner. A warning light came to life inside his helmet. Only twenty-five minutes of air left. *Blast. I don't have time to talk her down.* He took one cautious step forward.

"No!" the woman shrieked. "It's a trick! I know it!" He heard the air between them crackle and burn as a brilliant red beam leaped from the muzzle of her gun to strike Iron Man directly between his eyes.

Some variety of heat weapon, he guessed, feeling a slight burning sensation on his forehead. The laser was no match for his armor's shielding, though: epitaxially deposited diamond, coating a layer of high temperature enamel over a lattice of crystallized iron. Undaunted by the beam, he marched over and seized the rifle in his iron grip. The muzzle crumpled beneath his strength. He twisted it out of shape, then reached for her wrists, hoping to help her to her feet. She cringed as his metal gloves touched her. "Get away!" she cried out.

At times like this Iron Man wished his armored form was not so intimidating. "Please believe me," he said. "I'm not going to harm you."

Still trembling from shock or fear, she eyed him quizzically. "You're really Iron Man?" she whispered. He nodded. She peered beyond him, evidently assuring herself that he had come alone. She stood up gradually, gaining confidence, perhaps, because he hadn't killed her yet. Iron Man spotted the signs of stress and fatigue in her face. Dark circles drooped beneath her eyes. Her breath was short and ragged.

She's about to collapse, he realized. He reached out to steady her.

This time she didn't flinch. "You're going to help me?" she asked in hushed tones. "You're not with *him*?"

"Who?" Iron Man asked, anxious to discover the origin of her fear. "What happened here? Who did this?"

She breathed one word before sagging into his waiting arms, all strength and consciousness abandoning her:

"Modok."

CHAPTER 4

THURSDAY. 4:40 PM. EASTERN STANDARD TIME.

Stark One, Tony's private jet, was parked on the runway at Miami Airport when the woman woke up. Aboard the plane, his quarters included a working office and living area. Air conditioning kept the temperature a comfortable sixty-eight degrees. The rescued A.I.M. scientist was stretched out on an expensive leather couch, her head resting on a plush velvet pillow, her body covered by a burgundy-colored wool blanket imported from Scotland's Isle of Arran.

Iron Man sat across from the couch on a cast-iron chair specifically designed to support the four-hundred-pound-plus weight of his armor. He wished he could take his armor off. It wasn't that he was claustrophobic; over the years, he'd gotten used to wearing his iron suit for hours, sometimes days, at a time. Still, even though his armor had dried hours ago, he could still smell the salty residue, and his body felt tired and sweaty inside the gleaming metal suit. A warm shower would have been wonderful, but he could hardly risk revealing his dual identity to this unknown woman who did, after all, work for A.I.M.

She stirred beneath the blanket, then sat up abruptly, eyes wide with terror, crying out once again, "Modok!" Tony scowled at the sound of that name. He had half-hoped that he'd heard her wrong the first time.

Modok. The Mental Organism Designed Only for Killing. Next to the Cosmic Cube, Modok was A.I.M.'s most terrible creation. The creature now known as Modok, he recalled, had once been just another scientist in the employ of Advanced Idea Mechanics—until he was chosen at random to be the unwilling subject for an experiment in controlled mutation. Forcibly placed in A.I.M.'s "alteration chamber," he underwent extensive cellular irradiation and physical bioengineering. The result was a freakish super being whose grotesquely expanded brain was several times larger than his shriveled, atrophied body. Endowed with incredible psionic powers, Modok, as the newborn monstrosity was christened, had been intended to join A.I.M.'s abundant arsenal of super-weapons. Instead the hideous mutant had turned on his creators and one-time colleagues, seizing control of A.I.M. itself and marshalling all of the organization's human and technological resources in numerous attempts to conquer the world. Iron Man felt a chill as he remembered Modok's huge, distorted face, filled as always with rage and hatred directed at all of humanity. Still, Modok had supposedly died many months ago. . . .

The woman from the lab looked panicked for a minute, then her dark brown eyes took in her new surroundings and she seemed to relax a little. She swung around on the couch until her shoes hit the floor. She still wore her battered yellow uniform, but her face looked less exhausted than before. Iron Man noted, despite himself, that she was very attractive. She looked around, then let her gaze fall on Iron Man. "Where am I?" she asked. "How did we get here?"

"You helped me find that escape pod at the lab, remember?" *And a good thing too.* With close to two miles of ocean above their heads, he would have had a rough time getting her safely to the surface if not for the minisub docked in an subterranean cavern adjacent to the airlock. He wondered again why any of the other residents hadn't used the sub to escape. *Someone—Modok, I guess—never gave them the chance.*

"I think so," the woman said. She held her head in her hands, rubbing her forehead as though that would help her memories rise to the surface. "I remember the attack, hiding, then being trapped—" Her voice broke, and she had to take a deep breath before resuming. "Trapped in the dark, in the silence, all alone for what seemed like forever!" She lifted her head. "What day is it?"

Iron Man told her the date. "Five days then," she said. "I was stuck there for five whole days. There were emergency food tablets in the airlock, and hydration capsules, but still it was horrible. I thought I was buried alive. I *was* buried alive, until you came." She stared at him, searching perhaps for the humanity beneath his armor. "You *are* Iron Man, aren't you? The real Iron Man?"

"I'm not an adaptoid, if that's what you mean," he said. "And you are?"

She hesitated before answering. Iron Man recalled that she was probably wanted by the authorities for her activities with A.I.M. "Bright," she said finally. "Dr. Christine Bright."

"M.D. or Ph.D.?" he asked.

"Ph.D.," she said, smiling for the first time. "Specializing in plasma physics and alternative energy sources."

Iron Man nodded. He suspected he had gotten a taste of one of her alternative energy sources in a castle in England. Very impressive, in an apocalyptic sort of way. "I'm glad I was able to be of assistance, Dr. Bright. Are you feeling all right? If you want, I can call for a doctor." He had given her a superficial examination back on *Athena*. Aside from shock and fatigue, she didn't appear to have any major injuries. *Not bad for the only survivor of a massacre.* Christine Bright, Ph.D., was luckier than she looked.

"No," she said. "I don't think so." The smile vanished from her lips. "*He* didn't find me, unlike all the others."

Who is "he"? Iron Man wondered. *Modok?* "In that case," he said, "do you think you're up to telling me what happened?"

She nodded. "I think I can manage," she said slowly. Shivering once more, she wrapped the wool blanket around her shoulders, as if the warm, comforting fabric could protect her from the memories she summoned. "First off, the thing you have to understand is that there are *two* A.I.M.s. Two rival factions bitterly opposed to each other."

Interesting. He hadn't heard anything about Advanced Idea Mechanics splitting in two, and was willing to bet that neither Captain America nor S.H.I.E.L.D. were aware of this development as well. For the first time since arriving in Miami, he felt as though he was getting somewhere with his investigation. *Which faction*, he wondered, *sent the Spymaster droid into Stark Enterprises?* "What's the difference between the two?"

"Humanity," Christine replied. "The adaptoids took over part of A.I.M., rebelling against their human creators. The surviving humans, including myself, have managed to keep our own version of A.I.M. going despite competition from the adaptoids. Since the split, we and the adaptoids have been locked in a sort of arms race, both sides rushing to develop a new Cosmic Cube. Whoever created a Cube first would be able to conquer the other side once and for all."

Not to mention the rest of the world. Christine's adaptoid-versus-human scenario sounded all too plausible. He still remembered the time a Life Model Decoy of Tony Stark had tried to take over his life. The renegade android had almost succeeded in replacing him permanently.

Hostile adaptoids, however, paled before the threat of another Cosmic Cube. "Which side was winning the race?" he asked.

Christine frowned. "To be honest, we humans were lagging behind. After months of labor, the best we had managed was a crystalline chip capable of channeling vast amounts of pure energy from another dimension, and even that was stolen from us by—'' a suspicious look came into her eyes as she made the connection between War Machine and Iron Man ''—an associate of yours.''

''I know all about that chip,'' he admitted. ''Rest assured, it doesn't exist anymore.'' *And there's a big crater outside of London to prove it.* ''But where does Modok fit in? I thought he was dead.''

''That was the first Modok,'' she explained. ''This is Modok 1.5, a new and improved version of the same experiment, but, in theory, easier to control.'' She smiled ruefully. ''At least that was the idea.''

''You people never learn, do you?'' Iron Man said, remembering all the havoc generated by the original Modok. ''Why in heaven's name would you ever want to unleash another Modok on the world?''

''Why does Tony Stark keep recruiting Iron Men?'' she challenged him, unaware that Stark and Iron Man were one and the same. Like most of the world, she assumed that more than one man had served as Stark's armored bodyguard over the years; indeed, to maintain this deception, Tony had publicly ''fired'' and replaced Iron Man at least once. ''Besides, the adaptoids ended up with control of Modam,'' she said, referring to the Mental Organism Designed for Aggressive Maneuvers, one of A.I.M.'s later creations, designed along the same lines as Modok. ''We needed an effective countermeasure. We were sure we knew how to control Modok this time.'' Her voice grew more somber. ''We were wrong.''

And the rest of your colleagues paid the price, Iron Man concluded. But what was this new Modok up to now? And where did Stark Enterprises fit in? *For that matter*, he wondered, *why is she being so forthright with A.I.M.'s secrets?* Christine sat silently upon the coach, hugging herself tightly while her eyes stared back into her past, once more viewing the atrocities that she alone had survived. "I know this must be difficult," Iron Man said, "but I really need to know what happened next."

Christine nodded, her eyes still vacant and unfocussed. "It happened five days ago. Modok attacked SURF—the Submerged Undersea Research Facility—after going AWOL forty-eight hours earlier. He wanted to take over the lab, construct another energy chip, but our security forces tried to repel him. There was a battle. People panicked. There were bodies and explosions everywhere." The memory made her shudder. "We couldn't stop Modok. Nothing could. Then the dome was breached—I don't know by whom. Water started pouring in, flooding the lab. And Modok kept on coming, blasting people apart with psionic bolts, firing weapons from his hover-chair, shooting and killing and killing and—" she covered her face with her hands, overcome by the horrific images invoked by her words. After a moment, she forced herself to continue. "I ran for the airlock. There were some other people with me. Keith, Glenn, Lucienne. I guess they didn't make it."

So they had names after all, Iron Man mused, *despite their faceless uniforms and code numbers.* He felt another pang of regret at the thought of all those wasted lives. *And if not for my armor, Christine and*

I would be just two more bodies lost at the bottom of the sea. Which reminded him of something else. "There was a creature, a sort of octopus? It attacked me outside the lab."

She recognized his description of the monster. "NEMO," she said. "Neurologically-Enhanced Mega-Octopoid. A biological weapons experiment. It must have escaped from its holding cell during the chaos." She looked over Iron Man speculatively, as if searching his armor for suction marks. "Is it still loose?"

"No," Iron Man said. "I don't think it survived our encounter. Sorry." *NEMO, eh?* He marveled at A.I.M's apparent fondness for self-important acronyms. He was half-tempted to ask his guest what Christine stood for. Cold, Hungry, Rescued, Interesting Scientist-Technician Immersed in a National Emergency?

She shrugged. "I wasn't deeply involved with the NEMO project. As a physicist, all my efforts were devoted to rebuilding the energy chip."

"How far along were you with the new chip?" Iron Man asked. "Enough for Modok?"

"Maybe," Christine answered. "The knowledge necessary to create a second chip was already in place, as were the facilities. All we needed were the time and the materials. Conceivably, Modok could have obtained the data before or during his attack on SURF. With the lab destroyed now, he'll need to find some new facilities as well as the necessary components."

"Which are?" Iron Man prompted her.

The scientist fell silent, obviously reluctant to share any more A.I.M.'s secrets with one of the organization's oldest enemies. "Look, Dr. Bright," he said, "if that's your real name, I don't know what plans your particular chapter of Advanced Idea Mechanics had in mind for that chip, but your lab is trashed, your cohorts are all dead, and your schemes are pretty much defunct. Now you've got two options. You can cooperate with me—or you can let Modok get his hands on a new energy chip. Frankly, I don't think either of us wants that to happen. And if you *do* help me, it will prove a mitigating factor at your trial."

Christine glared at him angrily, taken aback by the harshness of his words, and seemingly surprised that Iron Man would turn her over to the authorities when he was done with her. Then she closed her eyes and took a deep breath before responding. "You're right, of course," she said. "Modok murdered my friends. The last thing anyone needs is for that monster to gain still more power. Besides, with all that's happened, a security leak is the least of our problems." She faced Iron Man steadily, her voice filled with new resolve. "The actual formula for the creation of the chip is too complicated to explain now; we're talking eighth-dimensional mathematics reconfigured to allow for the intersection of two parallel planes of reality. But the ultimate construction of the chip requires three rare substances: vibranium from Wakanda, a radioactive ore found on Wundagore Mountain, and an adamantium alloy that can only be manufactured in zero-gravity. A.I.M.—my A.I.M.—

had already established an orbital laboratory to produce the adamantium alloy. We intended to obtain further supplies of vibranium and the radioactive ore on the black market, but we still hadn't located a reliable supplier at the time of the attack. If Modok wants to build a new chip using our data, he's going to need all three components.''

And he has a five-day lead on us, Iron Man realized. "Obviously, I have to stop Modok from obtaining those ingredients, if he hasn't already.'' He rose from his cast-iron chair and looked down on the victimized A.I.M. researcher. "You don't know what he wants with the chip, do you?''

"No,'' she said, "but with that much pure energy at his disposal, he could accomplish almost anything.''

Maybe even re-create the Cosmic Cube.

"There's something else you need to understand,'' Christine insisted. "Even without the chip, Modok 1.5 is more powerful than you can imagine, much more deadly than either Modam or his predecessor. Back at SURF, he blew through our defenses like they were mosquito netting.'' Her intent gaze swept over his armor, examining him from head to toe. "You might not be able to stop him.''

"Don't worry,'' he said. "I'm not about to tackle this alone.''

While Christine took advantage of the jet's facilities to clean herself up, Iron Man contacted his allies. A wide television screen descended from the ceiling next to the abandoned couch. Despite *Stark One*'s extensive film library, Iron Man was not interested in an in-flight movie. Instead a splitscreen image connected him with both Jim Rhodes and Steve Rogers, at the Los Angeles and New York headquarters of WorldWatch and the Avengers, respectively. Although Captain America was in costume, as he usually was, Jim had, quite understandably, not donned his War Machine armor for the call. However, after entering a few commands into the console, the image flickered and changed into War Machine's black-and-silver helmet. Christine might come back into the cabin unexpectedly, and the fact that Jim Rhodes and War Machine were one and the same was only known to a select few.

"Are you sure this line is secure?" Cap asked. His traditional blue mask covered everything but his ice-blue eyes and resolute jaw. Small, symbolic eagle wings adorned his mask, sprouting just above his ears. A large capital "A"—for "America," naturally—was emblazoned on his forehead.

"Positive," Iron Man said. "I designed the encryption program personally." He was not surprised to find Cap in costume. After decades as a national icon and hero, the man on the right side of the screen had probably spent more time as Captain America than he had as just plain Steve Rogers. It was a testament to Steve's innate humanity, Iron Man thought, that his larger-than-life persona had not completely consumed the man himself.

Jim Rhodes, on the other hand, had a full-time career as the director of WorldWatch when he wasn't fighting the good fight in the most combat-ready suit of armor Tony had ever devised. Before assuming the identity of War Machine, Jim had also served a substantial tour of duty as Iron Man himself, subbing for Tony when his friend had been incapacitated by drink or disease. Those bleak days were long ago, but Tony could never forget how Jim Rhodes had held the fort when times were bad. He had no doubt that Jim—and War Machine—would come through this time as well. "What's up?" he asked.

Quickly and concisely, Iron Man filled the other heroes in on his adventure beneath the Atlantic, plus everything he had learned from Christine Bright. "I think we can trust that Dr. Bright's telling the truth, at least to some degree," he assured his comrades before they could ask. "She doesn't want Modok to get his hands on the chip anymore than we do, and with the undersea lab devastated, we're all she has."

"I still wouldn't let her outta my sight too long," Jim said.

Iron Man nodded in agreement, then continued: "There's no way to tell where Modok will strike next so we'd better cover all the bases."

"I'll take Wakanda," Captain America volunteered. "If Modok wants vibranium, he'll probably head straight for the source. Besides, I won't mind seeing T'Challa again." The hereditary king of Wakanda was both a reserve Avenger and an old ally of both Captain America and Iron Man.

"What about the Savage Land?" Jim asked, referring to a prehistoric jungle hidden in the frozen wastes of Antarctica. "I heard they had vibranium down there, too."

"Same name, different properties," Iron Man explained. "The vibranium found in the Savage Land is similar to the African isotope, but there are some significant differences in their subatomic compositions. Dr. Bright was quite emphatic that the energy chip can only be constructed with Wakanda vibranium."

"I guess I'll take Wundagore then," Jim suggested. "Even if this Modok thing turns out to be a wild goose chase, it will give me a chance to check out the human rights situation in Transia."

"Be careful," Iron Man warned him. "Wundagore Mountain has a long and infamous history. Strange things tend to happen there." As a scientist, Tony Stark scorned superstition, but he couldn't deny that Wundagore had seen more than its share of bizarre occurrences, and that the mountain was as known for its occult significance as for the unique radioactive ore found only on its peak.

"Don't worry," Jim said. "I'll stay on my toes— and inside my armor."

"That leaves A.I.M.'s space lab for me," Iron Man said. "Good. That works out fine. Dr. Bright can give me the coordinates and my space armor is well suited to this type of mission. Fortunately, there's a copy of the space suit stored aboard *Stark One*."

"Just in case you have to leave the planet in a hurry?" Jim asked him.

"In our line of work, you never know," Iron Man replied. It was true. As Iron Man, he had spent more time in space—and on alien worlds—than all of

NASA's astronauts combined. Hopefully, this present adventure wouldn't take him any further than in orbit around the Earth. "We're going to be scattered on and off the planet, so let's agree to update each other on any new developments until this crisis is resolved."

"Roger," Captain America said. As the television screen receded back into the ceiling, Iron Man heard a door slide open behind him. He turned around to see Christine Bright emerge from the jet's private bathroom.

"Thanks for letting me use your shower," she said, dabbing her shoulder-length black hair with one of Tony's monogrammed towels. One of the requirements of being a billionaire playboy was that Tony kept a closet full of female attire, in a variety of sizes and fashions, onboard *Stark One*. Christine had exchanged her well-worn A.I.M. bodysuit for a silk, saffron bathrobe embroidered with golden trim. The robe was cinched tightly around her waist and fell to just below her knees, exposing a pair of shapely calves and bare feet. "I feel much more human now."

Behind his golden mask, Iron Man caught his breath involuntarily. Fresh from the shower, recuperating from her five-day ordeal at the bottom of the ocean, Christine turned out to be strikingly beautiful. Her damp hair was sleek and lustrous, her newly-scrubbed skin shined like polished obsidian. Alert brown eyes, filled with humor and intelligence, looked for his through the narrow slits in his faceplate. *How did a nice girl like you end up in A.I.M.?*

he wondered. *And what am I supposed to do with you now?*

"What's next?" she asked, anticipating his concerns. She settled down on the leather couch, her bare legs tucked beneath her. A waft of perfume teased his nose. *Obsession,* he guessed. One of Bethany's favorite scents. For a second or two, he fantasized about getting out of his armor—and getting Christine out of her robe. Tony Stark was a notorious ladies' man, and had been long before he became a super hero. Old habits died hard.

None of that now, he scolded himself. The fate of humanity was at stake after all. "I need the coordinates of A.I.M.'s orbital laboratory," he said bluntly, all business. "Maybe there's still time to keep Modok from that processed adamantium."

"Of course," she said. A serious look came over her face. "Look, I realize you probably feel obliged to turn me over to the authorities. A.I.M. was involved in a lot of illegal activities, I admit that. But I know more about the energy chip and its construction than anyone else left alive. You're going to need me before this business is over. Let me help you."

She had a point. And yet . . . "A.I.M. was more than simply illegal," he pointed out. "Your colleagues have threatened me and the rest of the world more times than I can remember."

"The world is falling apart," she asserted. "A.I.M. offers the world a scientific and rational alternative to the corruption and chaos that is destroying this planet. Don't tell me you'd rather have the politicians and preachers running the show—they've made a mess of things for thousands of years. It's time for real scientists to take over and put things right. Only the systematic application of new technology can—"

"Don't spout the party line at me," Iron Man interrupted her. "I know what A.I.M. is. I know you have no respect for individual lives and freedom."

"What freedom? The freedom to behave irrationally? Freedom to be stupid and self-destructive?" Her tone grew more heated; Iron Man could tell this was an old argument for her, one she'd had many times before, perhaps even with herself. Her cheeks were flushed, fire flashed in her eyes.

Iron Man sympathized with her frustration at the ways of the world; he was enough of a technocrat to share her conviction that science held most of the solutions to the world's problems. Advanced Idea Mechanics had the wrong approach, though. Science couldn't force its answers on humanity; that way lay madness. To date, all A.I.M. had done was create new and more horrible weapons.

He started to say as much, but Christine surprised him by regaining her self-control. "Forget it," she said. "We could argue politics and ideologies all day, but that's not going to stop Modok from re-creating the chip." She stared up at Iron Man defiantly. "You said it yourself. Neither of us wants Modok to succeed. I'm offering you my help. The only question is: are you smart enough to accept it?"

Iron Man did not answer her right away. *Blast it!* He had a dozen different sensors built into his armor, monitoring everything from the atmospheric pressure to local police radio bands, but nothing that would let him peer into the heart and soul of the woman seated before him.

Can I trust her? he thought. The last time he'd accepted help from a beautiful woman he barely knew, back when Strucker held him prisoner, she'd turned out to be part of a virtual reality trap. At least Christine was real, or so he assumed; computerized holograms seldom asked for showers. He contemplated Dr. Christine Bright. In her gossamer bathrobe she'd seemed no match against his impervious iron shell. *What harm can she do?* he wondered. All of her colleagues, weapons, and equipment were lost beneath the Atlantic Ocean. *Too bad the original chip was destroyed before I had a chance to examine it thoroughly.* Then he wouldn't have needed Christine at all. And once this was over, he could remand Christine into federal custody.

"Okay," he said finally. "You can stay here, on this plane, until we settle things with Modok. After that—well, we'll deal with that then. I'm taking a risk by trusting you, Dr. Bright. I pray that's not a mistake."

"Call me Christine," she said, stretching sinuously upon the couch. Her long, svelte legs caught his gaze for several seconds. The silk robe fell open slightly, revealing a provocative display of cleavage. He had to tear his attention away. *Yes, that is definitely* Obsession *I smelled.*

The man inside the armor hoped he wasn't keeping her around for all the wrong reasons. "My name's still Iron Man," he said. "Don't forget it."

FRIDAY. 2:35 AM. WAKANDA ROYAL TIME.

The Avengers quinjet, a supersonic aircraft designed by Tony Stark, touched down on the runway. In the pilot's seat, Captain America brought the quinjet to a gradual stop. In the distance, beyond the lighted runway, a mountainous shape, drenched in shadows, loomed above the horizon. *The vibranium mound*, Cap realized. The source of Wakanda's prosperity—and Modok's presumed target.

The African nation of Wakanda has been described as a "technological jungle." More accurately, Central Wakanda, the nation's capital, was an oasis of high-tech comforts and conveniences nestled in the midst of lush, verdant greenery. Gazing out through the quinjet's windows, Captain America saw the bright lights and imposing buildings of a modern city. The controlled use of vibranium, as well as its carefully monitored export, had raised Wakanda's standard of living a hundredfold in just one generation, as had the vision and keen judgment of T'Challa, king of the Wakandans.

Born and raised in a previous era, Captain America never ceased to be amazed by the speed with which science and technology had changed the world. Nowhere was that change more dramatically demonstrated than in Wakanda.

He still remembered the first time he had visited Africa. It was 1942, only a few months after he volunteered for the top secret medical experiment that had transformed him into Captain America. He and Bucky Barnes, his kid sidekick, had chased the Red Skull halfway across the continent in search of stolen U.S. war plans. *We still called it the Dark Continent back then,* he mused. Africa had seemed like a completely different planet from the Brooklyn streets where he had grown up, an exotic and primitive realm out of an Edgar Rice Burroughs novel, seldom seen by American eyes except in newsreel footage of perilous safaris.

Now I think nothing of hopping a jet to drop in on an old friend, and the African jungle holds a scientific wonderland to rival anything found in the West. So much had changed since he first assumed the identity of Captain America. The war was over, and Bucky long gone, and only one thing in his life had remained the same: America still needed a champion to defend it against madmen like Modok.

He brought the quinjet to a smooth halt. Unbuckling his seatbelt, he stretched his stiff and weary muscles, readying himself for whatever challenges the future might hold. *I just hope I'm in time.* Who knew when Modok or his agents might make a grab for the vibranium?

T'Challa was waiting for him on the tarmac, accompanied by a handful of advisors and security personnel, most attired in traditional Wakandan robes. According to ancient custom, the king of Wakanda was also known as the Black Panther; T'Challa's ceremonial garb accentuated the king's identification with his royal totem. He wore a tight, black bodysuit

that clung to his athletic frame like a second skin. A
short black cape was held on by a strap across his
chest. Only his head remained uncovered. Cap rec-
ognized the face of his old friend and comrade. The
Black Panther had handsome, dignified features and
amber eyes that reflected the moonlight like a cat's.
Sacred Wakandan herbs and rituals had given the
Black Panther many of the physical characteristics of
his namesake, much as the late Dr. Erskine's Super-
Soldier Serum had transmuted frail and skinny Steve
Rogers into the perfect physical specimen known as
Captain America.

"Welcome back to Wakanda," T'Challa said
loudly as the door of the quinjet slid open and Cap
emerged from the plane. The African night was hot,
humid, and smelled of exotic jungle orchids. Cap
noticed the temperature difference the minute he
stepped out of the air-conditioned quinjet; the moist,
muggy heat hit him like a blast from an open fur-
nace. Somewhere in the distance a lion roared.
Clouds drifted across the moonlit sky. Completely
automated, the underbelly of the plane extruded a
collapsible stairway on which he descended to the
runway. The stairs retracted automatically as soon as
Cap's boots stepped onto the runway.

Like the Black Panther, Captain America had
come in uniform. Clad in patriotic red, white, and
blue, the hero looked like the very personification of
the American flag. A spotless white star was displayed proudly on his chest, nestled amidst a shirt
of blue, protective chain mail. Vertical red and white
stripes circled his muscular waist, while his hands

and feet were tucked into bright red gloves and boots. Cap kept his mask on; unlike T'Challa, his true identity was not a matter of public record.

Cap felt a strong kinship with the Black Panther. Both men had become the symbols and champions of their respective countries. The only difference between them was that T'Challa was also the political and spiritual leader of his people. *What a tremendous responsibility*, Cap thought. He did not envy T'Challa. He knew how hard it could be to live up to the expectations of an entire nation.

And the Panther is also a super hero, not to mention a technological genius on a par with Tony Stark. As a member of the Avengers, the Black Panther had fought evil alongside Captain America and Iron Man for several years, until the demands of ruling Wakanda forced him to abandon a full-time life of adventure. Cap just hoped that T'Challa, with his many roles and responsibilities, had managed to carve out some time for a private life as well. Searching his memory, he seemed to recall that T'Challa was engaged to be married—and to an American woman, no less. *Good for him,* Cap thought, just a bit ruefully. His own career as Captain America had often come between him and the women he had loved and lost over the years. Lady Liberty remained his one true bride.

"Sorry to disturb you at such a late hour," Cap said, shaking T'Challa's hand, "but the danger could be urgent."

"So you said," T'Challa confirmed. Cap had briefed the Panther by radio on his way to Wakanda.

"It is no hardship. You are always welcome here, regardless of the reason." The king of Wakanda spoke English with no trace of an accent, having been educated in the finest schools in the United States and Europe.

"Thanks anyway," Cap said. His gaze turned towards the imposing mountain to the north. The jagged peak of the vibranium mound could be seen above the city buildings stretched out between it and the airstrip. From a distance, the precious mound looked like any other mountain. "I'd like to check on the mound immediately, if you don't mind."

"Of course," T'Challa agreed. "I assumed as much. Tayete, Kazibe, the floating disk, please." The king spoke softly, but his subjects hurried to fulfill his command. The crowd of advisors around T'Challa parted and two men carried an unusual object over to Cap and the Panther. It was a flat metallic disk, copper colored and about four feet in diameter. Aluminum handlebars rose from the disk to the height of a man's chest. T'Challa stepped onto the disk and gestured for Cap to do the same. The disk was just large enough to hold two standing adults comfortably.

T'Challa manipulated a set of controls on the handlebars and the disk slowly rose off the tarmac. Cap gripped one of the aluminum bars for safety's sake as they ascended into the warm night sky.

Smoothly, silently, the disk carried the two heroes above Central Wakanda. A cool breeze provided some relief from the heat. Cap was no scientist, but he recalled that vibranium could absorb sounds and convert any sonic vibrations into energy. He assumed the noiseless floating disk was a product of Wakanda's vibranium-based technology. Glancing back over his shoulder, he saw the tiny figures of T'Challa's retinue shrinking away as the disk gained altitude. They looked no larger than ants. "What about them?" he asked.

The Panther shrugged. "I've already ordered that security at the mound be increased. There's no reason why all my staff should have to be running about at three in the morning." A gentle smile appeared on T'Challa's face. "W'Kabi, my security chief, will have a fit. He hates it when I run off without any bodyguards, but I think he's growing resigned to the fact that I'm used to looking out for myself." He adjusted the controls and the disk leveled off at about five hundred feet above the ground. "Besides, you and I have faced much greater threats with considerably less warning."

"I hope you're right," Cap said. Iron Man had sounded pretty concerned after his excursion to A.I.M.'s undersea lab. *Well*, he thought grimly, *we'll find out soon enough how serious the danger is.* Strapped to his upper arm, his famous shield waited in readiness, its twelve-pound weight a comforting presence in times of peril.

The shield, never far from his side, had been Captain America's primary weapon and defense for decades. Shaped like an enormous frisbee, two and a half feet in diameter, the shield featured the same patriotic coloring as its bearer and was quite literally indestructible. Two generations of spies, soldiers,

and super-villains had failed to dent, let alone penetrate, its impervious skin; the decorative stripes and
the great white star at the center of the shield looked
as bright and new today as they had when Cap had
first received the shield, during the darkest days of
World War II.

Once top secret, the exact composition of Captain
America's shield had been lost to history, but, he
suddenly recalled, both vibranium and adamantium
were rumored to be involved in its creation. Could
the blazing fury locked within A.I.M.'s energy chip
only be contained by the very elements that had held
his shield together against the most awesome of attacks? It was a sobering thought.

Hundreds of feet below, the capital city of Wakanda spread out. Despite his apprehension concerning Modok and his schemes, Cap couldn't help but
admire the view. Seen from this angle, T'Challa's
city was a masterpiece of architecture and urban
planning. Well-lit pavilions and promenades, gener-
ously provided with gardens and other greenery,
connected graceful modern buildings decorated with
traditional African designs. Panthers were a frequent
motif, as were stylized representations of the surrounding jungle. Marble monkeys posed in the
branches of graceful sculpted trees. Sparkling water
flowed from artificial fountains and waterfalls. The
few pedestrians still awake at so late an hour strolled
securely through the city streets. Peering down, Cap
glimpsed both modern and classical statuary amidst
the open public spaces.

Most striking of all was the immense crystal panther head that occupied the roof of T'Challa's royal palace. Carved from what looked like a single, enormous block of polished, black crystal, the great cat, its features as huge as the Sphinx's, looked out over Central Wakanda. *Amazing,* Captain America thought, *what one man's vision can accomplish, especially when that vision is devoted to the common good of a brave and resourceful people.*

Captain America smiled warmly at his companion. In a world full of malevolent and destructive forces like Modok, it was good to remember that there were also men and women like T'Challa. Although he had been created to preserve America in particular, Cap was proud to have an opportunity to defend Wakanda beside such a noble ally. If there was one thing he had learned in his travels about the globe, it was that freedom and individual liberty rightfully belonged to the decent, law-abiding citizens of every nation.

"You've built a wonderful city, T'Challa," Cap said to his companion. "Your royal ancestors would be proud."

"A city is only as great as its people," the Panther replied. "We Wakandans hope to have the best of both yesterday and tomorrow, respecting our ancient traditions while remaining open to the opportunities presented by new ideas and technologies. It's a delicate balancing act. Defeating a psychotic supervillain sometimes seems easier in comparison. Perhaps that's why I have never been able to quite give up the habit of adventuring. It beats regional planning meetings anyday." He shared a wry look with Cap. "And don't get me started on revamping our healthcare system. . . ."

"I think I can imagine," Captain America said, thanking heaven that he didn't have to actually run the country he had come to symbolize.

In time, the bright lights of the city faded into the distance as the massive vibranium mound grew ever larger before them. A crescent moon cast its light upon the dense jungle foliage, partially hidden in darkness, that concealed the base of the vibranium mound. Dimly seen shapes rustled through the underbrush as Wakanda's nocturnal wildlife went about their nightly rounds. A soft breeze cooled Cap's face amidst the heat of the night. It was hard to imagine that any evil lurked in such a peaceful setting. Sunrise remained hours away. Cap permitted himself a long yawn. He had been on the go for hours, without any chance to sleep. What time was it now in New York? Eight o'clock? Nine? He had just started to calculate the time difference when the disk he and the Panther stood upon dipped forward alarmingly.

Captain America grabbed onto the handrail with both fists. The copper disk wobbled beneath his feet; it was like standing on the deck of a small boat during a storm at sea. Fighting to maintain his balance, Cap looked over at T'Challa. The Panther's amber eyes were fixed on the disk's controls, his jaw was clenched in fierce concentration. "What's the matter?" Cap asked. The disk was losing altitude fast, diving towards the jungle at a steep angle.

"Something's jamming the sonic propulsion

unit," T'Challa said. Shaking his head, he looked up from the controls. "There's nothing I can do. We're going to crash." Keeping one hand on the handlebar, T'Challa reached back behind his neck and pulled a black mask up and over his head. The mask completed T'Challa's costume, transforming the human king of Wakanda into the man-shaped embodiment of a jungle cat. Slitted pupils gazed out from behind the featureless black mask. The pointed tips of cat-like ears rose above his skull. Cap was suddenly reminded of the giant stone panther god watching over the city behind them; T'Challa had become one with the statue guarding his palace, the living avatar of the panther god. "Get ready," the Black Panther said.

The primeval forest seemed to rush up at them. The hot air raced past his face. *Could be worse*, Captain America thought, immune to panic. *Could be cement.* The disk was tilted at nearly a forty-five degree angle. The flying platform was no longer holding him up; now it was dragging him down. His gaze moved quickly from the oncoming jungle to the long aluminum handlebars between him and the dark, leafy shadows ahead. *Those are only going to get in the way*, he decided. *Time to abandon ship.* Readjusting his shield, making sure it was securely strapped to his back, he caught the Panther's gaze and pointed down. The Black Panther nodded, understanding.

Cap dived left. The Panther dived right. They left the disk at the same moment, mere seconds before the falling contraption smashed into the waiting treetops. Cap heard the sound of wood and metal tearing each other apart.

He fell headfirst into the jungle. Wind and tree branches whipped past his face. Twigs and vines snapped beneath his weight. Gravity accelerated him towards the ground. Cap knew he had to slow his descent and fast. A massive branch, as thick as his arm, struck him just below his ribcage. The impact knocked the breath out of him, but his body responded automatically, rolling over the bough, then reaching out with both hands to grab onto the very same branch and swing back over it again. Like an Olympic gymnast on the uneven bars, Captain America swung in a loop around the gnarled bough, his outstretched legs ripping through the surrounding leafage while he regained a measure of control over his speed and direction. Then he cast off from that branch just before it snapped apart under the strain.

He soared through the air like a trapeze artist until his outstretched hands caught onto another serviceable bough and then another. Swinging and jumping, falling and swinging, he descended from tree to tree, each skillful acrobatic move diminishing his speed until there were no more branches, just empty air beneath him, and he fell feetfirst towards the jungle floor. His heavy red boots, flared at the top, pirate style, struck the earth.

For several moments, he crouched there, stunned but alive. The dense green bracken carpeting the jungle floor provided him with a mattress on which to recover. Then he stood up slowly, taking an inventory of his limbs and injuries. *Ribs feel bruised*, he decided, *but nothing broken.* The chain mail in his costume had protected him from some of the impact; his super-enhanced agility had done the rest. He stretched his arms experimentally, and grunted with satisfaction as they responded to his commands. He'd think twice about stepping onto one of those disks again, but, all in all, he appeared to have come out of the experience intact. This was not the first crash landing he had survived; he doubted it would be the last.

Now what? he thought. Squinting, his gaze searched the darkened jungle without much success. The pallid moonlight barely penetrated the thick, leafy canopy overhead. There didn't even seem to be a trail anywhere in sight. He stood knee-deep in leafy fronds and clinging tendrils. Dense groves of mahogany and ebony, mangrove and African teak stretched toward the sky. Tree trunks draped with moss and hanging vines hemmed him in on all sides. The humid air smelled of moist earth and fragrant blossoms. He removed his shield from his back, holding it at the ready while he waited for his eyes to adjust to the dark.

Where was T'Challa? For now, Captain America chose to work on the assumption that his fellow Avenger had survived the crash as well. If anything, the Black Panther was an even more talented gymnast than he was, although, Cap reluctantly conceded, no amount of acrobatics could have saved the Panther if he hit a tree the wrong way. Cap imagined T'Challa impaled upon a stout, jagged branch, then forced the bitter image out of his mind. "T'Challa?"

he whispered to the darkness. "Are you there?"

He was tempted to shout, but there was no way to know who else might be lurking in the shadows. *Someone* had sabotaged the floating disk from the ground. He couldn't believe the crash was an accident. A.I.M., he knew, was perfectly capable of jamming the sonic propulsion unit.

The jungle at night was full of noises. Monkeys chattered in the treetops. A boa constrictor, hissing angrily, slid over a twisted bough above Cap's head; Cap took a few steps back from the branch. Small animals rustled through the verdant bush, although nothing was growling just yet. *Thank goodness*, Cap thought. He wanted to find *the* Panther, not a panther. He remembered that somewhere in Wakanda there was supposed to be a jungle where real dinosaurs still walked the Earth. *I hope that's far from here*, he thought with a shiver. The last thing he needed tonight was to run into a tyrannosaur.

Of course, it wouldn't be the first time.... Since becoming a super hero over fifty years ago, he'd butted heads with just about everything at least once, from a crazed Nazi vampire to green-skinned alien soldiers, including the occasional berserk dino.

A twig snapped behind him. Cap spun around to confront a pair of glowing amber eyes staring at him from the midnight shadows between two moss-covered treetrunks. He peered into the darkness, saw sinewy muscles ripple beneath what looked like a coat of black velvet. "T'Challa?" he asked hopefully. "Is that you?"

Ivory fangs flashed beneath the amber eyes. A

low, rumbling growl erupted into a savage snarl as a large black leopard pounced at Cap. Three hundred pounds of jungle cat slammed into the Star-Spangled Avenger, knocking the breath from his lungs. The force of the animal's attack caused Cap to lose his grip on his shield. His faithful weapon went flying away into the underbrush.

The panther sank his fangs into Cap's shoulder, but the fierce jaws failed to penetrate the chain mail. The panther refused to let go of its prey, however; it stood on its hind legs, its sharp claws raking Cap's chest, its tail whipping the air. Cap staggered beneath the beast's weight, his knees almost buckling. He grabbed the panther by the back of its neck and pulled it away from his shoulder, the dagger-like points of the animal's fangs digging into his flesh even through the protective mail.

The enraged leopard snarled ferociously, its snapping jaws only inches from Cap's face. The creature's breath was hot and fetid; the stench made his eyes water.

"Sorry, Bagheera," he grunted at the great cat, "but I haven't come this far just to become your late-night snack."

The black, velvet fur was hard to hold onto. Cap knew he couldn't keep this feline predator away from his throat for long. Moonlight glinted off the panther's fangs and claws. *If only I had my shield.* His keen eyes sought out the polished metal disk in the dense foliage. For several heartbeats all he could see was the bush and the shadows, then there it was: lying upside-down less than three yards away, tantalizingly near yet beyond his reach. *How can I get my hands on that shield?* he wondered. The instant he let go of the scruff of the panther's neck, the carnivore's fangs would tear his face apart—unless he could get out of the way fast enough.

There was no other option. He would have to pit his own agility and speed, augmented by the Super-Soldier Serum in his blood and honed by decades of combat experience all over the world, against the panther's natural hunting ability. Yanking hard on the leopard's hide, he threw the animal to one side while he leapt in the opposite direction, toward his shield. *Move!* he commanded himself. He had to make every second count.

The panther was upon him immediately. He felt the beast's foul breath at the back of his neck, heard its feral growl next to his ears. The panther's paws struck his exposed back even as his fingers touched the brim of his shield. Lightning-fast reflexes took over automatically; Cap swung the shield back over his shoulder in an arc that caught the panther right between the eyes. The animal emitted a yelp of pain and sprang off its back and onto the jungle floor. In one fluid motion, Cap rolled away from the sound of the leopard's cry, then jumped to his feet, his shield extended between him and the jungle cat. "Back off!" he shouted harshly. "Back!" He held his shield the way a lion tamer holds a wooden chair to keep a snarling beast at bay.

Jaws wide, the panther hissed angrily. One blow had not been enough to discourage the cat. Predator and prey faced off against each other beneath a dense canopy of leaves and hanging vines. The panther kept its head low to the ground, its hind legs poised and ready to pounce.

Keeping both eyes fixed on the hungry carnivore, Cap ran one hand along the edge of his shield. One good blow to the panther's throat, he thought, and the big cat's neck might break. He hated the idea; it would be a shame to kill such a magnificent wild animal, especially when that animal was also the spiritual totem of the Wakandan people. It would be like killing an American bald eagle, only worse since he was a guest in this country. "Good kitty," he said softly. "Be a good kitty and just go away. I don't want to hurt you."

The leopard snarled in response. It hunched its shoulders, marshalling its energy for the attack to come. Cap kept his shield ready while his mind raced, searching for a humane way to resolve the standoff without endangering either himself or the panther any further. He considered rushing the panther, his shield out front, but that might only provoke the animal further. *What I really need is a bit of fire.* Unfortunately, he carried neither a lighter nor a match.

He had been an Eagle Scout, though. He unbuckled his belt with his free hand, then struck the metal belt buckle against the adamantium-vibranium alloy of his shield. "C'mon," he said under his breath. "Let's have a spark or two."

It was a good plan. It might even have worked, except that the panther didn't seem inclined to give it a chance. Filling the night with its cries, the great cat sprang at Cap, who saw the panther coming and ducked out of the way just in time. The beast landed on all fours only a few feet away from Cap. It came at him again the minute its paws hit the ground, changing direction with frightening speed. *This cat is obsessed*, Cap realized. *It's not going to stop until its turned me into raw meat.*

He snapped his belt like a whip. The metal buckle smacked the panther across its muzzle. The crack of the belt echoed through the jungle like a gunshot, startling the panther out of its attack. *Now I really feel like a lion tamer.* Its nose bleeding slightly, the panther circled Cap relentlessly, stalking through the underbrush intent on its chosen prey. The repeated crack of Cap's belt kept it at a safe distance for the moment, but the beast wasn't about to give up on him yet.

Okay, let's try this one more time. He snapped the belt again, just to keep the panther at bay for a few seconds more, then grabbed onto the buckle and scraped it hard against the impervious surface of his shield.

Blue sparks leaped from the intersection of buckle and shield. "Yes!" Cap exclaimed. He thrust the sparking shield against the mossy bark of the nearest tree. The clinging moss caught fire, orange flames and black smoke licking at the gnarled bark of the tree itself. Cap broke off a low-hanging branch and held it against the burning moss. *Careful, Cap*, he warned himself. *You want to ward off this animal, not burn down the entire jungle.*

The panther backed away from the burning tree-trunk. Its amber eyes reflected the dancing flames. As soon as the broken branch began to smolder and burn, Cap waved his makeshift torch at the panther. Smoke rose from the tip of the branch, irritating Cap's nostrils. A trail of floating sparks followed the torch like the tail of a comet. Cap took one step closer to the panther, then shoved the business end of the torch at the panther's head.

Flames singed its whiskers. The great black leopard let out an indignant hiss, then spun around and disappeared into the jungle without a backward glance, proving that the animal was merely stubborn, not actually rabid. Prey that fought back was one thing, apparently; fire was an entirely different matter.

I knew all those merit badges would pay off someday. Captain America permitted himself a sigh of relief. He peeled some more moss off the adjacent tree trunks and wrapped enough of the stuff around his branch to make a decent torch. Then he used his shield to carefully stamp out his original fire. Holding his torch aloft with one hand, unintentionally posing much like Lady Liberty herself, Cap propped his shield up against the base of an African teak long enough to thread his belt back through the loops of his trousers. *I wouldn't want to lose my pants before I make my way to the vibranium mound.*

The flickering flames of the torch cast dancing shadows on the surrounding trees. Even with the extra light, he couldn't see more than a yard or two in any direction. *What now?* he wondered. He wasn't eager to go stomping through the jungle without a compass or guide. The way his luck was going, he'd probably stumble right into the middle of a den or lions or something. For all he knew, that hungry panther might be the least of the predators lurking in this jungle. Cap's eyes scanned the vine-choked murk all around him. His ears listened intently for any hint of trouble.

Something rustled overhead. Turning around quickly, Captain America saw a single leaf fall from a banyan tree a few yards away. Had the panther come back again? Combat-trained muscles went on alert; this time he wouldn't be taken by surprise. He snatched up his shield by its edge, ready to fling it at the first available target with all his strength. He waited for the bloodthirsty growl of the panther.

"Hang on," a familiar voice called softly from the branches of a towering ironwood. "It's just me." Leaves rustled again, and Cap heard something drop lightly from the trees onto the jungle floor.

At first, he couldn't see anyone at all, only more black shadows in the night-shrouded vegetation. Then he spotted a pair of golden, catlike eyes glowing in the sylvan darkness and breathed a sigh of relief. *Now you show up*, Cap thought ruefully. "Glad to see you made it," he said.

"Likewise," the Black Panther said, rising slowly from a crouched position amidst the foliage. In his pitch-black costume, he was barely distinguishable from the other patches of darkness between the bushes and the trees. Cap had to squint to make out the Panther's silhouette.

"You found me quickly enough," Cap said. "I'm impressed."

The Panther stepped closer. Cap saw that one shoulder of T'Challa's costume had torn, revealing a few inches of brown skin. The Black Panther had also discarded his cape at some point, the better to bound through the trees. "Your scent is unmistakable," the Panther said, sniffing behind his mask. "No offense. Also, that star-spangled banner you're wearing definitely stands out in the jungle."

I suppose so, if you can see in the dark. He also imagined that the Panther probably knew the jungles of Wakanda like he knew the streets of New York City.

"If you say so," he conceded. The mission was what really concerned him now. "What about that crash anyway? I call that pretty suspicious, don't you?" he said.

"Absolutely," the Panther agreed. "I've used those flying disks dozens of times without any problems; I designed them myself. There's no way that the primary *and* secondary systems could have gone out at the same time unless there some sort of deliberate sabotage at work."

"That's what I figured," Cap said. Someone had gone to a lot of trouble to keep them away from the mound tonight. "Now I definitely want to check out that vibranium."

"Put out that torch," the Panther said, "and follow me."

He leapt effortlessly into the overhanging branches. Cap hesitated for a second, reluctant to relinquish the flames he had strived so hard to produce. Still, the Panther had a point; he could hardly swing through the trees with a lit torch in his hand. He extinguished the flames by squashing the burning branch into the ground, then stamped out the embers with the heel of his boot.

Strapping his shield onto his back, Cap jumped after the Black Panther. They moved swiftly through the shadowy jungle, leaping from tree to tree. Cap kept a close eye on the Panther, following his lead and struggling not to lose the black-clad figure in the darkness. The Panther never paused to orient himself; he clearly knew where he was going. They made good time, too. It was faster and easier to travel through the treetops than it would have been to fight their way through the overgrown greenery below.

Within minutes they reached the base of the vibranium mound. Cap had to crane his neck back to see the top of the mound, towering over them like the Matterhorn. Spotlights embedded in the earth illuminated the openings of mine shafts in the face of the mound, but Cap spotted no guards or miners. The scene struck him as curiously quiet, even for this early in the morning. Had the vibranium absorbed all the sounds in the vicinity or was something amiss?

A few branches ahead of him, the Panther came to an abrupt stop. He held up his hand, signalling Captain America. Then he dropped silently from a mahogany tree, landing on all fours like the jungle cat he emulated. Cap also jumped to the ground, his boots sinking into the moist, fern-covered earth almost as soundlessly as the Panther. "What is it?" he asked softly.

"Look," the Panther said. He led Cap to a patch of underbrush a couple of yards past the edge of the jungle. There, sprawled upon the ground, were the bodies of two youthful male Wakandans. The two men wore matching sashes and headbands, each imprinted with a leopard-skin design. Futuristic rifles rested in the high grass near their fingers. The Panther quickly placed his hand against first one man's neck, then the other's. Neither guard stirred as their king checked their pulses. "They're alive," the Panther said after a moment, "but they appear drugged." He sniffed the air. "Gassed, I think. There are still traces of it in the air."

"Then their attacker can't have gone far," Cap said. He had no doubt that the guards had been immobilized by the same party that had caused their flying disk to crash. Modok was not wasting any time, assuming that Modok was indeed responsible for this assault on the vibranium mound.

He stared at the nearest mine opening, partway up the side of the mound. A winding trail, carved out of the face of the rocky mount, led to the entrance of the mine. Shield in hand, Cap ran up the trail, leaving the guards' high-tech rifles behind; Captain America had never relied on anything except his own strength and shield. The Panther sprinted after him.

"There's a metal gate in place at the entrance of every mine," the Panther explained as they climbed the trail. At the outer edge of the trail, the side of the mound dropped away steeply; noting the absence of any guardrails, Cap kept safely to the center of the path. "I ordered all the gates closed and locked the minute I received your warning," the Panther continued. Cap was not reassured. A steel gate might stop most people, but not A.I.M. Anyone who could slip past Wakanda's borders undetected, and take out T'Challa's guards, was not going to be discouraged by any mere barrier.

Sure enough, when they reached the top of the trail, they found the gate torn asunder. The heavy steel gate, composed of overlapping titanium bars, was at least three inches thick, but someone had yanked it apart as though it were made of balsa wood. Gazing at the damaged gate, Cap and the Panther saw the indentations of ten powerful fingers. "By my father's spirit," the Panther said in disbelief, "the invader did this with his bare hands." He glanced at Captain America. "The Hulk hasn't joined A.I.M. recently, has he?"

"Not that I've heard," Cap said, although he couldn't deny the possibility. The Hulk hadn't been seen in months, not since he fought government troops in Chicago.

Unfortunately, the Hulk was hardly the only being on the planet capable of such incredible feats of destruction. It didn't look like Modok's handiwork, though. If the new Modok was anything like the original, the cyborg's abilities were more mental than physical.

Cap peered into the cavernous depths of the mine

and wished he'd thought to bring a flashlight. A couple of wooden crates were stacked along one side of the tunnel; mining supplies, Cap assumed. Beyond the spotlight fixed on the entrance, the tunnel gave way to utter blackness. Was their unknown enemy down there in the darkness somewhere or had he already come and gone with the vibranium he craved? There was only one way to find out. Fearlessly, Captain America took a few steps into the mine. The air within the tunnel was dank and musty.

The Black Panther started to follow Cap, then halted in his tracks. He cocked his head, as though his super-sensitive hearing had alerted him to a sound beyond the detection of ordinary human ears. He sniffed the air once, and his eyes grew wide. The Panther sprang at Captain America, knocking him to the ground. "Watch out!" he called.

Cap heard something *whizz* through the air exactly where his head had been before the Panther shoved him out of the way. A tiny green dart, less than an inch long, ricocheted off the wall of the mine. Cap ducked instinctively, but the dart bounced harmlessly onto the floor. He raised his shield to protect him and the Panther as they scrambled to their feet. "What the—!" he exclaimed. "Where did that come from?"

The Panther sniffed again. "Something oily," he said, then pointed decisively at the roof of the tunnel. "There!"

Cap couldn't see a thing where the Panther pointed, only shadows, but he heard an angry hiss and watched in horror as something leaped from the ceiling and attacked T'Challa. The Panther staggered backwards, into the light, and Cap saw a green, scaly figure grappling with the Panther.

He recognized the figure instantly. It was the Cobra, a.k.a. Klaus Voorhees, a professional super-villain and a charter member of the criminal organization known as the Serpent Society. It was the Serpent Society, he recalled, that had ultimately assassinated the first Modok. Could there be a connection between that murder and A.I.M.'s current operation?

Time enough to worry about that later. "Let go of him, Voorhees!" Cap shouted. He rushed to aid the Panther in his battle against the Cobra, who had wrapped both his arms and his legs around the Panther's torso, pinning T'Challa's arms to his sides. The Panther fought to stay upright, even as the Cobra snapped at his throat with sharpened teeth. So far, the Panther had managed to keep his exposed neck away from the Cobra's jaws, but how much longer could he evade the Cobra's bite?

Years ago in India, the bite of a radioactive cobra had mutated Klaus Voorhees, endowing him with the speed and flexibility of a serpent. Although Voorhees had remained human in appearance, he had advertised his new reptilian abilities by devising a costume that gave him the appearance of a human cobra. An elaborate mask and headpiece simulated the hood of a cobra about to attack, while an emerald suit composed of artificial scales covered most of his body. Captain America knew from experience that the Cobra's scales had been specially treated with a silicon and graphite-dust compound that made the Cobra incredibly slippery and difficult to hold onto. Suction devices on his hands and feet allowed him to stick to walls and ceilings. An articulated armor chestpiece, deep purple in color, completed the Cobra's costume, leaving the villain's arms and legs free while protecting his torso. Cap had fought the Cobra many times before so he knew what a deadly adversary he could be. He couldn't remember if T'Challa had ever challenged the Cobra in the past. There had been so many villains, so many life-or-death battles. . . .

He grabbed onto the Cobra from behind, trapping the serpent-man in an unbreakable headlock and pulling him away from the Black Panther. The cold-blooded villain felt slippery and unexpectedly cool to the touch. The Cobra's arms and legs let go of T'Challa as he struggled to extricate himself from Cap's grip. Cap felt the Cobra's well-lubricated body twisting and sliding in his grasp. "No way," he grunted, holding onto the Cobra with all his strength, "you're not going anywhere!"

"We'll see about that," the Cobra hissed. His sly, sibilant voice dripped with scorn and malicious humor. A distinctive accent betrayed his origins in Holland, although Cap recalled that the Cobra had chosen to become an American citizen.

Despite Captain America's best efforts, the Cobra's arms wriggled free of the headlock, stretching and twisting themselves as though they were made of rubber. Dislocating both shoulders without a qualm, the Cobra jumped away from Captain America, landing flat on his stomach outside the entrance to the mine. The loose gravel scattered beneath his torso; small clouds of dust were tossed upward. "Good try, Yankee Doodle," he hissed, "but there's no hold I can't slip away from!"

The Panther dived for the Cobra, pitting the speed and agility of his feline totem against the Cobra's reptilian powers. The Cobra slithered out of the way, sliding down the rocky trail on his belly, moving his body along without the use of either his legs or his arms, travelling at incredible speed through muscular contractions alone. Cap glimpsed a small snakeskin pouch affixed to the Cobra's belt. He could guess what it contained.

"He's got the vibranium!" he shouted to the Panther. He hurled his shield at the Cobra, flinging it like the enormous frisbee it resembled. Years of experience provided his aim with deadly accuracy. The shield struck the Cobra in the small of his back, bouncing off the villain's purple armor to lodge in a narrow crevice in the face of the mound. The Cobra let out a howl of anger and pain. He clutched his back, momentarily dazed by the force of Cap's throw. "Never underestimate the determination of a free man intent on justice," Cap said.

The delay was all the Black Panther needed. He lunged at the Cobra, throwing his body into the air without fear or hesitation. He crashed into the prone form of the Cobra and the two men went rolling down the trail to the jungle below, locked in a violent embrace, stirring up still more clouds of dust and gravel. Captain America's glance darted from the grappling pair to his shield, jammed into the mouth of a crevice several yards down the trail. The polished surface of the shield glinted in the night, reflecting the moonlight shining on Wakanda. Cap swiftly decided on his strategy. He'd retrieve his shield first, then join the battle below. "Don't let him get away," he called to the Panther. "I'll be with you in a second."

A growl from behind him interrupted Cap's plans. He spun around instantly, realizing even as he did so that both he and the Panther had overlooked an important fact: the Cobra was fast but only moderately strong. There was no way Klaus Voorhees could have shredded the mine's solid steel gate. The Cobra was not alone. There had to be someone else.

The big man stepped out of the shadows of the mine. He was much larger than Captain America, almost seven feet tall and probably over four hundred pounds. Unlike the Cobra, he had no elaborate costume, only a dull-green cotton suit and a short cloak draped over his shoulders. He didn't need a mask, for his face was fearsome enough: the skin stretched tight over his massive skull, the mouth twisted in a permanent grimace. His ruddy features were coarse and bestial, like a caveman's, and his bloodshot eyes were filled with rage. A shaggy, wild mane of tangled brown hair crowned his monstrous head. The hair was matted and greasy and smelled like it hadn't been washed for weeks. Captain America knew this ferocious face well. It belonged to the homicidal madman known as Mr. Hyde.

Despite the muggy African heat, a chill ran down

Cap's spine. As a small child, back in the 1930s, he had snuck into a matinee showing of the classic black-and-white movie version of Robert Louis Stevenson's *Dr. Jekyll and Mr. Hyde*. Fredric March's performance as the horrendous Hyde (and his tormented alter ego) had given the young Steve Rogers nightmares for a month. In reality, Cap knew, the creature stalking towards him was not really Stevenson's fictional monster brought to life. This Mr. Hyde was, in fact, an unscrupulous chemist named Calvin Zabo, who had invented a dangerous artificial hormone that dramatically increased his strength and mass even as it distorted and disguised his features. The Hyde of literature was a good man turned evil by forces he could not control. Zabo was bad to begin with, a heartless criminal who used his metamorphic potion to indulge his greed and anti-social tendencies. *Just another super-crook*, Cap reminded himself. *Nothing to be afraid of.* Still, somewhere deep inside him, a small child faced the return of a recurring nightmare.

"You!" Hyde snarled. His voice was rough and guttural, as though his vocal cords were no longer entirely suited to human speech. *If a gorilla could talk, he'd sound like Hyde.* "They told me you would be here!" He snatched up a piece of the shattered metal gate and twisted it in his big, beefy hands. Tortured metal shrieked in protest as Hyde turned the steel fragment into a vicious-looking club. He lumbered toward Captain America with murder in his eyes.

Who? Cap wondered. Who had sent Hyde and the

Cobra here, and warned them about his involvement? He had no time to speculate about the growing mystery. Moving surprisingly fast for one so huge, Hyde swung his makeshift club at Captain America. Cap nimbly evaded the blow. Ducking under Hyde's arms, he delivered a powerful uppercut to the villain's chin. "Who sent you, Zabo?" he demanded along with the punch. "Modok? A.I.M.? The Serpent Society?"

It was like slugging a boulder. Cap felt the impact in his knuckles even through the padding in his glove. Worse, the punch only angered Hyde. "My name is Hyde!" he shouted. Spittle spewed from his mouth as he growled in fury. Tossing his club aside, he snatched at Captain America with both hands, but the hero jumped through Hyde's arms before they could close in on him. He somersaulted in the air and landed on his feet beyond Hyde's grasp. The trick, he recalled, was to keep out of Hyde's clutches. The Super-Soldier Serum had vastly increased Captain America's strength, but he was nowhere near Hyde's league. Given a chance, Hyde could easily crush Cap's bones to jelly.

"You might as well give up, Zabo. I've beaten you before and I can do it again."

"My name is Hyde! Hyde!" Bellowing like an enraged bull, the furious villain charged at Cap, who now stood at the very rim of the narrow trail. Behind him, the face of the mound dropped away steeply.

This doesn't make sense, Cap thought, his mind racing even as he faced off against the immense, mutated monstrosity that Calvin Zabo had become.

Mr. Hyde and the Cobra used to be partners in crime, before the Cobra hooked up with the Serpent Society, but that had been years ago. Constant backstabbing had turned the former allies into deadly enemies, so what were they both doing in Wakanda now?

Clawing the air with his misshapen hands, Hyde came at Captain America, who waited until the very last minute, then dived out of Hyde's way. The monster's momentum carried him over the outer edge of the trail. Cap heard Hyde's growl become a shriek of surprise as he tumbled down the side of the mound.

Cap smiled grimly. *I can't overpower that brute*, he thought, *so I'll have to outsmart him*. His smile faded, however, when he recalled T'Challa's dire situation. How was the Black Panther faring against the Cobra?

He bounded over to the brink of the cliff. In the moonlight, he saw the Panther and Cobra still ensnared in each other's grip. The Panther, standing squarely on both feet, had one hand around the Cobra's throat and one fist clenched tightly around the Cobra's right wrist. Incredibly, however, the criminal contortionist had managed to stick both his legs between T'Challa's and bent his legs backwards at the knees in order to wrap his lower legs around the Black Panther's neck from behind. It hurt Cap's legs just to look at the bizarre posture the unbelievably flexible Cobra had assumed; still, the Panther seemed to be holding his own for the moment.

His response turned to dismay when he spotted

the Cobra lifting his free hand towards the Panther's face. At this distance, Cap remembered rather than saw the spring-loaded missile launchers on the Cobra's wrists. "T'Challa!" he cried out, but he was too late. The Cobra fired another green dart, no doubt dipped in cobra venom, at the Panther's head. The tiny projectile barely missed T'Challa, nicking the tip of one of the Panther's decorative cat ears. A minute piece of black fabric fell like confetti to the jungle floor.

The Panther tried to twist out of range of the Cobra's wrist-weapon, but there was little he could do with both hands already engaged in fighting off the villain's attack and the Cobra's scaly, distended legs still exerting a stranglehold on Panther's neck. From the top of the trail, Cap watched in alarm as a noxious green gas spewed forth from the nozzles on the Cobra's wrists, the same gas that had almost certainly been used against T'Challa's guards not long ago. Cap quickly judged the distance between his current perch and jungle below. Was there any way he could get to the Panther in time? He tensed his muscles, ready to jump for it.

A massive hand clamped down on Cap's ankle, squeezing it so hard that Cap could feel the bones in his foot grinding together. Clenching his teeth against the pain, he looked down and saw Mr. Hyde's grotesque face staring up at him. His ruddy complexion had turned almost purple with rage.

Hyde had not fallen all the way down the hill after all. He must have halted his descent somehow and laboriously climbed back up to where Cap stood watching the Panther fight for his life. Now the monstrous berserker hung beneath the edge of the cliff, one hypertrophied hand clutching onto an outcropping of rock, the other holding Cap's ankle in a bone-crunching grip.

"Ha!" Hyde laughed maniacally. Foam bubbled at the corners of his mouth. His once-brown eyes were now completely shot with red. *Good Lord*, Cap thought, horrified by Hyde's crazed appearance. The effect of Zabo's potion on the chemist's body were terrible enough; Cap couldn't help wondering what years of chemical abuse had done to Hyde's brain.

"You lunatic!" Cap said, spitting out the words in defiance of the pain in his foot. "What in God's name have you turned yourself into?"

He tried to pull his foot free from Hyde's grasp, even if it meant leaving his crimson boot behind, but Hyde would not let go. Indeed he seemed more intent on crushing Cap's ankle than in rescuing himself from his own precarious situation. "Fool!" he bellowed. "No one escapes the wrath of Mr. Hyde!"

Cap kicked the ground with his free foot, sending a spray of dirt and gravel into Hyde's face. He pounded on Hyde's wrists with both fists, hoping to force Hyde to release his aching ankle. Hyde ignored his efforts. He sputtered through the dirt and froth caking his lips. Letting go of the jutting stone with his other hand, he started to slide back down the hill, pulling Captain America with him. Only his hold on Cap's boot kept him from tumbling down to the bottom.

Cap felt the full weight of Mr. Hyde tugging on

him. He was going to go over the edge—and then what? Hyde seemed impervious to pain. Nothing Cap could do seemed to stop him. He looked about desperately, searching for a rock, a piece of scrap metal, anything he might be able to use to pry or hammer Hyde's hand off of him.

But it was no good. Mr. Hyde's makeshift metal club had landed several feet away, over by the entrance to the tunnel. There was nothing but gravel in reach. Hyde slid down the mound a few more inches and Cap winced in pain. His ankle felt like it was in a vise. His foot blazed in agony as both Mr. Hyde and the relentless pull of gravity put unbearable pressure on his bones and tendons. He couldn't hold out much longer.

"Come on down!" Hyde laughed. "I'll meet you at the bottom—and squash you like a bug! I'll dance on your broken bones until you're nothing but pulp! I'll smash in your skull and feed your brains to the monkeys!" Psychotic merriment twisted Hyde's features, making his bestial face even more repellent than before. "Here, little monkeys, have a piece of America! Ha, ha!"

Cap's captive foot was yanked out from beneath him. He fell backwards, smashing his spine into the gravel-covered rock. Refusing to acknowledge the pain, he jerked himself up to a sitting position. He dug in his heels against gravity's relentless pull, striving to keep from being pulled over the edge of the precipice. Using both hands, he tried to pry Hyde's hand away from his ankle, finger by finger, but Hyde only tightened his fanatical grip.

"Better men than you have tried to kill me, Zabo," Captain America said, "and with a lot better dialogue."

"Hyde!" the brute protested. "Call me Hyde!"

I won't give you the satisfaction, Cap thought. *Hyde was a monster from my childhood, and that was a long, long time ago. You may end up killing me, Zabo, but I'll never buy into your twisted fantasy. Never.* Cap faced death with his head held high. Something snapped in his ankle and he bit down on his lip, determined not to cry out. *I still don't understand. What are Hyde and the Cobra doing together? They hate each other.* His boots slid closer to the brink, his heels digging twin trenches in the gravel. Hyde cackled incoherently.

"Cap!" another voice called out. It was the Black Panther, apparently still in the game. "Catch!"

Captain America looked up into the sky. There, soaring through the moonlit sky, was his shield, spinning like a flying saucer manufactured in the heart of the United States of America. Cap felt his heart leap up at the sight of his most faithful ally. He almost wanted to salute.

The shield arced through the sky, descending toward him. With reflexes honed by decades of practice and combat experience, he plucked it out of the air. He raised the shield above his head, holding onto to its edge with both hands. The unbreakable shield hovered above Hyde's wrist like the blade of a guillotine. Cap knew what he had to do, but even still he hesitated. Could he really go through with this, mutilate another human being, even when that human being was as despicable as Hyde? It was Hyde, he recalled, who had once beaten Jarvis, the Avengers' butler, to the point of death. How could any brute subject such a fine old gentleman to such unspeakable violence and still expect mercy for himself? Cap's fingers tightened around the rim of the shield. Miraculously lightweight though it was, the shield suddenly felt very heavy.

"Do it!" Hyde taunted him. Flecks of saliva sprayed from his lips. His teeth gnashed together. Blood-red eyes bulged from their sockets beneath bony, apelike brows. "I dare you! Hyde never surrenders. Hyde and the Cobra will conquer you all!"

Hyde *and* the Cobra? Cap felt an itch at the back of his mind. His eyes lighted up as the pieces finally came together in his brain. *Of course*, he thought. Hyde and the Cobra would *never* get back together, not after all the times they've betrayed each other, and the Serpent Society had nothing to do with this caper. "I was wrong," he admitted to Hyde. "You're not Calvin Zabo at all."

"I told you!" the monster howled, still hanging onto the hero's ankle. "I am Hyde! Hyde!"

"No," Cap corrected him. "You're an adaptoid." He brought the shield down. Hard.

The shield sliced through "Hyde's" wrist, severing his hand from his arm. The adaptoid plummeted down the side of the mound, bouncing off its craggy exterior. He landed with a crash at the foot of the mound. The monster sprawled lifelessly amidst the fronds and creepers, stunned and possibly unconscious. Cap glanced down at the pseudo-

Hyde's gorilla-like hand, still clutching his ankle. He expected to see sparking wires and machinery jutting from its severed wrist. To his disgust, the wound looked more organic than that: dark, viscous fluid dripped from the hand, gradually transforming into a thick green syrup that smelled like melted plastic. The massive fingers twitched convulsively before releasing his ankle. Cap breathed a sigh of relief; he had half-expected the five-fingered abomination to fight on with a life of its own.

A hoarse groan disturbed the night. Staring down into the jungle, Captain America saw Hyde's prostrate form begin to stir. *Good God, won't anything stop that beast?* The adaptoid seemed almost as relentless as the real Mr. Hyde. Cap considered the mountainous hillside stretching between him and his foe. Bumps and boulders studded the face of the mound. Was there any way he could start a landslide? Thinking quickly, he ran for the entrance to the mine. Hyde's club still rested upon the tunnel floor, partially hidden by the shadow cast by the lip of the mine. *Perhaps, I can use the club as a crowbar.*

It was heavier than it looked. Cap needed both hands to lift the twisted length of steel. Remembering how easily Hyde had swung the club—with one hand!—Cap marvelled again at the creature's superhuman strength. Captain America didn't feel outclassed, though; he'd pit his own strength and skill, sustained by his enduring faith in the American Dream, against any foe, no matter how powerful. He started to charge back to the brink of the trail, then his gaze fell upon the stacks of wooden crates he'd spotted before. Dropping the club, he hurried to investigate the crates, a plan forming in his mind. Could he really be so lucky . . . ?

Yes! The crates contained blasting caps and sticks of dynamite, no doubt intended to be used in the further excavation of the vibranium mine. Cap snatched up a handful of dynamite and a few of the caps, and raced for the cliff. His hands hastily assembled a small but workable bomb. *Now this is the kind of technology I'm used to*, he thought with some satisfaction. He remembered handling similar explosives behind the front lines at Normandy. *Time for some good, old-fashioned fireworks!*

He hurled the dynamite at the edge of the trail, exactly where the adaptoid's amputated hand now rested atop the gravel, then threw his entire body in the opposite direction. The blast went off almost immediately. Cap felt a wave of concussive force carry him away from the site of the explosion, although the noise of the detonation struck him as strangely muffled. *It must be the vibranium*, he thought, *absorbing the noise of the bang.*

Noise or no noise, the bomb did the job. Flying through the air, Cap saw the explosion tear apart one side of the mound. Rocks and dirt were thrown up into the sky, then came crashing down on the side of the mound, joining a tremendous landslide that thundered down the hillside—straight towards the bogus Hyde. Cap glimpsed the monstrous adaptoid lurching to his feet, his savage face contorted by shock and fury, his severed wrist spraying fluid and plastic, before the rockslide careened into Hyde, concealing him in a cloud of dust and debris and carrying him away. *You wanted vibranium*, Cap thought grimly. *Have a couple of tons. . . .*

Twisting his body in the air, Captain America positioned the concave underside of his shield directly beneath him only heartbeats before he came crashing into the side of the mound, several yards east of the rockslide. Drawing his knees up against his chest, and holding onto the sides of the shield for dear life, he crouched in the shallow bowl of the shield, riding it like a sled down the face of the mound.

It was a wild and bumpy ride. The shield skipped off boulders and craggy outcroppings of rock, sometimes going airborne for seconds at a time, gaining speed as it rocketed down the hillside. The wind blew in Cap's face so hard that he had to grit his teeth and squint against the dust and dirt being thrown up. The shield spun like a top so that a 360-degree view of the mound and the jungle raced before his eyes. His heart pounded. Bumps and jolts rattled his bones. It was terrifying and exhilarating at the same time.

And then it was over. The shield reached the bottom of the hill and slid through the underbrush for over fifty yards before slowing to a halt. Cap rose slowly, more than a little dizzy, and stepped out of the shield. The dizziness passed quickly, a testament to his amazing recuperative powers, but his injured foot still hurt when he put his weight upon it. He lifted his shield from the tall grass, blossoms, and shrubs and inspected its bright, multi-colored surface. It wasn't even scuffed.

"Cap?" The Black Panther strode gracefully through the underbrush, alive and quite evidently intact. His midnight-black costume was torn and one ear of his mask was ripped and hanging loosely from top of his head, giving T'Challa the appearance of a grizzled old jungle cat who had seen more than his share of nature in tooth and claw. "How are you, my friend?"

"Okay, I guess," Cap grunted. He took a step toward the Panther and winced. "I think Hyde may have broken my ankle, though." He glanced around quickly. The Cobra was nowhere in sight and neither was his grotesque partner-in-crime. *Or reasonable facsimiles thereof*, he corrected himself. "Hyde?" he asked of T'Challa.

"Over there," the Black Panther said, pointing to a huge pile of broken rocks lying at the base of the towering vibranium mound. Clouds of dust still drifted above the rockpile, and tiny pebbles rolled down from the top of pile, disappearing into the cracks and crevices between the larger chunks of stone. Silence clung to the pile as well, where once the ferocious growls of the artificial Hyde had violated the sanctity of the night. "More of a monument than he deserves," the Panther commented, "although appropriately lacking in beauty."

Cap wondered if the creature could conceivably still be alive under the rocks, if an adaptoid could truly be said to live. "If I were you I'd have that rock pile carefully dismantled, stone by stone, by an armed security team. Just in case.'' He explained to the Panther the true nature of the being who had appeared to be the infamous Mr. Hyde. Cap looked over the scene again, taking in the Panther's less-than-pristine appearance and the puzzling disappearance of the ''Cobra,'' whom he assumed had been an adaptoid as well. ''What about you?'' he asked T'Challa. ''I thought the Cobra gassed you?''

''I've gotten very good at holding my breath,'' the Black Panther explained. ''Remind me to tell you about the time a fiend named Solomon Prey buried me alive.''

''I see,'' Cap said. Apparently, the demands of kingship had not entirely eliminated adventure from the Black Panther's life—nor diminished his considerable survival skills. ''And the Cobra? Or rather that adaptoid *duplicate* of the Cobra?''

The Panther shook his head sadly. He took Cap's arm and draped it over his own shoulder, helping to take Cap's weight off his broken ankle. ''Come over here,'' he said, leading Cap towards the vibranium mound. The Star-Spangled Avenger limped beside his friend to the narrow crevice where his shield had lodged right before his fight with the artificial Hyde. The crevice was about six inches wide and penetrated deep into the mound itself. No human being alive could have slipped through that skinny crack.

Except, Cap realized, *a creature who, like the genuine Cobra, could twist his super-flexible body through just about any opening.* ''Blast,'' he swore, although he knew that he shouldn't be too surprised.

The Cobra, real or otherwise, was nothing if not one of the the world's best escape artists.

"This crevice connects with any number of underground caverns and fault lines," the Panther said. "If he can squeeze through cracks of that size, and I wouldn't have believed it if I hadn't seen it with my own eyes, then he could be anywhere by now."

"Yes," Cap agreed. He could easily imagine the sinuous Cobra working his way through an intricate maze of subterranean fissures, ultimately emerging from the earth miles from where he eluded Cap and the Panther. When would the adaptoid rendezvous with Modok, who had presumably sent him to Wakanda, and was there any way to stop him? For the moment, he and T'Challa appeared to have run out of options. "He's gone," Cap said. "With the vibranium."

The two heroes considered all the implications of Cobra's escape as they stood quietly in the moonlight beneath the scarred face of the vibranium mound. The monkeys chattering in the treetops seemed to mock their efforts, as if rooting for Modok and his adaptoid operatives. Finally, after several long minutes, the Panther broke the silence. "Come," he said. "Let's return to the palace and have that ankle looked at. My healers are well trained in both Western medicine and traditional Wakandan remedies. Some of our native herbs have truly astounding restorative properties. Trust me, I've found them quite invaluable over the years."

"That sounds fine with me," Cap said. Despite this latest setback, he wasn't about to give up yet.

Things had sometimes looked bleak during the Big One, too, but the courageous hearts of brave men and women had prevailed in the end. The sooner he got back on his feet, the sooner he could take the fight to Modok.

I just hope, he prayed, *that Iron Man and War Machine are having better luck than we are.*

CHAPTER

6

FRIDAY. 3:05 AM. TRANSIA MEAN TIME.

War Machine zoomed over Europe. Twelve microturbines, six in each iron-plated boot, generated over two thousand pounds of thrust, propelling the armored figure through the sky at speeds in excess of 250 miles per hour. Exhaust fumes jetted from the soles of his boots as he flew in a rigid horizontal position, arms outstretched before him for maximum aerodynamic efficiency. His built-in computer system monitored his surroundings on various visual and electromagnetic frequencies, protecting him from unwanted collisions although he was unlikely to encounter any birds or flying debris at his current altitude, roughly twenty thousand feet above sea level. *Don't want to bump into any passenger flights, though,* Jim Rhodes thought, encased in his metallic alter ego.

The War Machine armor resembled Iron Man's, albeit with different coloring and a lot more visible weaponry. Designed by Tony Stark for heavy-duty combat situations, the armor bristled with a rocket launcher, minicannon, chain gun, flamethrower, and other artillery. A matte-black finish covered the chestplate, boots, and gauntlets while his arms, legs, and faceplate had a distinct silvery sheen. No brightly-colored Golden Avenger, War Machine was the intimidating embodiment of modern military hardware, all packed into a single one-man arsenal.

War Machine wondered how many military treaties he was violating just by zipping through the airspace of the various countries below.

Tough, he thought. Sometimes the greater good meant breaking a few rules; that's what War Machine was all about. As a human rights activist, Jim Rhodes tried to work within the system, relying on politics and public relations whenever possible. Sometimes, though, diplomacy broke down and direct action was required to avert or avenge some ghastly crime against humanity. Then, as now, Jim donned his black-and-silver armor and meted out justice first hand. A.I.M., after all, was hardly likely to respond to pamphlets or petitions.

His chain gun and missile launcher were stowed in their standby position, locked in place upon his back. War Machine didn't anticipate any trouble right away. A heavy layer of cloud cover concealed the landmass below. Dark, turbulent thunderheads billowed ominously, lit up sporadically by strobelike flashes of white electricity. War Machine flew above the storm, intent upon his mission.

As he rocketed through the night, he reviewed the available information on his destination. Tony had e-mailed all the Avengers' files on Wundagore Mountain to Jim before War Machine left Los Angeles; now, micro-TV units built into his headpiece projected both text and images so that the files appeared to float in front of his face. The projectors responded to the slightest movements of his eyes, allowing him to scroll through the material at will.

It was quite a story, he conceded. Tony hadn't

been kidding when he said that Wundagore Mountain had a long and colorful history. So far, Transia had escaped the bloody civil wars that had engulfed so much of the Balkans over the last few years, but Wundagore had seen more than its fair share of life-or-death struggles. For an overgrown hill in an obscure East European nation, this particular peak had been the site of a surprising number of momentous and frequently mind-boggling events.

According to the files, the saga began in the sixth century A.D. when Morgan Le Fay (yes, *the* Morgan Le Fay, he read, the sorcerous half sister of King Arthur himself) confined the elder god Chthon to the very substance of the mountain. Centuries later, an enigmatic scientist built a massive research complex, also known as Wundagore, atop the mountain in order to conduct radical experiments in artificially accelerated evolution. Although the scientist's true name had remained unknown, he eventually assumed the title and guise of the High Evolutionary. A sort of high-tech Dr. Moreau, he successfully created a race of sentient, humanoid beings evolved from apes, dogs, and even a cow. The High Evolutionary and his animal-people eventually abandoned the planet to seek an unknown destiny in outer space, but not before Wundagore played a crucial role in the lives and careers of Earth's various super humans.

Miss America, a heroine of World War II, ultimately died on Wundagore, giving birth to a stillborn monstrosity. Years later, one of the High Evolutionary's experiments transformed a young girl named

Jessica Drew into Spider-Woman, the first of two different women who had fought evil under that name. Wundagore also witnessed the birth of former Avengers Quicksilver and the Scarlet Witch, mutant heroes who were only later revealed to be the long-lost children of Magneto, arch-foe of the X-Men.

Nor was the High Evolutionary the only individual to discover the unique radioactive and mystical properties of the mountain's native earth; the Puppet Master, a longtime adversary of the Fantastic Four, had sculpted his mind-controlling mannequins from clay stolen from Wundagore Mountain.

Whew, War Machine thought, as the data scrolled past his startled eyes. Spider-Woman, the Avengers, the X-Men, the Fantastic Four—were there any super heroes around whose fates had not been linked to Wundagore in some way? *Guess it must be my turn.* He hoped he'd fare better than the unfortunate Miss America. *I wonder if Cap knew her. . . .*

In recent years, after the departure of the High Evolutionary and his creations, the abandoned complex had been reduced to ruins by a series of super-powered battles, including, most recently, a clash between the Avengers and the Acolytes, a cult of mutant terrorists devoted to the cause of Magneto. Since then, in theory, both ruins and mountain had been left alone—until A.I.M. decided to get its grubby hands on some of that rare, radioactive earth. *Not if I have anything say about it.*

To be honest, he found parts of Wundagore's recorded history a little hard to believe. That whole business about Morgan Le Fay sounded more like a fairy tale than anything else. Like Tony Stark, he tended to take magic and mysticism with a grain of salt. Still, he reminded himself, he'd seen stranger things in his career as War Machine. Besides, if Iron Man and the other Avengers took it seriously enough to include it in their official database, then maybe there was something to it. . . .

His ruminations were interrupted by the sight of a craggy, snow-capped mountain rising out of the clouds. Switching off the text display, War Machine consulted his suit's navigational computer. Yep, this was the place all right: Wundagore Mountain. He prayed that he'd arrived in time to prevent Modok from completing his recipe for the energy chip.

Storm clouds, black and billowy, hid most of the mountain from sight. Only the very top of Wundagore Mountain poked out from beneath the roiling clouds. Lightning flashed every few minutes, followed by booming peals of thunder that shook Jim even through his suit. He turned down the volume on his audio receptors. Drawing closer to the mountain, he saw that the peak still bore the scars of the cataclysmic battles that had been fought upon it. The very tip of the mountain had crumbled inward to form an immense crater, giving the mountain the look of a long-dormant volcano. Smaller craters, now filled with snow, marred the face of Wundagore Mountain; it was amazing, he thought, how much damage a couple dozen super beings could do.

He descended into the churning maelstrom of the storm. Fierce winds whipped against him while lightning crackled all around. Grateful for the electrical insulation built into his suit, War Machine took advantage of the storm to recharge his armor; energy conversion units in the outer layers of the suit absorbed the raw electricity surging through the thunder clouds and filled his capacitors to their utmost. *Too bad I can't recharge myself so easily.* The long flight across Europe had taken a lot out of him.

War Machine dropped out of the clouds. Icy rain mixed with snow cascaded against his armor, but the watertight suit kept him warm and dry. His chest beam cast a brilliant halogen light over the scene below. He cruised over the snow-covered mountain, watching carefully for any indication of suspicious activity. At first he spotted nothing unusual, then he noticed some flickering lights on one side of the mountain, just above the treeline where a dense pine forest gave way to unbroken sheets of white. According to the map loaded into his computerized navigational system, the lights were coming from exactly where the High Evolutionary's laboratory had once stood. *Ground zero*, War Machine thought. *I might have known.* Bootjets firing, leaving a trail of exhaust across the sky, he zoomed toward the lights.

Traces of the devastated installation still protruded from the snow. Twisted steel girders supported empty air or else lay uselessly amidst the snowdrifts. Large chunks of rusting, rime-coated metal were strewn haphazardly along the edges of yet another gaping crater. War Machine spotted a cracked computer monitor half-buried in the snow, along with what looked like part of an operating table, but most of the debris had been rendered unrecognizable by time and happenstance. The wreckage provided far too many hiding spots, War Machine noted unhappily. The ruins of Wundagore looked like the perfect spot for an ambush. He flew slowly over the crater, but he could not locate the source of the mysterious lights he had glimpsed from a distance. This close to the ruins, he could see only the shadows cast by the demolished steel structures.

To make matters worse, the lightning, thunder, and snow interfered with his scanners, making it all but impossible to detect any telltale life signs amidst this atmospheric tumult; how was he supposed to detect a heartbeat or a body temperature in the middle of an electrical storm and blizzard? *So much for aerial reconnaissance.* He'd have to search the ruins on foot.

Steam rose where his boots sank into the snow. The wintry, white carpet was packed at least seven inches deep. He looked around for tracks, but the falling flakes had quickly eliminated whatever footprints his quarry may have left. He trudged through the snow toward the center of the crater, his halogen spotlight showing him the way. Thunder rumbled overhead as he walked beneath and between two semitoppled walls. The bottom half of one rusty steel wall was supporting another wall that had fallen on top of it, forming a triangular tunnel between them. Winter winds had carried the snow into the tunnel, covering the ground with over three inches of frozen precipitation.

War Machine was halfway through the tunnel when he heard the unmistakable sound of heavy footsteps on the other side of the sloping metal wall directly above him. *Uh-oh.* Jim took a deep breath. Acting on instincts honed in his years as an Army pilot, he threw himself to the right.

A laser beam, neon red, pierced the propped-up metal wall, narrowly missing War Machine. The beam sizzled past him to burn a hole in the snow in front of his boots. *That was too close for comfort.* He wasn't about to give the shooter another chance.

Servomotors whirred within his armor as War Machine reached up with both hands to give the wall a tremendous push. Super-amplified strength overcame the fallen wall's inertia and sent it toppling backwards, away from War Machine and on top of the would-be sniper. War Machine heard a hoarse cry of surprise, then the ringing crash of the wall smashing down on something hard and metallic. His bootjets flared to life, lifting him six feet off the ground. A retractable minicannon emerged from the gauntlet on his right hand.

"All right, whoever you are!" he bellowed. The microphone in his helmet amplified and distorted his voice; he sounded like Darth Vader in a bad mood. "Don't try anything tricky. I have you covered."

A groan came from beneath the wall. For a second, War Machine wondered if he'd have to lift the wall off the sniper himself. Then five robotic fingers, seemingly encased in overlapping rings of metal, curled around the top of the wall. With a shove and a grunt, the heavy steel wall was lifted off the snow and a figure dragged himself out from under the huge sheet of metal. Lightning flashed in the distance.

War Machine saw the light coming through a dime-sized hole in the wall; the sniper's laser had cut through the solid steel plate in less than a heartbeat. He didn't want to think about what the laser might have been able to do to his armor. Tearing his gaze away from the hole, War Machine was surprised to see exactly who had fired upon him. "Holy shit," he said out loud. "Deathlok?"

The figure before him, climbing back onto his feet, couldn't have been anyone else. A cyborg developed by Roxxon Industries, one of Tony Stark's less scrupulous competitors, to be the ultimate soldier of the future, Deathlok was a frightening mixture of man and machine. The cyborg's face illustrated his dual nature dramatically: one half of his face was a polished metal skull, with a lighted camera lens where his left eye should have been; the other half resembled a dead man's rotting visage, the skin grey and pasty, his hair nothing but a thin layer of stubble covering the right side of his scalp. An insulated electrical wire ran along the temple of his human side, connecting the optic nerve in his one remaining eye to the computer lodged beside what was left of his brain. A dull red uniform covered Deathlok's torso. His prosthetic limbs consisted of reinforced steel cables approximating the musculature of a well-conditioned human body. It was an unnerving sight: scarred human tissue mercilessly welded to lifeless machinery. *I just call myself a War Machine. Deathlok's the real thing, poor bastard.*

He was confused, however, by the cyborg's unexpected appearance here, not to mention Deathlok's unprovoked laser attack. Despite his horrific appearance, War Machine knew, Deathlok was one of the good guys. He and War Machine had fought together to liberate the African nation of Imaya from a brutal dictator. Although designed to be a weapon of destruction, Michael Collins—the man trapped inside Deathlok's ghastly form—had long ago overcome Roxxon's programming and subjected the cyborg's augmented abilities to the restraints of his own human conscience. War Machine didn't get it. Shooting people without warning was not Deathlok's style.

"What the hell are you doing here, Michael?" War Machine demanded. "You could have killed me."

"Don't sell yourself short, buddy," Deathlok replied. The cyborg's voice was as hoarse and raspy as a cancer victim. His dead skin smelled faintly of formaldehyde. "I'm sure your armor's tougher than that. I'm sorry about the close call, though. What with the dark and the storm, I thought you were one of the bad guys."

"A.I.M.?" War Machine's jets cooled, slowly lowering him to the ground. The heat of the boots's exhaust turned the snow to slush.

"Who else?" Deathlok replied. The human half of his face made a disgusted expression. "I uncovered a link between Roxxon's 'dirty tricks' division and Advanced Idea Mechanics. The trail led me here."

Sounds plausible enough, War Machine thought. Unlike Stark Enterprises, Roxxon seldom let ethics get in the way of profits. "Seen anyone snooping around?"

Deathlok shook his head. "Just you so far. But let me show you what I have found." He removed a palm-sized electronic instrument from a pack on his back. "A portable geiger counter," he explained. "I had just come up with some promising readings when I heard you stomping through the snow. I assumed you were one of Modok's agents, following me to get to the uranium."

"Uranium?" War Machine asked. He must have overlooked that in his research. "Is that all?"

"Not just any uranium," Deathlok said. "Apparently, it's some sort of unique isotope that's only found on this mountain. It's supposed to have mystical properties, too."

"So I've heard." War Machine activated his own radiation sensors. The readouts indicated a sizable concentration of radioactive material less than a meter to the east. "I guess A.I.M. can't just dig up any old bucket of dirt to get what they want."

"It's not that easy, lucky for us," Deathlok said. He raised the miniature geiger counter. The device emitted a clicking noise which grew louder as Deathlok pointed it towards the east. "The way I figure it, we find the uranium, we find Modok's stooges."

"Sounds good to me," War Machine said. "Come on."

"Mind if I recover my gun first?" Deathlok asked. War Machine noted that the thick rubber holster attached to the cyborg's hip was empty. Deathlok must have lost his weapon when War Machine pushed the wall down on top of him. War Machine walked over to the fallen wall and grabbed it by the side. The thick layer of ice coating the metal wall made it slippery and hard to hold onto; still he succeeded in lifting it off the snow with one hand. Deathlok's laser pistol was there all right, pressed into the frozen snowbank.

"Go ahead," he said. Deathlok retrieved his weapon. He shook the snow off it, then inspected the gun with both his human and cybernetic eyes. "You ready now?" War Machine asked.

Deathlok hefted the futuristic-looking pistol. A bloodthirsty gleam came into his organic eye. "Yeah," he said with a feral grin. "Now I am."

Damn, Michael, when did you become such a gun nut? Jim frowned, then caught himself. *Look who's talking*, he thought ruefully. *The walking ammo dump.* "Let's go," he said.

Following the radiation signals, the two armored soldiers trekked through the snow. The clicking of the geiger counter led them to a circular depression at the center of the crater. *Ground zero*, War Machine thought again. He wondered who had caused the explosion that had so obviously carved this crater out of the face of Wundagore. The Avengers? The X-Men? *Anybody I know?* It was odd to realize just how many of his personal acquaintances were capable of blasting a mountain apart.

"Right here," Deathlok announced. "This is where the readings are strongest." War Machine's own sensors confirmed Deathlok's conclusion. *Makes sense.* Most of the topsoil here had already been blown away, exposing the uranium ore underneath the surface.

Deathlok drew his pistol and fired on the spot. The fiery red laser beam melted the snow covering the depression. Steam rose from the beam's target and tiny rivulets of icewater dug canals in the frozen crust around the melting snow. "What are you doing?" War Machine asked.

"I want to get a sample of this stuff," Deathlok said. "See what all the fuss is about." Returning the laser pistol to its holster, he knelt beside the depression and dug his bionic fingers into the exposed earth. The artificial hand easily ripped out a fistful of a dark, claylike substance. The geiger counter in Deathlok's other hand started clicking like mad as the cyborg placed the uranium in a storage compartment mounted to his shoulders. War Machine reminded himself that Michael Collins had been a scientist before Roxxon turned him into Deathlok; still, it made him uneasy to see Deathlok shovel handful after handful of the rare substance into his pack.

"Do you really need that much?" he asked.

"This?" Deathlok responded. "We're talking less than five pounds probably."

Before War Machine could reply, thunder rumbled once more, and he felt the arctic chill of the mountain seeping through his armor, into his bones. He adjusted the temperature controls of his suit, directing more energy to the internal heating units, but it didn't seem to do any good. He shivered inside his iron casement. "Is it just my imagination," he asked Deathlok, "or is it really getting colder out here?"

"Cold enough," the cyborg answered cryptically. He placed one last handful of uranium ore in his storage compartment, then sealed it shut with a loud snap. He stared past War Machine, as if addressing someone standing further away. "Now," he said.

Something slammed into War Machine from behind. He fell forward into the snow. Dazed and surprised, it took him a moment to recover. He felt a burning sensation at the back of his neck. Heat induction circuits in the armor tried to disperse the heat, but not fast enough; the metal neckpiece connecting his helmet to the rest of the armor was growing increasingly hot to the touch. *Deathlok's laser*, he realized. *He's trying to burn through my armor.*

"What kind of dirty game are you playing, Michael?" War Machine grunted through the pain, confused and angered by the cyborg's treachery. "Why are you doing this?"

"That's my little secret, buddy," Deathlok replied. "Too bad you'll never figure it out."

He had a point, War Machine admitted. Now was not the time to figure out Deathlok's motives. He started to stand up, only to experience another jolting blast that knocked him to the ground. Deathlok was not alone, he realized, but who else was attacking him? These force blasts felt familiar, like he'd endured them before. The searing pain at the back of his neck made it hard to concentrate. He had to do something fast, or Deathlok's laser beam would penetrate his armor—and slice right through his throat.

Rather than trying to stand up again, War Machine simply activated his bootjets.

Rockets flamed beneath his heels, and War Machine took off straight across the ground, tearing through drifts of accumulated snow and ice like a runaway snowmobile. Zooming facedown through the ruins of Wundagore, War Machine waited until he was at least a hundred yards away from his foes, then he veered up off the ground into the sky. The wind and falling snow pelted his armor, but the harsh weather did not slow him down for more than a second. A double loop followed by a barrel row brought him flying back toward Deathlok and—

"What the hell?" War Machine couldn't believe what he was seeing.

Cold Warrior?

Increasing the magnification of his telescopic lenses, he zoomed in on the pale white figure standing near Deathlok. He saw another cyborg soldier, of even cruder design than Deathlok. Sheets of grey metal were bolted to the man's body in no discernible pattern. An icy white glaze coated him from head to toe, while labels written in the Cyrillic alphabet betrayed the cyborg's Russian origins. A halo of frozen air seemed to shimmer around him. The figure looked just like the crazed Russian super soldier War Machine had battled several months ago. *But that's impossible. They told me he was dead. I killed him.*

The Cold Warrior had been the willing victim of a Soviet medical experiment in the 1950s. Preserved in cryogenic suspension until recently, he had never accepted the fall of the Soviet Union. The Cold Warrior could drain heat from his environment and convert the kinetic energy into blasts of concussive force. *I knew I'd felt those blasts before.* Unfortunately, the same circuitry that gave the Cold Warrior his offensive capabilities had also sustained his unnatural existence. When War Machine, assisted on that mission by the super hero known as Hawkeye, defeated Cold Warrior, he unwittingly ended the Russian cyborg's life.

Then again, he reminded himself, *I never saw the body.* The Cold Warrior could have faked his death—and apparently did. But what was Deathlok doing with a fanatic like the Cold Warrior? It made no sense, although Jim felt surprisingly relieved to see Cold Warrior alive and well. As a semiprofessional War Machine, he already had too many deaths on his conscience.

"Welcome back, Frosty," he announced through his loudspeaker. "Let's rumble."

Ready for combat, he rocketed through the wind and snow. High speed positioning rails on his back shifted his missile launcher and electric chain gun from their standby positions to their fully active modes. They locked in place upon his shoulders. The muzzle of his minicannon extended from his right gauntlet. His other glove could produce either a laser-powered saber or flamethrower. Both functions were fully operational. Automated loading systems offered him a wide variety of ammunition and missiles, including everything from tear gas to armor-piercing rockets with spent uranium cores. In short, War Machine was loaded for bear and ready for anything either Deathlok or Cold Warrior could throw at him. *Last time*, he thought, keeping his sights on Cold Warrior, *I needed Hawkeye's help to whomp your butt. This time you're all mine. . . .*

Cold Warrior saw him coming. "Imperialist stooge!" he shouted over the thunder in a heavy Russian accent. "Running dog lackey of the capitalist oppressor!"

That clinches it. This has to be Cold Warrior. No one else talks like that these days. "Give it a rest, comrade!" War Machine said, increasing the volume on his speaker system. "The Berlin Wall has come down. The Cold War is over!"

"Never! Not while I live to embody the spirit of the Glorious October Revolution!" The Russian cyborg raised both fists and pointed them at the oncoming War Machine. The air around his fists seemed to thicken and waver, like the ripples one sometimes sees above hot blacktop. Then a burst of pale white energy leaped from the Cold Warrior's hands, heading straight for War Machine. "Feel the icy rage of the proletariat!" he cried. "You have nothing to lose but your miserable, counter-revolutionary life!"

What did he do? War Machine wondered. *Swallow a truckload of Marxist pamphlets?* Refusing to deviate from his course, War Machine braced for impact. Cold Warrior's blast slammed into War Machine, throwing him backwards a few feet. His armor absorbed most of the jolt, though, leaving the man inside largely unharmed. Shaking off the punch, he dove again for Cold Warrior, weapons blazing. The electric chain gun mounted on his left shoulder fired multiple rounds of 3.9mm, caseless, electrically-primed ammunition. Each bullet contained its own rocket-powered propulsion unit, as well as a drop of restrained mercury that vaporized on impact with a target, propelling the spent-uranium core through just about any armor on the planet. War Machine sincerely doubted that Cold Warrior's crude, Krus-chev-era armor plating could stand up to state-of-the-art firepower.

It's ironic, he thought. *Cold Warrior, Deathlok, and I are all war machines: human weapons designed expressly for combat.* He clenched his fists as he flew at his enemies. *May the best war machine win.*

"Incoming!" he taunted his adversaries.

At over a dozen rounds a second, a barrage of bullets tore up the snow and frozen earth in front of Cold Warrior and Deathlok. *That's just a demonstration. Don't make me use this on you.* A repulsor blast from his left gauntlet knocked Deathlok off his feet, while the missile launcher over his right shoulder fired a projectile tear gas canister at Cold Warrior.

"Give it up, boys!" he called out, his amplified voice drowning out the thunder. "I have you both outgunned." He found himself hoping desperately that the pair of cyborgs would take the hint and surrender. *Please, don't force me to kill you.*

While both Iron Man and Captain America rigorously refused to kill, War Machine took a more pragmatic approach to crime-fighting. Although he tried to avoid taking another person's life, he was willing to do so in self-defense—or to prevent a greater atrocity. This time around, though, he found himself determined not to resort to deadly force. Deathlok, no matter what madness had possessed him, was an old friend and ally. And Cold Warrior . . . well, War Machine really didn't want to have to kill the man *twice*.

"If I were you, I'd surrender right now." His amplified voice boomed above the thunder and lightning.

The tear gas missile detonated a few feet away from Cold Warrior. The pale cyborg staggered backward a couple of paces as noxious orange fumes poured out of the missile. War Machine expected to hear Cold Warrior coughing and sneezing helplessly, but something else happened instead: the tear gas fumes proved unable to penetrate the aura of frozen air surrounding Cold Warrior. The minute the orange smoke came within a few inches of the Soviet madman, the fumes began to drift down to the ground, staining the snow an ugly shade of orange without inflicting any harm on Cold Warrior. With a shock War Machine realized that the Russian cyborg had drained the kinetic energy from the gas, causing it to shrink and solidify rather than expand. *Hmmm. This could be trickier than I thought.*

"Hah!" Cold Warrior barked. "Is that the best you can do, bourgeois pawn? A true worker's hero has no need to fear the petty policeman of a decadent, capitalist regime. I will bury you!" He fired another concussive blast at War Machine.

War Machine met the attack head on, then returned fire with his repulsor rays. "Put a sock in it," War Machine taunted him. "You people couldn't even catch moose and squirrel."

He kept one eye on Deathlok. The other cyborg had scrambled back onto his feet and was now speaking into what looked like a communicator on his wrist. Jim furrowed his brow in concentration. What was Deathlok up to now? Calling for reinforcements? War Machine didn't want to find out. He fired another tear gas missile, this time at Deathlok. The cyborg's computerized reflexes reacted immediately to the new threat. Roxxon had clearly gotten their money's worth where Deathlok's targeting computer was concerned; his laser beam sliced the missile in half before it came anywhere near him. Tear gas spilled harmlessly from the bisected missile, contaminating the air between War Machine and Deathlok and hiding the American cyborg from sight. War Machine made sure his own ventilation system was closed, just in case the wind blew any of his own gas back at him.

"You can't hide from me, Michael!" he shouted at Deathlok. "I've got sensors here that make your implants look like tinker toys."

The repulsor rays had stunned Cold Warrior, but not stopped him. *Damn.* Another blast of force pounded his chestplate. The halogen spotlight flickered briefly before coming back online. War Machine's repulsors jolted Cold Warrior right back, but the Russian cyborg stayed on his feet, filling the chill night air with outdated rhetoric. "From each, according to their abilities!" he ranted. "To each, according to their doom!"

War Machine did his best to tune out Cold Warrior's seemingly inexhaustible supply of warmed-over propaganda, preferring to focus on his adversary's fighting abilities. Apparently, Cold Warrior's freezing aura functioned as a sort of force field, draining the energy from War Machine's assaults—and converting it into a potent counterattack. *He's turning my own firepower against me.* He deactivated his repulsors and took evasive action to dodge Cold Warrior's latest force-blast. "Screw that," he muttered. This situation called for a whole new strategy.

He hovered several yards above the snowy ruins, hopefully out of range of Cold Warrior's energy-sapping field. A force blast zipped harmlessly over his head. "Your aim's as misguided as your politics," he told Cold Warrior. "You should have stayed frozen in your time capsule." Captain America, he recalled, had also spent decades in suspended animation, but Cap had managed to adjust and come to grips with modern times; Cold Warrior remained mired in the international rivalries of the past. War Machine almost felt sorry for the deluded cyborg.

But what is Deathlok's problem?

"Foolish American," Cold Warrior shouted back. "The future belongs to me. The inexorable forces of dialectical materialism will compel the true communist state into being. You are doomed to the dustbin of history—and to the gnawing criticism of the rats!''

Another frigid blast of energy came at War Machine. He deftly evaded it—only to feel a sudden burst of heat sear the sole of his foot. *Deathlok's damn laser,* he realized instantly. *Hell, they've got me in a crossfire.* The flying jets in his left boot cut out abruptly, and he began spinning in the air. *Deathlok's deliberately targeting my bootjets, the sneaky sonofabitch.* He tried to arrest his spin, using the repulsor units in his palms to compensate for the lack of propulsive thrust from the damaged boot. It was trickier than it sounded, like walking on stilts with a rocket on your back—and in the middle of a firefight.

Cold Warrior and Deathlok took advantage of War Machine's flight difficulties to turn him into a moving target. A concussive bolt struck War Machine in the side, bruising his ribs, while a crimson laser beam gave him another hot foot, this time in his other boot. Despite himself, War Machine was impressed by Deathlok's aim. *I don't know what sort of sighting mechanism Deathlok's got built into that phony eye of his*, he thought, *but Stark had better look into getting the specs.*

The jets in his working boot conked out. For a heartbeat, War Machine hoped that the microturbines's automatic restart system would kick in, but no such luck. He dropped out of the sky, accelerating toward the snow-caked wreckage. As he fell, he fired his repulsor beams at random, attempting to give himself some cover. Maybe he'd even get lucky and blast either Deathlok or Cold Warrior where it would hurt most.

He hit the top of a huge, rusty generator, then bounced off into a snowdrift. The pile of snow cushioned his fall a bit, but the crash landing still rattled his teeth and bones. "Die!" Cold Warrior shouted from somewhere far too close by. A heavy weight landed on his back, driving his faceplate further into the snow. "Death to the oppressive tool of American industry!"

Cold Warrior's hands clamped down on War Machine's shoulders, shoving him deeper into the accumulated ice and snow. The cyborg's metal-plated knees scraped against the side of War Machine's armor. Even worse, Jim realized, the minigun and rocket launcher on his shoulders were pointed the wrong way, into the ground. *Great, I couldn't blow Frosty away even if I wanted to.*

A numbing, glacial cold seeped into his armor, leeching the strength from his body and the power from his suit: Cold Warrior's doing, no doubt. He tried to shake the crazed Soviet off him, but the servomotors in his armor refused to come to life. The suit's environmental controls hummed loudly, struggling to keep Jim warm inside the armor, but Cold Warrior drained the heat even faster than the suit could manufacture it; the energy-draining field quickly overloaded his armor's thermocouple, plunging the man inside into a frozen torture chamber. *Brrrr*, War Machine thought, shivering violently, *I haven't felt this cold since*—his mind raced backward through his memories—*well, since the last time Cold Warrior had his icy mitts on me.*

That time Hawkeye had come to the rescue with a well-timed thermite arrow, directed not at Cold Warrior but at War Machine himself. The flaming arrow had restored strength and mobility to War Machine when his armor had seemed hopelessly frozen. As far as he knew, Hawkeye was nowhere near Transia tonight, but maybe he could manage some fireworks of his own.

It took all his remaining strength, but War Machine managed to lift his left arm enough to point his own gauntlet at himself. A frozen elbow joint shrieked in protest. A thin layer of hoarfrost cracked over his arm, then quickly reformed, locking the arm in its new position. He had lost all feeling in his fingers and toes. A blinking red alert suddenly flashed before Jim's eyes: WARNING. SYSTEM FAILURE IMMINENT.

Now or never. With a cybernetic command, he activated the concealed flamethrower in his left gauntlet. A blazing stream of bright orange fire gushed from his wrist, melting the ice over his armor and restoring warmth and sensation to his aching flesh. Energy conversion circuits, located beneath the heat exchange piping in his armor, transferred the heat to raw electrical energy and conducted it throughout the metal suit. The warning message disappeared as status reports came back online and vital systems powered up again. *Going to be a hot time in the old town tonight*, War Machine thought jubilantly. His toes and fingertips stung like mad as the blood rushed back into the frozen tissue, but Jim didn't mind the pain; it was proof he was still alive.

Flames, red and golden, crackled over War Machine's prone form. Astride the fallen hero, Cold Warrior screamed in pain and anger. War Machine realized he had only seconds before the cyborg's freezing aura dampened the flames as well. He had to get Cold Warrior off his back—and before Deathlok could rejoin the fray.

Fortunately, he still had a few tricks up his metal sleeve. The laser sighting system affixed to the right side of his helmet, for instance, was fully capable of directing a targeting beam either backwards or forward. War Machine activated the laser, blinding Cold Warrior with an incandescent beam of coherent light. Then, while the refrigerated cyborg was still reeling from the unexpected ray of light, War Machine switched both his shoulder weapons back to their standby positions. High-speed rails rushed the missile launcher and the electric gun right to where Cold Warrior was now sitting. The heavy weapons slammed into the surprised cyborg like freight trains, hurling Cold Warrior off of War Machine.

War Machine sprang to his feet. He shook his head to clear the packed snow away from his eye slits. Cold Warrior was sprawled in a snowdrift a few yards away. His cold-field must have protected him from War Machine's flamethrower; the cyborg looked angry but unharmed. *Careful*, War Machine thought, backing away from Cold Warrior. *I can't let him get close to me again.* He tried to ignite his bootjets, but found they were still inoperative. Deathlok's precision laser blasts had really done a number on his propulsion system; War Machine was grounded until he could effect repairs. *Terrific.*

Keeping one eye on Cold Warrior, War Machine looked for Deathlok. He still couldn't figure out what Deathlok, a straight shooter if ever there was one, was doing with Cold Warrior. For that matter, he wondered, why was a dyed-in-the-wool ideologue like Cold Warrior running errands for A.I.M.? It didn't make sense. The world was full of super-powered mercenaries willing to sell their services to the highest bidder, but Cold Warrior's frozen heart clearly belonged to the old Soviet Union. Why would either Deathlok or Cold Warrior work for A.I.M? *Unless,* it occurred to him, *they weren't really who they appeared to be.* Hadn't Tony said something about an android copy of Spymaster?

Before he could pursue this notion, he spotted Deathlok standing on a snow-draped rise several yards away. An unusual aircraft was descending through the wind and snow toward Deathlok. The vehicle was shaped like more like the head of a submarine than a conventional airplane. A matte-black finish covered its sleek design, while opaque windows concealed its interior from view. War Machine recognized the ship instantly. Deathlok called it the *Dragonfly*, and War Machine had last seen it soaring over the desert sands of Imaya. Deathlok could control the ship by remote control, he knew; the cyborg must have summoned it using his wrist communicator. *Damn! He's making a break for it—with the uranium.*

"Don't do it, Michael!" he yelled, at the same

time wondering who or what he was addressing. How was he supposed to tell the difference between a cyborg and an adaptoid duplicate of a cyborg? It was a subtle distinction, but a crucial one. His missile launcher slid up onto his shoulder. He didn't want to use it, not against a friend. "Talk to me, Deathlok!"

The cyborg did not reply, but another voice shouted above the thunder. "Yankee imperialist!" Cold Warrior screamed as he lunged at War Machine. His freezing hands reached for his enemy's armor. "You should have stayed in your own decadent country!"

War Machine could feel the waves of cold radiating from Cold Warrior. *Uh-uh.* No way was he letting Cold Warrior drain his heat again. He dived away from the cyborg's outstretched hands, landing in a bank of packed snow a bit further down the hill. He rolled twice before springing to his feet. The laser target-designator on his helmet located Cold Warrior. An infrared beam picked out a target on the center of the cyborg's chest. War Machine's missile launcher was ready to fire.

He quickly considered his options. It was tempting to blow the rime-caked figure apart with one of the antitank missiles, but he still wasn't sure whether he was facing a living human being or a cleverly constructed simulacrum of a man. If only there was some way he could know for certain! The flame and explosive missiles were no good, too; Cold Warrior would just absorb their energy and make himself stronger. Already, the Soviet-built cyborg was running down the snowy slope toward War Machine, intent on draining every last calorie of heat from the armored hero. *Suppose I take the opposite route, and fight this freak on his own terms?*

He made his decision. Keeping his laser sight fixed on the approaching cyborg, he cybernetically selected the appropriate missile and fired. Propelled by a built-in solid fuel rocket, the missile leaped from the launching mechanism above War Machine's shoulder. Forward-looking sensors in the head of the missile locked onto the target designated by the laser beam. About the size of a road-flare, and travelling at a speed exceeding Mach 1, the missile hit Cold Warrior almost instantly, knocking him off his feet.

There was no explosion, however; no release of excess heat or energy. Instead a fire-suppressant foam escaped from the core of the missile, spreading over Cold Warrior and coating his body from head to toe. *You like it cold?* War Machine thought grimly. *Try this on for size.* The foam, developed by Stark Enterprises, absorbed both oxygen and heat from its surroundings, swiftly lowering the temperature around any incendiary situation. Of course, Cold Warrior was already leeching the warmth from his environment, and running his cyborg body with the stolen energy, so the foam combined with Cold Warrior's own cold-inducing aura to freeze the very air around him, trapping him in a man-shaped shell of solidified air and foam. Pale blue energy crackled briefly around the cyborg's fists, as he tried to use his concussive blasts to free himself from his icy prison, but the foam had drained too much of his power from him. His blasts lacked the power they needed to crack the shell confining him.

And, best of all from War Machine's point of view, no sound escaped the frozen foam, meaning he wouldn't have to listen to any more of Cold Warrior's doctrinaire political rantings.

For a second, he wondered if, caught like a fly in amber, Cold Warrior had enough oxygen or energy to stay alive. Then he remembered that the real Cold Warrior, if that's who this truly was, managed to survive three decades in cryogenic suspension. Adaptoid or not, a few more hours on ice weren't likely to do him much harm.

War Machine turned his attention back to Deathlok. Guided by its autopilot, the *Dragonfly* now hovered less than two feet off the ground. The right side of its black carapace peeled upwards, inviting Deathlok inside the ship. The American-made cyborg stepped towards his ship, the storage compartment on his back stuffed with radioactive earth from Wundagore, one of the vital ingredients in Modok's recipe for a new energy chip. War Machine knew he had to stop him.

"Hold it right there!" he shouted at Deathlok, turning his speaker up to full volume. "Deathlok—Michael—think about what you're doing! Remember Imaya? We fought on the same side there. Don't turn your back on me now!"

War Machine cursed his sabotaged bootjets. Even with the assistance of motorized muscles, there was no way he could run uphill through a snowstorm in a four-hundred-pound suit of armor and still get to Deathlok in time to stop him from getting into the *Dragonfly* and taking off. *And if he's really just an adaptoid duplicate of Deathlok, complete with a duplicate* Dragonfly, *then I'm wasting my breath trying to reason with him.* His laser sight found Deathlok. The muzzle of his minicannon slid out of his gauntlet. "Talk to me!" he yelled again. "What's all this about?"

The cyborg ignored his cries and stepped into the *Dragonfly*. For an instant, before the sleek black carapace came down again, sealing Deathlok inside his ship, War Machine glimpsed the cyborg seated behind the *Dragonfly*'s controls. His minicannon was loaded with lethal ammunition. *One good shot. That's all it would take.* All he could see was Deathlok's right profile, the human half of his face. Although grey and desiccated, with the shriveled flesh of a corpse, it was still the face of a friend. But was this really his old ally—or only a fraudulent imitation? The gun waited his command to fire, but War Machine hesitated. *I can't do it*, he realized. *God help me, but I can't take the chance that this is really Michael Collins.*

The door of the *Dragonfly* slammed shut, concealing Deathlok from view. Unseen engines roared as the ship lifted itself away from the mountain. War Machine fired his repulsor rays at the *Dragonfly*, hoping to disable it, but the beams bounced harmlessly off the ship's refractory coating. His rocket launcher weighed heavily on his shoulder, filled with antiaircraft missiles that could conceivably bring the ship down and reduce both Deathlok and the *Dragonfly* to flaming wreckage. The ship was gaining speed. War Machine remembered how fast the *Dragonfly* could fly, eluding fighter jets over the African desert. If he was going to launch his missiles, he knew, it had to be now.

The moment passed. The *Dragonfly* disappeared into the distance, becoming a small black dot above the horizon. War Machine's shoulders slumped wearily, the missile box sliding back to its standby position. He felt torn by conflicting emotions. He had not killed anyone today, but one of the bad guys had gotten away. *I'm really going to feel stupid, if that Deathlok turns out to be an adaptoid.* Still, he couldn't blame himself too hard for erring on the side of mercy. Better to let a machine escape, perhaps, than to take the life of a good man. He could live with that.

War Machine trudged through the snow to check on Cold Warrior's immobile form. The storm seemed to be letting up a little. *About time,* he thought, wondering where in Transia he could get his boots repaired. He stared at the sky, but the *Dragonfly* was long gone, along with Deathlok and the uranium. War Machine kicked the snow angrily, hoping against hope that his fateful decision hadn't doomed Tony and the others.

FRIDAY. 5:35 PM. EASTERN STANDARD TIME.

Iron Man walked clumsily across the runway. As always, his special space armor felt large and cumbersome in normal gravity, reminding him of the bulky metal suits he'd worn at the beginning of his career as Iron Man. The space armor, containing all the life support equipment needed for an extended stay in outer space, was easily twice as heavy as his regular, more streamlined armor. He felt like a refrigerator with arms and legs. He stomped across the tarmac in iron boots big enough to fit the Frankenstein monster. *The better to blast off with*, he thought.

His helmet swiveled atop the massive armor suit as he glanced back at *Stark One*, where Christine waited for him to complete his mission in space. He had considered installing her in a penthouse suite in Miami, but his private jet was probably just as luxurious and a good deal more convenient—and secure. In effect, she was under house arrest aboard the plane; even someone who could successfully channel the alien energies of another dimension, as Christine had done, would have a hard time against a state-of-the-art Stark Enterprises security system.

Besides, he reminded himself, there wasn't a moment to waste. Modok had a five-day head start on Iron Man and his allies, although Iron Man took comfort in the fact that he had foiled the adaptoid

Spymaster's raid on Stark Enterprises. He still wasn't sure exactly what the adaptoid had been up to, but hopefully the droid's failure had thrown off Modok's timetable.

Then again, fear of his plan's exposure might encourage Modok to speed up his diabolical operation. *For all I know, Modok's pawns may be on their way to the space station right now, if they haven't already come and gone.* He looked up at the gorgeous blue sky. No clouds obscured the sunshine on this beautiful Florida afternoon. A.I.M.'s orbital laboratory was up there, he knew. Christine had given him the coordinates, assuming she wasn't really sending him on a wild goose chase. *The truth is out there, just like they say on TV.*

He fired his bootjets, being careful not to activate the full nuclear thrusters until he was safely away from the airport. A mixture of regular air and ignited liquid oxygen fueled his ascent, lifting him off the runway and into the sky. Cool-air venting ringed the sole of each boot, mixing a very cold layer of air with his jet exhaust in order to keep Iron Man from roasting everything—and everyone—in his wake.

Miami spread out beneath him, shrinking so fast that soon he could no longer make out the airport, let alone his own plane. He flew higher, relying on his regular jets until he reached the upper stratosphere, over seven miles above the surface of the earth. Then he cut off the jets and switched instantaneously to the nuclear thrusters built into his oversized boots.

The difference was immediately noticeable. Tony's body slammed into the padded inner layer of his armor as he experienced the pull of multiple g-forces. He gritted his teeth and silently endured the strain of the blast-off. The acceleration was awesome; Iron Man zoomed through the stratosphere in seconds, then through the ionosphere into orbit around the planet itself. The thrusters went offline exactly on schedule, and Iron Man found himself floating in an empty black vacuum. Far beneath him, many miles away, Earth sat serenely in the heavens. It looked like a vast blue hemisphere, mottled with clouds and occasional masses of green and brown. Iron Man thought he could make out the continent of North America. *Christine's down there*, he thought, mildly surprised at her prominence in his thoughts, *along with everything else I know and cherish.*

His stomach gave a tiny flip. The sudden shift from superacceleration to zero-gravity was disorienting, but Iron Man had spent too much time among the stars to succumb to space sickness now. He tore his gaze away from the Earth's grandeur and searched the surrounding darkness with every available sensor. According to Christine, A.I.M.'s secret space station should be somewhere nearby. In theory, it was shielded from earthly surveillance by advanced stealth technology, but he should be able to locate the satellite from his current elevated location.

His gravimetric sensors spotted it first, alerting him to the location of a sizable accumulation of mass forty degrees sunward. Using his regular bootjets to navigate through the void, he headed toward the source of the signal. Soon, less than five minutes later, the spotlight from his chest projector fell upon a large object drifting in the Earth's shadow. *Score one for Christine.* The coordinates she'd provided had certainly proved genuine. Jetting closer, he got a better look at the station.

The sight of the station produced a distinct sense of *déjà vu*, along with a savage surge of indignation. A.I.M.'s orbital laboratory, floating before him, was clearly modelled on *Ad Astra*, Tony Stark's own experimental space station. A huge spinning wheel revolved around a long, cylindrical central core, providing artificial gravity for the station's living quarters. The de-spun labs, where zero-gravity conditions were maintained for experimental and manufacturing reasons, were located in a smaller, stationary ring further down the core. A.I.M.'s station was significantly smaller in scale than Tony's had been, but the design was basically the same. It was the twisted geniuses of Advanced Idea Mechanics, he recalled, who had sabotaged *Ad Astra*, infecting the entire station with a genetically-tailored space microbe, turning his state-of-the-art showcase for the scientific and industrial potential of extraterrestrial research into an $800 million pesthole in space. His blood burned when he remembered how A.I.M. had corrupted the dream of *Ad Astra*.

Maybe I'll have a chance to return the favor today. He didn't try to hail the station. Knowing A.I.M., he could hardly expect a friendly welcome, so it seemed better to preserve the element of surprise, if possible. He wondered if Christine could have deliberately sent him into a trap. *At least there's not likely to be any mega-octopuses lurking around.* He made sure his repulsors were charged and ready.

First things first, though. He had to find a way in. Fortunately, A.I.M.'s shameless appropriation of his designs made it easy to locate the docking/extravehicular activity segment attached to the core. The segment was equipped with two EVA hatches, both leading to a sealed airlock. He pried the hatch open with iron fingers, then welded it shut behind him before opening the airlock and making his way into the core of the station.

Now where—? he wondered. If Modok wanted a special variety of adamantium, he reasoned, of a type produced only in space, he'd look for it in the zerogravity laboratories in the small ring. Iron Man decided to head there first, bypassing the habitation ring. As he hurried down the corridor, he considered the nature of Modok's prize:

Adamantium was the most indestructible metal known, extremely rare and colossally expensive. The mutant X-Man called Wolverine had claws made of adamantium, while a murderous adamantium robot named Ultron had resisted all the Avengers' attempts to destroy him. *Too bad the stuff's so hard to find, or I'd seriously consider renaming myself Adamantium Man.* He wasn't too surprised to find adamantium involved in the creation of A.I.M.'s astounding energy chip; it would take an extremely durable substance to contain that much raw power for as long as it did.

The narrow corridors of the core were filled with silence. Ceramic tiles covered the floor while banks of instrumentation covered the walls. OBEY ALL SAFETY REGULATIONS, said a sign posted at regular intervals along the corridor, VIOLATERS WILL BE TERMINATED.

Harsh, Iron Man thought, but almost understandable; space could be a remarkably unforgiving environment. The sign was written in English, with no translations into other languages provided; apparently, A.I.M. required that all its operatives speak the same language. *So much for multiculturalism.* He imagined that in a world ruled by A.I.M., cultural differences and idiosyncrasies would be the first to go: too irrational and inefficient for the new "scientific" government. *Wonder how Christine feels about that?*

Iron Man was surprised at how quiet the station seemed. He'd expected that his arrival would set off every alarm and attract security teams from all over the station, but so far, nothing. For awhile, he thought the station had been deserted—until he found the first body. A dead A.I.M. technician, still wearing the standard yellow uniform, floated lifelessly in the null-gravity confines of the core. Iron Man checked the body. Judging from the burn marks upon the corpse's clothing and flesh, he guessed the man had been electrocuted. He glanced around quickly. There were no exposed wires or other electrical hazards in sight; Iron Man doubted this was an accident. *Am I too late, or just in time?*

He hurried down the corridor as quickly as his

bulky spacesuit would let him. He wished there was an easy way to shed the space armor until he needed it again, but that would have left him completely unprotected from whatever—or whoever—had killed the technician.

He found more bodies hanging eerily in space, and noticed a peculiar pattern to the killings. The body of one victim was charred and black, as though he had been burned alive. The next victim had been frozen to death: frost covered her uniform and beneath her headpiece and gloves, her lips and fingertips were blue. Yet another victim appeared to have been slammed into a bulkhead with great force; his skull had been reduced to a gory mess. The latter body was still warm. His killer could not have gone far.

Electrocution. Flame. Cold. Force. The varied means of execution ran through Iron Man's mind as he made his way to the de-spun laboratories. The pattern was familiar to Iron Man; he had a sneaking suspicion he knew who he was going to find in the lab—or, more precisely, who it would *appear* to be. *First Spymaster, now him. I should have expected this. . . .*

The metal door guarding the lab had been ripped violently from its hinges, almost as if the station had been hit a by hurricane or a tornado. *Or a vortex,* Iron Man thought. His theory grew more plausible every minute. *That's the problem with adaptoids. They lack imagination. They can only imitate, never create.* And he had a pretty good idea who was being imitated now.

A scream, followed by the sound of breaking glass, came from inside the laboratory ring. Iron Man charged into the lab, repulsors at the ready. "All right, you phony Mandarin, where are you?" he demanded. The wedge-shaped lab compartment showed all the signs of a brutal search or struggle. Shattered test tubes and beakers drifted in zero-gravity, above an overturned centrifuge resting motionlessly on the tile floor. Reluctant to inhale any of the drifting bits of glass and plastic, Iron Man made sure his air intake filters were operational. Microwave and infrared scanners stood abandoned by A.I.M.'s scientists, their digital displays flashing uselessly. An electric buzzer droned on and on, with no one available to shut it off. Broken petrie dishes spilled their contents, globs of protein gel spun weightlessly in the air. Iron Man wondered for a second whether the space-bred microbe that had rendered *Ad Astra* uninhabitable had been developed in this very lab.

Then his attention was seized by the imposing figure standing on the other side of the lab, in front of a circular porthole looking out onto the starry reaches of deep space. He was a tall Chinese man, approximately six feet two, resplendent in ankle-length robes of aquamarine silk. An ornate mask, covered with dozens of iridescent purple scales, hid the upper half of the man's face. Above his brows, the mask tapered off into two sharp points, suggesting the presence of demonic horns. Purple boots, also covered with glittering scales, poked out from beneath the figure's robes. Amethysts studded his earlobes. A dense black goatee and a mustache worthy of Fu Manchu could be seen below the rim of his mask, giving his face an even more satanic appearance. One hand held up a shiny metal sphere about the size of a baseball; the other hand was wrapped around the throat of a hapless A.I.M. technician.

"Ah, my oldest and greatest foe," the man observed. His voice was deep and commanding. "I should have anticipated your interference in this affair." His fingers loosened from his captive's neck. Iron Man watched in horror as the yellow-garbed body was tossed gracelessly into the air, floating amidst the other wreckage, the person's head hanging at an impossible position. Iron Man clenched his metal fists.

"I was just thinking the same thing," he said. The *real* Mandarin was indeed one of Iron Man's most persistent foes: an insidious mastermind determined to restore the vanished glories of imperial China—and remake the rest of the world in the process. Iron Man had lost count of how many times he had protected the entire planet from the Mandarin's megalomaniacal ambitions.

The *real* Mandarin, not the bloodthirsty counterfeit facing him now. "Look," Iron Man said. "I know you're really an adaptoid, you know you're an adaptoid, so why bother with this charade?" He gestured at the figure's flowing green robes. "I mean, look at you. The real Mandarin hasn't worn that outfit in years."

It was true. The genuine Mandarin had gone

through numerous costume changes over the years, as well as several more serious changes. In recent months, the Mandarin had renounced the super science he had once relied on and turned to sorcery instead, eschewing technological weapons in favor of occult spells and wizardry. *That* Mandarin would have disdained the contents of A.I.M.'s laboratory; this adaptoid was obviously working from out-of-date information. *Good.* It was reassuring to know that Modok was still capable of making a mistake.

"How dare you mock the invincible Mandarin?" the adaptoid raged. Long, pointed fingernails wrapped around the metal sphere in his left hand. Iron Man felt an unexpected thrill of nostalgia. This creature looked and sounded exactly like the imperious villain he had first encountered in China's "Valley of the Spirits" so many years ago. *Just like old times.*

His gaze was irresistibly drawn to the rings adorning the adaptoid's fingers. There were ten rings, one for each finger, each one with an intricate symbol, each echoing an identical ring worn by the genuine Mandarin. Discovered amidst the wreckage of an alien spacecraft, the original rings were the true source of the Mandarin's power, every ring equipped with a different deadly weapon, ten lethal modes of attack in all. *It's probably too much to hope that the adaptoid's rings are just cheap costume jewelry.*

Then he remembered the corpses he found throughout the station. *No*, Iron Man concluded with a sigh. The evidence strongly suggested that this Mandarin's rings were fully functional.

"I take it that's the adamantium," he said, pointing to the silvery sphere clutched between the ersatz Mandarin's fingers. *I got here just in time. Modok must have mobilized his forces the minute he heard about my visit to the undersea lab.*

"A product of your debased Western civilization," the adaptoid conceded, "but useful nonetheless." It was hard to think of him as anything except the Mandarin; the impersonation was *that* convincing. He appeared unconcerned by the bits of glass floating in the enclosed atmosphere of the space lab. Was he depending on his robes to protect him, or was one of his rings emitting an electrostatic field that repelled the drifting debris? "As you see," the Mandarin continued, "I have relieved these unworthy persons from the burden of its keeping."

"You mean you butchered them," Iron Man said angrily. The toppled centrifuge crumpled beneath his boots as he stepped toward the false Mandarin.

This pie-shaped compartment on the laboratory ring made for a cramped, confined battlefield, Iron Man noted. Thin aluminum walls hemmed in the antagonists, while broken and battered equipment floated weightlessly above the tile floor. Sealed, airtight doorways, one on each side of Iron Man, connected this segment with other sections of the ring. Ventilation grilles ran along the ceiling; he could hear built-in fans keeping the air moving. Metallurgical apparatus, including high-intensity welding torches, a diamond-tipped drill, ceramic crucibles, and a cracked electron microscope, were held down by strips of velcro atop shining metal counters that jutted from the walls in orientations that sometimes left the worktables perpendicular to each other, the better to make use of space in null-gravity. Iron Man's bootjets and superior maneuverability counted for little in this compact environment. *I guess I'll just have to make do, no matter what stunts this imposter pulls.*

"You have no more claim to this sphere than I do—and significantly lesser need," the adaptoid pointed out. The folds of his blue-green robes did not drape over his body as they would in normal gravity; instead they spread out about him like a silken halo.

"You mean Modok needs it. Your master," Iron Man said. He wondered how this copycat Mandarin could cope so easily with the lab's lack of gravity. *His boots must be magnetized*, he guessed.

The adaptoid's face twitched, perhaps from the strain of holding onto its borrowed identity in the face of Iron Man's persistent challenges. "I am the Mandarin!" he insisted. "I need not explain my purposes to you." The artificial creature seemed determined to stay in character.

Maybe, Iron Man speculated, *that's because it has no personality of its own beneath the façade.* For all he knew, the adaptoid might genuinely believe itself to be the real Mandarin. *There must be some way to exploit that.*

The adaptoid raised his right hand and extended the index finger toward Iron Man, who glimpsed a purple, star-shaped gem decorating that finger's ring. It began to glow.

Impact beam, Iron Man realized, bracing himself. He had long ago memorized all the Mandarin's rings and their disparate functions. The beam pounded him in the chest, striking with the concussive force of over 350 pounds of TNT. His sensors identified the beam as a stream of fast-moving neutrons, very similar in nature to his own repulsor rays.

His chestplate was up to the pounding, though. A magnetic field held the components of his armor together, reinforcing the natural strength of the advanced iron alloy. In fact, every inch of the armor's surface consisted of microscopic layers of exotic materials and circuitry sandwiched together to form a tesselated link of high-tech "chain mail." His boots firmly planted on the floor of the lab, Iron Man stood firm against the relentless pressure of the Mandarin's impact beam. He wasn't about to just stand there, though, and provide the adaptoid with target practice. *Time to take the offensive.*

A violet beam shot forth from the ray projector in Iron Man's palm. The ray snagged the adamantium sphere in its powerful magnetic grip. Grunting in surprise, the false Mandarin tightened his hold on the sphere, but the magnetic pull was too strong. The sphere escaped from his fingers and flew across the laboratory, coming to rest in the palm of Iron Man's crimson gauntlet. "Thief!" the adaptoid shouted with the Mandarin's voice. "Base, dishonorable villain!"

"Sticks and stones," the Golden Avenger replied, holding the adamantium sphere in a iron grip. Lifting his free right hand, he blasted the adaptoid with a strong dose of repulsor rays.

Before the beam could strike this Mandarin, however, an aura of white light enveloped the adaptoid. Brilliant flashes of energy were discharged when Iron Man's repulsor ray met the Mandarin's protective aura, but the duplicate Mandarin appeared unscathed. Iron Man stared angrily at the golden ring embracing the thumb of the Mandarin's left hand. A pill-sized amber disk marked the ring. The white light it generated, Iron Man knew, could be used as a tractor beam. Or a force field.

"You will have to do better than that, old foe," the adaptoid said, pretending a long association that didn't actually exist. "All the godlike powers of my sacred rings are arrayed against you. You cannot hope to defeat me."

Iron Man tried to guess what ring the phony Mandarin would employ next. The ice blast? The disintegration ray? What would the *real* Mandarin do? He considered the metal sphere he had snatched from the adaptoid's clutches. *Freeing up his left hand might not have been one of my smarter moves.* Now the adaptoid had the Mandarin's entire arsenal at his disposal.

He was ready to use them, too. A bolt of lightning leaped from the middle finger of the adaptoid's left hand, striking Iron Man between his eyes. *Electroblast*, Iron Man realized. Another of the real Mandarin's favorite weapons. Despite his protective lenses, the blinding flash hurt his eyes. Unable to rub his eyes through his heavy metal helmet, he blinked the tears away. He saw spots before his vision. He fired off another burst of repulsor rays to keep the adaptoid at bay while he recovered from the lightning bolt. *Thank God for the protective insulation in my helmet, or I would have been in for some unauthorized electroshock therapy.*

The adaptoid then charged at Iron Man, the heel of his open left hand raised high above his head. The armored Avenger remembered too late that the actual Mandarin was also a master of karate and other martial arts. White light outlined his fingers, the force field adding to the protective callus built up on this Mandarin's hand. The karate chop came down on Iron Man's right shoulder. He felt the blow even through his armor. *A few more of those*, he thought, *and my suit might actually crack.* He had to strike back—and fast.

His right arm still felt numb from the Mandarin's powerful chop, so he swung his left arm up and pounded the adaptoid in the side of the head with the unbreakable adamantium sphere. The sphere may have rendered weightless by the zero-gravity, but it still had plenty of mass. The adaptoid's force field cushioned the blow, yet the would-be Mandarin still let out a cry of pain. The impact cracked the amethyst earring in the adaptoid's exposed right ear. "I'll bet that hurt," Iron Man said. "How do adaptoids cope with pain?"

Very badly, apparently. The creature's artificial eyes glared with hatred. His imitation teeth gnashed together. He grabbed Iron Man's right arm by the wrist, pushing it away from his skull, while his other hand brought a ringed finger up against Iron Man's helmet. His vision slowly returning to normal, the hero saw a glowing amber cube on the golden band surrounding that finger.

The disintegration beam, he recognized. A weapon capable of dissolving the molecular bonds holding together any substance it strikes. Pressed close against his helmet, the ring was likely to disintegrate his headpiece entirely, along with most of his head. Fortunately, this particular ring took a second or two to charge up. *Forget it. I want to hang onto my head.* This called for drastic action.

The tri-beam projector in his chestplate flared to life, pummeling the Mandarin with a combination of heat, light, and force at nearly point-blank range. Even the adaptoid's white light aura couldn't withstand such an onslaught. He staggered backwards, his body silhouetted against the starry backdrop of space as seen through the large circular porthole. Scorch marks marred his elegant silk robes. Iron Man smelled the odor of burning fabric. *Remember*, he reminded himself, *this is just an adaptoid. I don't have to hold myself back.*

The disintegrator ring flashed ominously. A dangerous weapon to use onboard an enclosed space environment; no wonder this recycled version of the Mandarin had preferred, at least at first, to use that ring when he was very close to Iron Man. "You have defied me for the last time, Avenger," he barked. "Now feel the full and unforgiving wrath of unstoppable glory that is the Mandarin!"

Boy, he's really getting into this. Caustic, coruscating radiation shot out of the amber cube on the ring, heading straight for Iron Man. The armored warrior responded by forming a shield of electromagnetic energy between himself and the corrosive orange ray. The energy shield looked like a sparkling yellow wall hanging in the air in front of Iron Man; it popped and crackled with electricity. When the disintegrator ray hit the shield, the orange radiation blended and merged with the shield, streaking the golden field of sparks with fiery traceries of red and orange before dissipating entirely. *Quite a light show*, Iron Man thought appreciatively. He recalled, with an audible sigh of relief, that the Mandarin's disintegrator ring required twenty minutes to recharge after being used. The same, he assumed, applied to the adaptoid's duplicate ring. This Mandarin, after all, was nothing if not a slavishly faithful reproduction of the genuine article.

"Nice try, pretender," he told the adaptoid. "Almost as good as the real thing."

The false Mandarin seethed visibly behind his purple mask. His jowls grew flushed and livid. "Give me that sphere!" he demanded, his voice hoarse with rage. A stray beaker drifted in front of the adaptoid's face. He brushed it out of the way with a wave of his hand. "Surrender it unto me!"

Iron Man released the adamantium ball. It hung suspended in the air. "Come and get it," he said.

The purple star on the index finger of the fake Mandarin's right hand glowed once more. An incandescent azure ray crossed the laboratory to take hold of the sphere. *Not so fast*, Iron Man thought. He knew full well that the Mandarin's impact beam could produce a magnetic effect. He matched the adaptoid's ray with his own artificially produced magnetism. The metal sphere wobbled in the air, torn between two equal and opposing forces. The adaptoid upped the pull of his ring; Iron Man poured more energy into his magnetic beam. *This has to be made of adamantium.* Any lesser metal would have been ripped in half by now.

Unfortunately, the adaptoid had nine more rings—and two hands to work with. While his right hand maintained the attractive force tugging at the sphere, the false Mandarin pointed the ring finger of his other hand directly at Iron Man's head. A turquoise gemstone, shaped like a diamond, glittered before his eyes.

Blast! The mento-intensifier. If the adaptoid's ring was anything like the original, it would amplify its bearer's psionic capacity, allowing him to place another person's mind under his telepathic control. The real Mandarin's ring could be used on only one individual at a time, and only at a distance of less than ten feet. *In other words*, he realized with alarm, *in conditions exactly like these.*

At that very instant, he heard the voice in his head. *RELEASE THE SPHERE*, the voice commanded, sounding just as though they were his own thoughts, only more commanding, more compelling. *RELEASE THE SPHERE.*

"No, blast it! No!" Iron Man said loudly, struggling to hear his own thoughts over the voice in his mind. *RELEASE THE SPHERE.* The arm projecting his magnetic beam shook spasmodically; it was all he could do to keep from deactivating the ray as the voice commanded. *RELEASE THE SPHERE.* "Never!" he shouted. It was the only way he could hear himself think. *RELEASE THE SPHERE.* "I am Iron Man, damn you. Iron Man!" *RELEASE THE SPHERE.* "I have never surrendered to the real Mandarin—" *RELEASE THE SPHERE.* "—and I am sure not going to submit—" *RELEASE THE SPHERE.* "—to some cheap, mechanical imitation!"

But how long could he really resist? *RELEASE THE SPHERE.* The voice seemed to be growing louder with every heartbeat. *RELEASE THE SPHERE.* The vital distinction between his own mind and the invading voice grew harder and harder to maintain. *RELEASE THE SPHERE.* The metal ball bounced in the air in synch with the trembling of his arm. *RELEASE THE SPHERE. RELEASE THE SPHERE.* His will was dissolving into the voice, becoming one with the voice. *RELEASE THE SPHERE. RELEASE THE SPHERE. RELEASE THE SPHERE.* There was no more Tony Stark, no more Iron Man, there was only . . .

RELEASE THE SPHERE!

"Sure," he said. A final spark of defiance lit up inside him. He released the sphere—and then some. He reversed the polarity of his magnetic beam which, in tandem with the adaptoid's own magnetic pull, sent the ball of solid adamantium hurling into the adaptoid's open hand with the force of a meteor. His white light aura was not enough to protect him from this adamantium cannonball. The sphere smacked into the ersatz Mandarin's hand, pulverizing his artificial bones and flesh.

"Yarrrgh!" he screamed in agony. The striking sphere almost knocked him off his feet, but his magnetized boots held fast to the steel supports beneath the tile floor. He could not hold onto the speeding ball; it slipped from his fingers and continued through the air, its momentum only slightly diminished by its collision with the adaptoid's hand. A body in motion tends to stay in motion, especially in zero-gravity, and the adamantium sphere kept going until it left a dent in the steel bulkhead behind the adaptoid.

The adaptoid's shock and pain broke his hold over Iron Man. The alien voice fell silent immediately. *Thank God.* He shook his head to clear his mind of the last vestiges of the adaptoid's telepathic presence. His heart was pounding. His body was soaked in sweat, exhausted from his inner struggle. *That voice!* he recalled in horror. *Is that what schizophrenics experience all the time? The uncontrollable voices shouting inside their brains?* He made a mental note to sink more funds into psychological research and treatment programs, then took stock of the scene confronting him.

The adaptoid impersonating the Mandarin was clutching his injured hand, which had swollen to twice its normal size. The golden rings on his fingers had almost disappeared into his bruised and purpled flesh. As Iron Man looked on, the adaptoid treated his injury with the ice blast function of the tiny ring on the little finger of his good left hand. The false Mandarin numbed the pain with a wave of intense cold, then formed an icy cast around his fractured hand by freezing the very moisture in the air. Iron Man hoped for a second that he'd knocked the fight out of the adaptoid. "Ready to give up?" he asked.

No such luck. The false Mandarin glared at him with vengeful eyes. He left his fingers uncovered by the frozen sheath covering the rest of his right hand. "You!" he accused. "Demon of flesh and steel! How dare you defile the divine hand of the Mandarin!"

"The way I see it," Iron Man replied. "You got just what you asked for. Too bad you couldn't hold on to it." His eyes scanned the laboratory, searching for the metal sphere. There it was, he saw quickly: levitating only inches away from the crater-shaped dent it had left in the bulkhead. *Good thing it didn't hit the porthole. Explosive decompression can be very messy.*

His first aid complete, the adaptoid turned his ice ring against Iron Man. The air froze in the path of the frigid blast, forming an icy battering ram, but Iron Man was not taken by surprise. His chest beam melted the frozen air before it came close to him. Steam rose in the confined atmosphere of the lab where the beam met the adaptoid's arctic blast.

"Sorry, mister, but I've seen that old trick before." Iron Man fired his palm repulsors at the adaptoid, eager to end this fracas once and for all. The white light enveloping the fake Mandarin resisted the repulsor rays, flaring up like flashbulbs wherever the force field blocked the repulsors, but Iron Man kept the pressure on, hoping to overpower the adaptoid's defenses by sheer persistence and power. "Who's on the receiving end now, adaptoid? Think you can take it?"

"I am the Mandarin!" the deluded android insisted. "My victory is preordained. It cannot be opposed!"

"Try me," Iron Man said. The phony Mandarin called off his ice blast, but the armored hero did not give the adaptoid a moment's respite. He barraged Modok's murderous killing machine with both repulsors and his chest beam. At the same time, he kept one eye on the adamantium sphere. Bursts of energy lighted up the metallurgical laboratory, reflecting off the polished metallic walls. Iron Man stepped across the lab, pressing the attack, coming ever closer to both the adaptoid and the floating sphere.

Noticing the stars through the porthole, Iron Man wondered for the first time exactly how the adaptoid had come to the space station. He hadn't seen any vehicles docked at the EVA segment. Teleportation? Long-distance matter transference was numbered among the real Mandarin's many abilities; could the adaptoid have simply beamed himself to the station? If that was the case, then why hadn't the adaptoid beamed away the minute he captured the adamantium sphere? There was no explanation for why Modok's inhuman servitor had remained on the station to battle Iron Man.

Unless, he thought suddenly, *the adaptoid really*

thinks he's the Mandarin on some level. Maybe the artificial being had become so caught up in his role-playing that he could not resist the opportunity to challenge "his" archenemy. *He's sticking around just to fight me—because that's what the Mandarin is supposed to do.*

All these thoughts raced through Iron Man's mind as the obsessed adaptoid continued to work through the Mandarin's deadly repertoire.

Flame blast. The ring on the adaptoid's left index finger, marked by four bands of ruby quartz, produced a red-hot ball of fire that raced over Iron Man's armor, licking at the hero's gold and crimson sheen, trying to find a way to burn the man inside. The high-temperature enamel coating his iron suit, as well as his internal temperature controls, protected Tony from the voracious flames, but the the fireball's heat ignited a vial of chemical reagents affixed to one of the worktables. The vial exploded, spraying glass and boiling liquids at Iron Man and the duplicate Mandarin. On the opposite wall, on an upside-down table whose acid-pitted top faced the floor, a plastic container of cleaning solution also detonated. The dual explosions rocked the lab, and the air filled with toxic fumes and swirling mixtures of gas and liquid and solid debris. Iron Man switched off his repulsors; he was more likely to hit some floating chemical spill than the adaptoid.

How could the false Mandarin breathe in all this? *Did* the adaptoid need to breathe? He searched the smoky lab with his chest beam functioning only as a spotlight. "Where are you, adaptoid?" he called out. "Show yourself!"

"I will show you the face of fear," the imitation Mandarin declared. Iron Man glimpsed his enemy's face through the swirling fumes. The adaptoid raised his injured right hand. A small pink pearl flashed between the tip of his swollen thumb and the frost-covered block of ice encasing the hand. Iron Man took a deep breath. He knew what that harmless-looking pearl could do.

Matter rearranger. Possibly the Mandarin's most versatile weapon, capable of reordering the atoms and molecules of almost any substance. The magnetic field enveloping his armor shielded Iron Man from the ring's direct effects, but the real Mandarin had always found many ingenious ways to employ his matter rearranger against his archfoe. This ring was not entirely the Philosopher's Stone of myth and ancient lore—it could not literally transmute elements—but it could convert solid matter to liquids, solidify vapors. . . .

Or transform a compartment full of noxious chemicals, fumes, and debris into an all-encompassing trap for Iron Man.

Tiny fragments of glass, roiling clouds of smoke and gas, globs and puddles of floating chemical solutions all melted together to form a black, gummy substance that clung to Iron Man on all sides, falling from the ceiling and solidifying around his arms and legs. He tried to blast the goo away with his repulsors, but it was impossible to focus his beams on any one location. The viscous goo was everywhere, encasing him, cutting him off from the outside. Soon he was unable to move at all. The thick, gluey sludge held on tightly to his limbs. It was like being trapped inside an enormous tar baby. None of his sensors, visual or otherwise, could penetrate the darkness; he was effectively blinded. His space armor, equipped for long periods in a vacuum, had plenty of oxygen for him to breathe, but how long could he last stuck inside this morass? And what was the adaptoid up to while he was imprisoned? Iron Man felt the substance hardening about him, growing thicker and more solid. *If I wait long enough, this resin-like mucilage might become brittle enough that I can break my way out, but who knows how long that could take? What I wouldn't give for a good universal solvent!*

Inspiration struck even as the goo tightened its grip on Iron Man. *Wait a sec*, he thought. He had long since pretty much eliminated all need for lubricants in his ordinary armor; indeed, his regular suit was collapsible enough that it could be folded to fit into a standard-sized briefcase—and without leaving so much as an oil stain. His space armor, however, was another matter entirely; the countless minute moving parts in its expanded life-support and blast-off systems required liquid protection from the wear and tear of friction. Iron Man used polyultraxene, a synthetic nonconductive fluid developed by Stark Enterprises, to lubricate the specialized hardware in his space armor. The fluid, suspended in a colloidal solution, also served as a form of antifreeze, protecting the armor's mechanisms from the overwhelming cold of outer space. In theory, the stuff could be used as a solvent as well.

It was worth a try. Iron Man issued a cybernetic command to his armor, opening a valve on the exterior of his oversized boots. Micropumps squirted the lubricating fluid into the surrounding mass of coagulating black jelly. Iron Man was reminded of his very first adventure when, trapped inside a clunky, cast-iron suit, he had defeated a villainous warlord by spraying a thin stream of oil from his armor— and then setting it afire. He didn't plan on anything quite so pyrotechnic this time around, but maybe a stream of lubricant could save him once more.

It seemed to be working. The polyultraxene began to dissolve the dense black tar. He could feel the hold on his limbs loosening as the goo deliquesced rapidly. He took one step forward. The black slime still tugged on him, but not enough to really slow him down. Viscous, ebon fluid ran like syrup along the length of his armor, pooling in an amorphous, floating puddle that hung in the air behind Iron Man. The goo streamed away from the lenses over his eyes. He saw the ersatz Mandarin retrieving the adamantium sphere from where the weightless ball had finally come to rest.

"Hands off," Iron Man said loudly. "This ball game isn't over yet." He shook off the last few globules of dissolved goo. "That adamantium is not going anywhere, except with me."

The adaptoid glared at Iron Man. "Such arrogance!" he declared. "I swear by the spirits of all my honored ancestors that I will humble you yet!"

"Your only ancestor was a test tube," Iron Man replied, "unless you're counting Modok, and, if I were you, I wouldn't be so quick to claim him as a relative."

An angry snarl escaped the adaptoid. He wrapped his long fingernails around the sphere. A pale blue pearl glowed on the middle finger of his right hand. Iron Man grabbed quickly onto one of the steel lab counters jutting from the walls. He knew only too well what was coming next.

Vortex. Using his ring, the phony Mandarin seized control of the air itself. A miniature tornado, about seven feet tall and two feet across at its top, formed within the confines of the metallurgical laboratory. The whirlwind ripped apart the floating blob of semi-liquid goo and splattered the black slime against the walls. A powerful gust of wind battered Iron Man. He planted both boots squarely onto the tile floor and clung to the metal tabletop with all his strength. The vortex wanted to carry him out of the lab and away from the adaptoid and his prize, but Iron Man wasn't going anywhere. The wind made it impossible to advance, however, so he wasn't getting any closer to the adamantium either. *Have to squash this storm*, he thought, *and fast.* He couldn't afford to wait for a change in the weather.

A desperate, drastic strategy occurred to him. *I wouldn't dare try this stunt if there was anything human still alive in this lab. The adaptoid doesn't count.*

Still hanging onto the tabletop with both hands, Iron Man aimed his chest beam at the circular porthole beyond the fake Mandarin. Set at maximum strength, a repulsor blast stabbed across the lab. The adaptoid flinched involuntarily, but he wasn't the beam's real target; the crimson force-beam slammed into the transparent window separating the lab from the empty void outside. Three inches of solid, reinforced plastic shattered, the pieces tossed into space by the force of the repulsor ray. The clear fragments twinkled as they spun off into the void, each shard reflecting the light of distant stars.

Iron Man had little time to admire the sparkling lights. Explosive decompression struck instantly, sucking everything not bolted down into the gaping maw that had opened in the bulkhead. The false Mandarin's artificial vortex didn't stand a chance against the pull of the vacuum outside the space station; the whirlwind was sucked out through the open porthole, along with the rest of the air in the lab.

A high-pitched siren started blaring, hurting Iron Man's ears even through the protective insulation of his headpiece. Flashing red lights came to life above every doorway. A metal sheet slammed down over the entrance to the lab, cutting the laboratory ring off from the rest of the station. "*Warning! Warning!*" a pre-recorded voice boomed above the siren. "*Hull breach in Sector Three. Repeat: hull breach in Sector Three.*"

Iron Man doubted if there was anyone alive on the station to respond to the computer's alert. He remembered the bodies left behind after the massacre at the undersea lab, then added the crew of this space station to the growing list of casualties that could be laid at Modok's stunted feet. *You'll pay for this*, he vowed, *one way or another*.

The pull of the vacuum lifted him off his feet. His fingers dug into the stainless steel surface of the lab table. He was stretched out in the escaping air, his armor-clad body parallel with the floor below. Looking over his shoulder, he saw first the adamantium sphere, then the adaptoid go flying through the open porthole. Jagged pieces of plastic, still lodged in the porthole's frame, snagged onto the false Mandarin's flowing robes as he passed through the porthole. The sound of tearing silk could scarcely be heard over the blaring siren and the thunderous roar of air rushing out into the depths of space. The magnetic boots had not been enough to save the adaptoid; he went tumbling head over heels against a backdrop of faraway stars. Would the icy void of space be enough to stop the adaptoid? Iron Man hoped so, but there was only one way to be sure. *Everybody out*, he thought, and let go of the table.

He flew feet first out of the station, his burnished metal shell snapping off the last jagged shards still lodged in the porthole. As soon as he was clear of the opening, he activated his boot jets, stabilizing his flight and regaining control over his speed and direction. He was not alarmed to be thrust out of the safety of the station; this airless void was exactly the environment his space armor had been designed to function in.

He spotted the adaptoid at once, drifting in space in front of the vast blue globe that was the Earth. A brilliant white aura still surrounded the creature's body. Had the force field been enough to shield the false Mandarin from the rigors of space, Iron Man wondered, or was its android form naturally resistant to the cold and vacuum? For whatever reason, the adaptoid had clearly survived its forcible ejection from the station.

The artificial Mandarin moved slowly through space, using his impact beam to adjust his course when necessary. Iron Man was horrified to see that the adaptoid had already caught up with the adamantium sphere. Jets blazing, he zoomed toward the apparently indestructible android. He increased the magnification of his lenses just in time to see the fake Mandarin wiggle the little finger on his right hand. Eight small black gemstones decorated the ring on that finger. Iron Man glimpsed the gems for only a heartbeat. Then they disappeared from sight, along with everything else.

Even the stars went away. Iron Man found himself engulfed in all-encompassing darkness. For a second, he thought he was back inside the sticky, black goo, before he remembered the terrible power of the Mandarin's tenth and final ring.

Black light. Although this term was often used to describe mere ultraviolet radiation, the light-devouring phenomenon projected by the matching black gemstones was far more than that. More akin to the mysterious ''darkforce'' wielded by such super beings as Cloak, Darkstar, and the Shroud, the Mandarin's black light could create an area of absolute blackness which no light could penetrate. Suddenly, Iron Man could not even see his own gauntleted hands when he held them up in front of him, let alone the Mandarin, the metal sphere, the space station, or even the looming presence of the Earth itself.

But he did not stay disoriented for long. The adaptoid was fooling himself if he thought this trick alone was enough to stop Iron Man; the real Mandarin would have never made that mistake. Ignoring the darkness for now, Iron Man simply used his radar to locate both the Mandarin and the adamantium. He aimed his repulsors accordingly.

The neutron beams worked even better in a vacuum than they did underwater or in the air. The rays travelled faster and packed more of a punch when they arrived. In the soundless reaches of space, Iron Man could not hear the adaptoid cry out when the repulsors struck home, but the black light field disappeared the instant the rays should have reached the adaptoid's radar-reported location, suggesting that the blow had, at the very least, broken the false Mandarin's concentration. The Golden Avenger heard himself sigh in relief when the Earth, along with the endless canopy of stars, came back into view. Despite the unquestioned efficacy of his radar and other sensors, it was good to actually see again. The Shroud, he recalled, lived in perpetual darkness; he tried to imagine what it would be like to be a blind super hero, if such a thing was possible, and decided he was glad he didn't need to know, at least not yet. *I've already been crippled, alcoholic, homeless, and dead. Blindness is probably only a matter of time.* He wondered how hard it would be to develop artificial eyes.

Maybe I can find out from the adaptoid, Iron Man thought, *after I've taken him apart.* He rocketed at the imitation Mandarin, who inadvertently set himself tumbling again when he tried to fire his impact beam at the onrushing Avenger. Iron Man laughed at the adaptoid's error. The adaptoid had put some distance between him and Iron Man while the hero had been trapped in the black light, but Iron Man anticipated no trouble in catching up with the duplicate Mandarin. He had to assume that his space armor, bulky though it was, gave him an advantage in this environment.

The adaptoid took only a few seconds, though, to halt his headlong spinning. Clutching the sphere to his chest, he oriented himself in space so that he faced Iron Man directly. Ragged strips of silk, hanging loosely from the fake Mandarin's shredded robes, drifted around the adaptoid like the tentacles of the mega-octopus. *Looks like he's not giving up that ball without a fight. That's fine by me.*

He ran through the Mandarin's arsenal in his head, trying to predict the adaptoid's next move. *Fire blast. Electro-blast. Ice blast. Vortex.* None of those would work well in space, especially at a distance. Nor was there much in the way of gases, liquids, or solid material for the matter arranger to manipulate. The black light ring had already failed to stop Iron Man, as had the mento-intensifier. The adaptoid needed the impact beam to navigate and the white light aura to protect him from the hazards of space, so all it had left to fight with was. . . .

The disintegration beam, he realized with alarm. He focused his telescopic lenses on the ring finger of the adaptoid's right hand. An amber cube glowed orange atop a golden ring. "Blast!" he cursed out loud. Had it been twenty minutes already?

Unless he wanted his own molecules dispersed throughout the solar system, Iron Man had to move quickly. Firing off another volley of repulsor rays to give himself some cover, he executed evasive maneuvers, zigzagging through empty space faster than the adaptoid's inhuman eyes could follow him. *I need to take advantage of all this three-dimensional space*, he thought, his mind racing to find the right tactics. *He can't possibly maneuver as easily as I can. Maybe I can attack him from behind or below. . . .*

An incandescent ray of sparkling orange light shot from the adaptoid's ring. The beam missed Iron Man by several yards, passing far above his head. Tony Stark grinned savagely. *That was it.* The disintegrator ring was dead for another twenty minutes, more than enough time to take both sphere and pseudo-person into custody. He looked at the drifting figure of the false Mandarin. The adaptoid's lips were moving, but no sound reached Iron Man's audio receptors. *In space, no one can hear you rant*, he thought, grateful for small favors.

The adaptoid began pointing with one long finger, a triumphant smile on his demonic face. *What's he up to now?* The finger in question bore the disintegrator ring, but he could hardly be menacing anyone with that so soon after its last discharge.

The adaptoid seemed to be pointing past Iron Man. Slowing his acceleration toward the fake Mandarin, the armored Avenger looked back over his left shoulder. Behind his protective lenses, Tony's eyes grew wide with horror. *Dear Lord, the beam wasn't wasn't aimed at me at all.*

The adaptoid's disintegrating ray had struck the space station instead, severing one of the spokes connecting the habitat ring with the station's cylindrical core. The huge metallic wheel wobbled alarmingly as it tried to complete its rotation around the central core. Unseen gravitational forces buffeted the wheel. Iron Man prayed there was no one left alive aboard the habitat ring.

In complete and eerie silence, the space station began to tear itself apart. The other spokes, subjected to unexpected stresses, buckled beneath the strain. The habitat ring smashed silently into the side of the core. Huge sheets of radiation shielding were scraped away from the sides of the station. Trailing bits of wire and cables, they floated around the collapsing space station like gigantic pieces of confetti. Hull breaches occurred all over the station, blowing bursts of gas and debris into the vacuum. He saw the laboratory ring crumple like an empty eggshell crushed by an invisible hand.

Appalled by the senseless destruction, Iron Man had to look away. Never mind that the station had been built by A.I.M. from pirated Stark designs; the station had been a triumph of technology and human ingenuity. He couldn't bear to see it collapse into so much space garbage. It was like losing *Ad Astra* all over again.

His angry gaze found the adaptoid, floating weightlessly several hundred yards away. The would-be Mandarin executed a mocking bow in zero-gravity, then waved the hero good-bye. The white aura around him was replaced by a coruscating golden glow. He hefted the adamantium sphere in his left hand, even as his image grew wavery and indistinct. To his distress, Iron Man discovered that he could see the stars *through* the adaptoid's flickering form. *He's teleporting, and there's nothing I can do about it.*

The adaptoid's directive to fulfill the mission assigned to him by Modok must have finally overpowered his compulsion to emulate the real Mandarin. Perhaps, Iron Man speculated, destroying the space station had been enough of a symbolic victory to satisfy the adaptoid's artificial ego. Or was there more to it than that?

Steeling himself against the awful sight, he turned again toward the demolished space station. It was just as bad as he expected. The once-graceful design of the station had given way to an ugly mass of twisted metal and broken dreams. The entire station, or so it seemed from Iron Man's perspective, had slipped its moorings and fallen upwards toward the great cloud-speckled dome of the Earth, ascending closer to its ultimate place of origin.

In other words, he realized with a start, *it's falling out of orbit. It's going to hit the Earth!*

Small wonder the phony Mandarin had looked so smug before beaming away to parts unknown. The damage wreaked by his disintegrator beam had been sufficient to disturb the space station's delicate dance with Earth's gravity. Now several hundred tons of scrap metal were aimed at the planet and its inhabitants. *How perfectly diabolical. The real Mandarin couldn't have done anything more fiendish.*

Using his armor's built-in computer, Iron Man tried to quickly calculate the station's final landing place. *It's probably too much to hope that it's going to land harmlessly in the middle of an ocean somewhere,* he thought bitterly. *Life couldn't be that easy.* Taking into account the station's estimated mass, its apparent rate of acceleration, and the rotation of the Earth itself, he calculated that the falling station was heading straight for a collision with . . . Miami, Florida. *Right on top of Christine.*

"Blast!" he swore. There was no point in alerting Miami, no time to evacuate an entire city. He had to put the wrecked station back into orbit—if that was still possible. He flew through space, determined to put himself between the satellite and Earth, while simultaneously programming his computer to monitor the gravitational forces at work and to calculate the precise angle and altitude he would need to reach in order to lift the station back into a steady orbit.

Thank heaven I brought the space armor along. The boosters in his regular armor would have never been able to generate the kind of thrust he was going to need in a few more minutes. But were the spacesuit's nuclear thrusters powerful enough to push this colossal ruin back into place? They had only been designed to lift one armored super hero into space, not an entire orbital laboratory. He had faith and justifiable pride in his own technological creations, but he also knew the limitations of his machines better than anyone else. *No guarantees*, he thought grimly as he positioned himself in front of the midpoint of the cracked and crumbling station core.

He placed his palms against the wall of the core. If A.I.M. had copied his designs as closely as they appeared to have, then this region would be the most structurally sound—and the section least likely to come apart when he started pushing. He consulted his internal optical display; a digital readout at the lower lefthand corner of vision would give him a minute-by-minute report on the satellite's trajectory. Tony took a deep breath. Everything was set. Now he just had to do it.

And pray that he didn't fail.

"Three . . . two . . . one," he counted. *Blast-off!* The nuclear-powered thrusters built into his oversized iron boots surged to life. The force of the sudden acceleration rammed the top of Tony's head into the rubber parietal padding in his helmet. He gritted his teeth and pushed against the underside of the core. *With any luck, I'll lift the station and not tear my way through it.*

The strain was enormous, only slightly less challenging than carrying an ocean liner around on your shoulders. At this altitude, the station had not yet regained its full weight, but it was heavy enough;

Iron Man felt like Atlas holding up the sky. At first, he didn't seem to be making any headway. The station was too big. It was falling too fast. He couldn't overcome its accumulated momentum. He needed more thrust. *I can't fail. I have to do this. For Christine, not to mention the rest of Miami.*

He pushed his nuclear thrusters beyond their recommended safety thresholds, thresholds he himself had established based on comprehensive testing and analysis. The internal cooling systems began to overload. He could feel the temperature climbing in his boots. Perspiration poured from his skin, to be soaked up by the interior padding and osmotically pumped into collection cells. In theory, the captured sweat would be cooled and used to dampen the heat of the exhaust system. In fact, he was sweating like a pig and the suit was only growing warmer every second.

I can't take this much longer, he thought, checking the optical display. He saw that he had managed to halt the station's descent, but not enough to stabilize it. The minute he stopped pushing the satellite away from the planet, gravity would bring it crashing down again. *Christine*, he thought, anguished. *I wanted to get to know you better. . . .*

Slowly, he fought the relentless pull of the Earth, pushing A.I.M.'s devastated space station upward an inch at a time. He lost all track of the time. It seemed like he had been holding up the station for a lifetime and would keep on supporting it for yet another lifetime. There was only the weight above, the Earth below, and his own fading strength keeping them apart. He cursed Modok, he cursed the adaptoid, and he cursed himself for having the sheer *hubris* to attempt such an insane and manifestly impossible task. He was going to die here, he knew, his heart bursting until only his cold and lifeless body was left to continue holding the satellite aloft for all eternity. Maybe he was dead already and in purgatory, doomed to an endless Sisyphean torment. No doubt he deserved such an awful fate for letting the false Mandarin escape with the adamantium.

Finally, long after he had given up any hope of ever seeing home again, or doing anything except push against the considerable weight of the space lab, he noticed a tiny blue light flickering at the periphery of his vision. It was his digital display, he remembered, keeping track of the station's relative position to the Earth. According to the read-out, the station required only a few more seconds of lift to attain a stable orbit once more. Iron Man could hardly believe his eyes. He blinked, but the numbers stayed the same.

He'd done it.

Iron Man waited, holding his breath, until his computer reported that the station was safely stowed in orbit. He cut off his nuclear thrusters, content to drift in space for a time. His muscles ached and his armor, reporting a dozen minor malfunctions, gradually cooled down. A.I.M.'s top secret orbital laboratory, now nothing more than a zero-gravity graveyard, floated away from him. He was glad to see it go.

He turned slowly to contemplate the Earth spinning slowly above him. Somewhere on that fragile blue world Modok remained, spinning his inhuman schemes and plotting to subject the whole world to his heartless and megalomaniacal rule. Iron Man knew he had to return to Earth and stop Modok before A.I.M.'s berserk creation made more people suffer.

But first he needed to rest, if only for a minute or two.

FRIDAY. 8:14 PM. EASTERN STANDARD TIME.

The screen was split between two images. A close-up of War Machine, in full armor, took up the left side of the screen. Iron Man saw snow falling in the background. Captain America and the Black Panther, also in costume, occupied the other side. Leafy green fronds waved behind their heads. Iron Man, back onboard his private jet at Miami Airport, marvelled at the new reality of instantaneous global communication. He had exchanged his cumbersome space armor for his everyday, all-purpose suit. A reinforced chair supported the armored figure's weight.

The news was not good. According to his fellow heroes, they had also been unable to prevent Modok's adaptoids from absconding with both the Wakandan vibranium and the uranium from Wundagore. He had brought them up to speed on his frustrating encounter with the duplicate Mandarin, including the way his foe had escaped with the adamantium sample. "I should have stopped him," Iron Man concluded. "Then we wouldn't be in this mess."

"And if you hadn't decided to check up on that undersea lab we wouldn't even know Modok was up to something," War Machine said. "Don't beat yourself up. I'm sure you did your best. An adaptoid Mandarin, eh?" He whistled appreciatively; Jim Rhodes had fought the real Mandarin as both War Machine and Iron Man. "That must've been rough.

Have you noticed, though, how each of us ran into adaptoid versions of our own sparring partners? It's like they knew we were coming, and who was going where.''

"Hyde said something to that effect," Captain America confirmed. "The bogus Hyde, that is."

"In that case," the Black Panther commented, "I'm surprised I didn't run into replicas of Killmonger or Klaw." Iron Man recognized the names as two of the Panther's greatest foes.

"Modok didn't necessarily know you were going to get involved in this matter, T'Challa," Iron Man pointed out. "Apparently he did know that Cap was on his way to protect the vibranium; hence, Mr. Hyde and the Cobra." Although he kept his gaze on the screen, Iron Man was acutely aware of the presence of Christine Bright, seated on the couch behind him. Christine had been left alone aboard *Stark One* while he and the other heroes had scattered across (and above) the globe to guard the energy chip's components. Could Christine have communicated with Modok in their absence and notified him of their plans? He knew Cap and the others had to be nursing similar suspicions; who else knew which hero was going where? It was possible, he supposed, that Modok could have somehow tapped into their encrypted transmissions, but was that more or less likely than Christine betraying them? She was an A.I.M. scientist, after all, but Modok had killed all her friends and left her for dead in that undersea lab. Why in the world would she want to help Modok?

"Watch yourself, ShellHead," War Machine said

to Iron Man. He knew exactly what Jim meant. He must not let Christine's beauty and scientific brilliance blind him to her potential as a threat. *God knows it wouldn't be the first time I left myself vulnerable to a pretty face.* The Black Widow. Madame Masque. And Kathy Dare, his most psychotic "fatal attraction," the would-be assassin who nearly killed him. The names and the faces ran through his brain, along with the dangers each had subjected him to. *"Watch yourself,"* indeed, Tony.

"The only good thing I can see," he said to the screen, "is that the timing of the attacks suggests that we have forced Modok to speed up his timetable. He had a five-day head start, but apparently he didn't really start worrying about getting the necessary materials until we got on the case."

"He probably intended to rely on smugglers and the black market," Christine volunteered, "just like my people did." She got off the couch and walked over to Iron Man's side. "When you investigated the attack on the lab, he must have decided to go after the substances directly."

"But how did he know I visited the lab?" Iron Man asked. He looked directly into her face, examining her expression for any traces of guilt. Christine met his gaze without any apparent qualms. Out of all the elegant fashions available in his closets, she had put on one of Bethany's security uniforms: a tight blue vinyl bodysuit with matching boots and gloves. It looked good on her.

"Modok would know," she answered confidently. Her brown eyes found his. Her voice did not quaver.

"We built him to know everything about his enemies, to have the perfect tactical mind. Mental Organism Designed Only for Killing, remember? He must have left some device behind at the lab, monitoring any comings and goings. I can't imagine he could have overlooked the arrival on the scene of one of A.I.M.'s greatest adversaries."

Flattery will get you nowhere, Iron Man thought, *or at least not very far.* She didn't seem like a traitor to him, but how was he supposed to know for sure? He was an engineer at heart; he understood machines better than people. He had even turned himself into a machine, if only on the outside. He liked Christine's exterior, but who could tell what she was hiding inside? Maybe the Shadow knew what evil lurked in the hearts of men; Iron Man didn't have a clue.

"Things still sound bad to me," War Machine said. "Even if we forced Modok to jump the gun a bit, he still got every item on his shopping list. Now he has everything he needs to make another of those damn energy chips."

"Except," Christine observed, "the facilities to manufacture one. The undersea lab was wrecked beyond repair. And, according to Iron Man, the orbital lab is in even worse shape." She looked from Iron Man to the screen and back again. "He can't construct the chip without a highly-advanced construction facility."

Iron Man took her by the shoulders, being careful not to crush her beneath his iron gauntlets. "Tell me the truth, Christine. We need to know: does A.I.M.

have another hidden laboratory that Modok can use?''

''My A.I.M. or his A.I.M.?'' she asked, a bit too evasively for comfort.

''Either one.''

She shook her head. ''Not that I know of. There are other labs, of course. Hundreds of them, all over the world. Only the Supreme Scientist—and maybe Modok—knows where all of them are. But you can't make my chip in just any lab. It's an astonishingly complex procedure, involving incredibly sophisticated equipment. And, frankly, most legitimate research facilities are hardly up to A.I.M.'s standards.'' She shrugged her shoulders, slipping away from Iron Man's grip. ''That's partly why I hooked up with A.I.M. To work with the most up-to-date equipment, the kind of research tools that legitimate labs are too blind or too impoverished to even dream of. The stupid governments of the world throw away their money on frivolities and bureaucracy while true scientific research goes begging for measly amounts of small change. Things are different with A.I.M. They have the right priorities, the right attitude. Science comes first, not—''

Iron Man cut off her impassioned diatribe. As much as he admired her faith in science, an ominous thought had occurred to him. ''What about Stark Enterprises?''

''What?'' she said, apparently caught offguard by the question.

''Stark Enterprises,'' he repeated. He thought of HOMER, and of the state-of-the-art automated systems he used to manufacture his own armor. He recalled the phony Spymaster snooping around his headquarters in Silicon Valley. "Is Stark up to snuff? Could Modok build a chip using Stark's best equipment?"

"Perhaps," she replied slowly. Her eyes roamed over his armor, as if evaluating the workmanship. "Yes. I think so. Definitely. Stark's scientific accomplishments have impressed even A.I.M.'s top researchers. Given time, I'm almost positive Modok could adapt Stark's labs to suit his purposes.

"Then I need to get back to California right away," Iron Man decided. He checked the chronometer in his armor. "I can be there in a couple of hours."

"Maybe you should wait for the rest of us," War Machine said. His silver-plated helmet hid his face, but Iron Man could hear the concern in his voice.

Iron Man shook his head. "There's no time. By the time you folks make it back from Africa and Eastern Europe, Modok could have already added the chip to his arsenal."

"Start without us if you have to. We'll hurry back as fast as we can," Captain America said, "just in case you need reinforcements." War Machine nodded in agreement.

"I will accompany you," the Black Panther said. "The security of Wakanda has been compromised. That takes precedence over affairs of state."

"Thank you, T'Challa," Iron Man said. "I appreciate your help. Look for me at Stark headquarters in Silicon Valley. You all know the address." With luck, Cap and the others would arrive to find everything business as usual at Stark Enterprises. Deep down, though, he doubted they would be that fortunate. He began to sign off.

"Be careful," Captain America said gravely. "The first Modok was dangerous enough; I should know, I fought him plenty of times. I hate to think what the new and improved model is like."

"Just as ugly," Iron Man guessed, "and twice as nasty. Thanks for your concern, Cap. I won't get cocky." Captain America didn't bother, he noted, to try and talk Iron Man out of confronting Modok on his own; Cap understood the risks required to preserve liberty. He just wanted Iron Man to do so in a prudent and judicious manner. Not for the first time, Iron Man thought Cap would make a great commander-in-chief if ever he decided to stoop to politics. Indeed, he had been approached to run for President once, but turned it down. "Over and out," he said.

The screen went blank, leaving Iron Man and Christine along in the lavishly appointed passenger compartment of *Stark One*. He notified the pilot by intercom that he wanted to depart immediately for SE headquarters. *I might be able to fly back faster under my own power, but I ought to conserve my energy for the battle ahead, if there is one.*

Iron-clad fingers manipulated the controls of the communication console. *Best to warn Stark Enterprises right away.* He tried paging Bethany Cabe, his head of security, but got only a busy signal, even on her priority line. *What's going on?* he wondered anxiously. *Why can't I reach Bethany?* Mrs. Arbogast, his executive assistant, was similarly incommunicado. So was Felix Ricardo Alvarez, Vice President and Chief Operating Officer of Stark Enterprises; Dr. Abraham Zimmer, Director of Engineering; Dr. Erica Sondheim, Director of Medical Research; and so on. He checked his chronometer again. It was only 5:45 in Los Angeles; surely everyone couldn't have left work already. Besides, what about the swing shift? And beepers? Bethany, in particular, always made sure she could be reached at any time of the day. *Something's wrong.*

There was always HOMER, of course. HOMER was a computer program; he never slept, he never left Stark Enterprises, and he was never too busy to answer a call. If HOMER didn't respond, then Stark Enterprises itself might as well have disappeared. With a definite sense of anxiety, Iron Man requested direct access to HOMER.

After a second's delay, HOMER's voice came over the speakers. Stark Enterprises's corporate logo appeared on the screen. "Hello, Iron Man. What can I do for you?" HOMER knew Iron Man's secret identity, naturally, but he had been carefully programmed not to address Iron Man as Tony Stark when there was any possibility that a third party might be listening.

"Just checking to see if everything is okay back at headquarters." Iron Man was reassured to find HOMER available and online, even though he remained concerned about Modok's apparent interest in Stark Enterprises. Maybe Modok had not yet attacked the Stark labs?

"Everything is satisfactory," HOMER replied. "There are no unusual circumstances to report."

"Are you sure?" Iron Man said, aware that it was a funny question to ask a computer. "I have reason to suspect that Stark Enterprises may soon be invaded or infiltrated by Modok and his minions."

"Everything is satisfactory," HOMER repeated. "There are no unusual circumstances to report."

Odd, Iron Man thought. Even though he was only an artificial intelligence program, HOMER's responses sounded strangely mechanical. HOMER's dialogue was usually more spontaneous. "Please alert Security anyway. For some reason, I can't get hold of Bethany."

"Bethany Cabe is otherwise occupied," HOMER stated flatly, "but I will deliver your message. Is there anything else I can do for you?"

Yeah, stop sounding like a blasted bank machine. "No, I don't think so," Iron Man said. "Thank you."

The Stark logo vanished from the screen as he ended the transmission. Iron Man leaned back into his reinforced chair. Iron-clad fingers stroked a sculpted metal chin. Despite HOMER's reassurances, he felt a lingering sense of unease. Something was not right.

"Why don't you try contacting Tony Stark himself?" Christine asked. Startled, Iron Man sat up straight. Concerned as he was over what was happening to his company, he hadn't noticed what careful attention Christine was paying to his actions, nor that she was standing quite so close. He felt her hand drop lightly onto his metal shoulder. The smell of perfume teased his nostrils.

"I happen to know that Mr. Stark is attending a vital business conference in Hong Kong," he said, improvising shamelessly. "Trade negotiations, that sort of thing."

"Then shouldn't you be there as well, guarding his person?" Christine reclined against him, resting her weight upon his iron frame. He wasn't sure what unsettled him more: her curiosity about his alter ego or this casual intimacy. *You've saved her life twice already*, he reminded himself, counting the satellite's near-collision with Miami. *That's bound to affect her feelings toward you.*

"Sometimes my bodyguard duties extend to saving the whole planet. Mr. Stark understands this." He tried to dismiss the subject with a joke. "I have a *very* flexible job description."

"He must have a great deal of faith in you," she said softly. Beneath their feet, the plane began to move slowly down the runway; the pilot had obviously received clearance to take off.

Christine's voice grew huskier. "I know how he feels. I'd trust you anywhere, with anything."

How bizarre. Tony Stark was the debonair playboy, not Iron Man. He was used to being pursued by beautiful women (and vice versa) in his other identity, but not when he was wearing his metal suit. *For all she knows, I look like the Phantom of the Opera under my helmet.* Still, Christine's behavior sort of made sense, considering her passionate devotion to science and technology. Iron Man was nothing if not the heroic embodiment of scientific progress.

The jet accelerated down the runway, gaining speed rapidly. Iron Man made a show of turning away from her while saying, "Perhaps you should sit down, and fasten your seatbelt."

Christine picked up on the change in his mood immediately. "What's the matter?" she asked. Her striking brown eyes searched his faceplate, as if hoping to discern some expression on the rigid iron helmet.

Watch yourself, ShellHead. What did he really know about Christine Bright? Only that she was a devoted member of an international criminal organization. Could she be running some sort of Mata Hari number on him? He experienced a phantom pain where Kathy Dare's bullets had ripped apart his spine. Kathy had been very affectionate too. . . .

The plane leveled off, maintaining a fixed altitude. Christine, meanwhile, figured it out. Her eyes grew cold. Her jaw tightened. Her mouth became a thin, unforgiving line. "You don't trust me, do you?"

"Not entirely," he admitted. *Who had alerted Modok to our plans?* "I can't help wondering—"

"Of course you can't!" she interrupted him. "You're one of the good guys, an Avenger, a noble defender of the status quo, and I'm just another no-good mad scientist, who doesn't realize that she's supposed to play by the rules and accept things the way they are. Hell, I'm no better than an adaptoid, aren't I? Another mindless pawn of Advanced Idea Mechanics.'' Iron Man started to protest, but she turned away angrily. ''Don't say anything,'' she said. ''I don't want to hear it.''

Blast. That couldn't have turned out any worse. He wondered if he should have left Christine behind with the authorities in Miami. It was not too late to exit the plane and fly to California on his own power. He'd probably get there ahead of the jet, especially if he went high enough into space to take advantage of the Earth's rotation. But no, he decided after mulling it over; in the long run, it was better to keep Christine at hand, just to keep a close eye on her. Besides, he might still need her scientific expertise where the energy chip was concerned.

He gazed at Christine. She had retreated to the couch on the other side of the compartment. She kept her back turned to him. He couldn't see her face. The plane bounced awkwardly in the sky.

This is going to be a long flight. He seriously considered that Christine had deliberately sent him and the other heroes on a wild goose chase around the world—simply to get Iron Man away from Stark Enterprises. While he had been duelling with a duplicate Mandarin aboard A.I.M.'s orbital laboratory, had Modok been helping himself to Tony Stark's technological toystore? It was a scary thought.

SATURDAY. 2:25 AM. PACIFIC COAST TIME.

Stark Enterprises looked dark and abandoned. Not too surprising, considering the hour. Tony Stark often worked through the night, burning the midnight oil, but he encouraged his employees to have lives and interests outside of work. Fulfilling social and family lives made for happy, healthy, productive workers. *Cuts down on overtime, too*, he reminded himself.

Iron Man flew silently over the main laboratory building. He had left Christine waiting on the ground outside Stark Enterprises while he conducted an aerial reconnaissance of the plant and the surrounding buildings. The grounds appeared deserted, the buildings silent and shut down for the night. Security at Stark Enterprises was deceptively inconspicuous. Most of Tony Stark's major enemies would not even be slowed down by a chainlink fence or a roaming night watchman, so he had not bothered with such pedestrian defenses. The grounds below were monitored by a complex array of motion detectors, radar sensors, concealed cameras, and automated force field projectors. Among his many talents and responsibilities, HOMER made a better security guard than any retired ex-cop; it was a tribute to the ingenuity and skill of the bogus Spymaster that the adaptoid had managed to avoid setting off any alarms for as long as he had. Even as he soared above Stark Enterprises, Iron Man suspected that he was being tracked by dozens of computerized warning systems. For a second, he wished that he had donned his special "stealth" armor instead, but why should he have to sneak up on his own corporate headquarters?

From above, HOMER's reassuring report seemed entirely justified. Stark Enterprises hardly looked under siege. He remained disturbed, however, that neither Bethany or the others had returned any of his calls yet. Certainly, they all knew how to contact him on *Stark One*, and Bethany Cabe, who had long been aware of his dual identity, could transmit a message directly to the communications antenna in his armor. Why had no one responded to his inquiries?

He circled over the installation and headed back to the street where he had left Christine. The lovely A.I.M. scientist had not yet forgiven him for his lack of trust; the trip from the Los Angeles airport had been filled with angry glares and tense, icy silences. Iron Man regretted the barriers that had risen between them, but he needed to ensure the safety of Stark Enterprises before he could consider anything else. Assuming Christine wasn't a double agent to begin with.

As he descended toward Christine, he was surprised to see three figures surrounding the unarmed woman. *Uh-oh*, he thought, wishing for a second that he had provided Christine with a weapon, despite his doubts. The circle of figures tightened around her, blocking off all avenues of escape. In the dark, Iron Man could not make out any details about the figures, although they seemed determined not to let Christine get away.

His chest beam cast a brilliant white spotlight upon Christine and her assailants. The figures on the ground looked up at him, startled by the sudden glare. Iron Man saw a fearsome figure encased in black-and-silver armor, another man dressed all in black and wearing the face of a jungle cat, and a walking icon dressed in red, white, and blue. "Avengers Assemble," he breathed out loud, reciting the super team's traditional battlecry.

Captain America waved his shield at Iron Man. "Good to see you, ShellHead," he called out. "We weren't sure what Ms. Bright had done with you." Behind Cap, Christine scowled at the implied accusation.

"Nothing yet," Iron Man informed him. Exhaust sprayed from the nozzles of his boot jets as he lowered himself onto the sidewalk. He dimmed the glare of his chest-beam now that he was close enough to see the others easily. "I don't understand. How did you all get here so fast?"

"Never underestimate the maximum speed of a quinjet," Cap answered, "nor the resourcefulness of good men united in a common cause. T'Challa showed me how to use vibranium to jump start the quinjet's engines up to a higher level of power and efficiency."

I'd like to see that trick myself. Tony Stark's scientific curiosity was piqued by the idea. "You're going have to show me how you did that someday," he said to T'Challa.

"It will be my pleasure," the Black Panther said, "but now is probably not the right time."

War Machine shrugged his armor-plated shoulders. "Me? I just blasted off into the upper atmosphere and let the earth's rotation bring California underneath me. Then I dropped back to earth just in time to hook up with Cap and T'Challa."

Of course. A suborbital parabolic maneuver. It was a risky but effective way to travel, and one that Tony had personally taught to Jim Rhodes. *A lucky break for me, or something more suspicious?* An ominous notion occurred to him. *How can I be sure that one or more of these heroes are the real thing?* The adaptoids could duplicate anyone, even an Avenger.

Unfortunately, he couldn't think of a way to verify anyone's identities here and now. *I'm not sure that I could demonstrate that I am the real Iron Man if any of them challenged me.* It was even possible that War Machine was the genuine article while Cap and the Panther were fakes. Or vice versa. *I'm just going to have keep my eyes open—and be ready for anything.*

"I may not need you," Iron Man said to the others. He explained how quiet the installation seemed. "Let's give the place a thorough inspection, though. Follow me."

The sun had not yet begun to lighten the Silicon Valley sky. Dew covered the neatly manicured lawn in front of Stark Enterprises. Freeway traffic could be heard in the distance and the air smelled faintly of smog. Iron Man led the others along cement walkways that connected the various buildings that made up Stark Enterprises's California headquarters. Palm trees lined the walkways; moonlight cast their shadows upon the path. Despite their antagonism, Christine kept close to Iron Man, who assumed that she trusted the other heroes even less. War Machine guarded the rear, his chain gun mounted and ready on his left shoulder. Iron Man fought the urge to keep checking behind him. *I hope that's really you, Jim.*

No alarms blared as they walked between the buildings. Iron Man's armor emitted a constant identification signal that acted as an electronic skeleton key to the facility's various computerized defenses. The signal provided Iron Man and his party with unimpeded access to the entire Stark Enterprises installation. It was a good system; so far, no spy or super-villain had been able to mimic the signal.

Finally, they came to the primary construction laboratory, where HOMER manufactured the prototypes of Stark Enterprises's most sophisticated new inventions. Signs printed in thirteen languages declared the laboratory, "RESTRICTED. EXECUTIVE CLEARANCE REQUIRED FOR ENTRY." The laboratory was shaped like an immense geodesic dome. Unlike most of the other buildings surrounding them, the lab had no windows—for security reasons. Besides, HOMER could see through cameras stationed all over the complex; he was not likely to feel deprived by the lack of a view from inside the laboratory. Iron Man approached the main entrance. A signal from his gauntlet unlocked the door, which swung open automatically. Artificial light escaped the open door-way. Iron Man heard the hum of machinery coming from within the building.

I have a bad feeling about this. He stepped forward, eager to enter the lab and find out what was going on. *Could be just a routine experiment,* he reminded himself. *HOMER never sleeps, after all.* Deep down inside, though, he knew that trouble was brewing beyond the door. He raised his gauntlets, palms up, repulsors ready.

"Wait," Captain America whispered urgently. He ran forward, placing himself between Iron Man and the open door. "Let me check things out first. I'm not wearing a heavy metal suit. I should be able to sneak up on whomever's in there."

"I suppose," Iron Man said. He didn't quite see the need for secrecy. *It's not like we're breaking and entering. I own the entire building.* He suddenly noticed that Cap had not limped once since his arrival; hadn't he broken his foot during his fight with the counterfeit Mr. Hyde? "How's your ankle?" he asked the venerable hero.

"Good as new," Cap declared confidently, "but thanks for asking. Wakanda's herbal medicine can work miracles."

"This is true," the Black Panther confirmed. "I owe much of my strength and agility to a rare, heart-shaped herb that grows only in my homeland."

"So you've told me," Iron Man said, frowning behind his golden mask. He had known the origin of T'Challa's abilities for years; why had the Panther felt obliged to explain his secrets again? And why was Cap so keen on entering the laboratory first? Iron Man felt an itch at the back of his consciousness. *Am I just being paranoid, or is there really something odd here?* He had no solid reasons to suspect Cap and the others.

And yet . . . how had his fellow Avengers really gotten here so quickly? He had designed the quinjet's engines personally; how in the world would you use vibranium to make the ship fly faster? Granted, T'Challa was a genius in his own right, but it didn't make sense from an engineering perspective. The speed of the quinjet was limited by the basic realities of its design: the materials, the tensile strength, the vulnerability to wind resistance and internal friction, etc. Vibranium? It was possible, he supposed, but he couldn't see how. Then again, he had never figured out exactly how the adaptoids worked either.

And War Machine's suborbital maneuver? That was certainly plausible enough, he had to admit. Could it be that War Machine was exactly who he appeared to be? Or were the adaptoids even more convincing then he had ever feared?

He eyed his companions warily, assuming that his helmet hid the suspicious expression on his face. Three adaptoids, he recalled, had escaped from Iron Man and his allies: the Cobra, Deathlok, and the Mandarin (or reasonable facsimiles thereof). Furthermore, an adaptoid was always capable of changing its form to impersonate someone else. Three heroes, three adaptoids.

A frightening theory formulated in his mind.

Captain America still stood between Iron Man and

the door. "Hang on," the Golden Avenger said. "I have an idea." He looked at War Machine. "Why don't you use your armor's special camouflage abilities?"

"Camouflage?" War Machine said slowly. "I'm not sure I follow you, ShellHead."

"Sure," Iron Man said. "Use your holographic projection units to interface with the crystallized extraluminal refractory properties of your armor to simulate an external, multidimensional, metaphoric transmogrification." He spotted Christine out of the corner of his eye. She looked slightly taken aback by his outpouring of technological gobbledygook. Then she got it; her eyes narrowed slightly as she peered cautiously at the other heroes. "You remember, War Machine, you used that trick to outwit Blacklash and the Thermodynamic Man during that battle in Seattle?"

"Right!" War Machine nodded enthusiastically. "I remember now. It's been a while since I pulled that stunt."

"It sure has," Iron Man agreed. "So why don't you turn yourself into the spitting image of the standard-model A.I.M. technician. Modok will never expect that."

War Machine looked uncertainly at both Captain America and the Black Panther. Iron Man saw Cap nod almost imperceptibly. War Machine took a few steps backwards in response. He stood stiffly at attention, his arms at his sides, then he began to *change*.

Iron Man's eyes grew wide beneath his helmet.

He heard Christine gasp out loud. War Machine was changing before their eyes. The solid-looking armor covering his body had started to dissolve. It flowed like liquid mercury, rearranging itself into new shapes and patterns. War Machine's forbidding metal helmet became a tall, cylindrical hood much like a beekeeper's. His body armor assumed the folds and contours of a suit of fabric. The massive armaments mounted on his back and shoulders receded into his body. The texture changed next, going from a shiny metallic gleam to that of fresh yellow cloth. War Machine's height diminished by an inch or two. An identification number appeared on his hood: X758D. Iron Man wondered if War Machine had invented the number at random.

The entire transformation took less than three seconds. When it was over, War Machine was gone, replaced by a man in a yellow technician's uniform. Iron Man was impressed, but not the way the former War Machine had probably hoped for.

Captain America reacted first. "Good Lord," he exclaimed. "He's an adaptoid!"

He sounded truly surprised, Iron Man noted. And if Cap was for real, then the Panther must be genuine as well. *That's a relief. Maybe I'm not as badly outnumbered as I feared.* He aimed his palms at the uniformed adaptoid. "Don't move a muscle," he warned.

"So," the adaptoid said angrily. "It was all a trick. I should have known. War Machine's template contained no such camouflage ability, but you made me suspect that my data may have been incomplete.''

"That's right," Iron Man said. "War Machine's armor is good, but it's not that good. Only an adaptoid could change his shape so readily."

"The template was not discarded," the adaptoid intoned, "only stored in my molecular memory. Readapting now. . . ."

To his alarm, Iron Man saw a silvery sheen spreading over the bogus technician's yellow uniform. The adaptoid grew in mass and height even as the others watched. Repulsor rays struck the evolving adaptoid, but it was difficult to tell if they were having any effect. Synthetic steel contorted beneath the impact of the rays, yet the transformation continued. *This looks like trouble.* "Cap, Panther, watch out for Christine."

"A-okay," Cap responded. Iron Man heard Cap moving behind him, then the hero's voice took on a harsher tone. "Halt your attack immediately, Iron Man, or the female dies."

Blast, Iron Man thought. *Fooled again.* Switching off his repulsors, he spun around to see the being he had assumed to be Captain America holding on to Christine from behind, the edge of his shield poised above her throat. Christine stood frozen in Cap's grasp, afraid to move, her wide eyes crying out to Iron Man. *Guess I wasn't paranoid enough.*

Cap sneered, confirming all of Iron Man's worst fears. He had never seen such a malignant expression on the real Captain America's face. "Do not attempt a rescue, Iron Man," the adaptoid said. "My reflexes

217

are as swift as the original Captain America. I can kill the woman in an instant." His companion, the bogus Black Panther, stalked toward Iron Man with menace in his stride. *Three against one. Bad odds. Especially after that phony technician finishes changing back into something more powerful.*

"Fine," Iron Man said. "This is your game for now." He pointed at the lighted doorway. "What's going on in there?"

The false Cap scowled in a very out-of-character fashion. "You might as well see." He addressed his fellow adaptoids. "Come. Let us present our prisoners to the Master." Maintaining a tight hold on Christine, he stepped inside the laboratory. The imitation Panther gestured for Iron Man to follow. Iron Man nodded, keeping his eyes on the phony Cap and his hostage. *Let's play along for now, and learn what we can about the adaptoids' plot.*

He glanced back at the third adaptoid. As he'd feared, the creature was swiftly discarding his disguise as an ordinary lab worker. The substance of his uniform had melted away, reversing his earlier transformation. Yellow fabric transformed into gleaming steel. A chain gun and missile launcher sprouted from his shoulders. *Great*, Iron Man thought bitterly. *Just what we didn't need: the return of the duplicate War Machine.* Cap and the Panther were only human; despite the adaptoids' borrowed abilities, that pair of imitation heroes weren't in the same league as Iron Man with all his augmented strength and weaponry. The War Machine armor, on the other hand, was a match for his own. *I should know, I built them both.*

The adaptoid Panther shoved him roughly between the shoulders, and Iron Man turned his attention back to the open doorway. Light spilled out of the laboratory, casting the phony Cap's shadow onto the walkway. Iron Man walked over the adaptoid's shadow on his way into the lab. He wished he was stomping over the real thing.

A circular path, maintained for the convenience of HOMER's human visitors, divided the lab into two work areas: a series of work stations that ran along the outer circumference of the circular floor, and a larger area spreading out from the very center of the floor.

The centerpiece of the lab was a gigantic dome-shaped tank made of dense, transparent plastic and holding a transparent, turquoise-colored fluid. The huge, liquid-filled dome fit inside the larger dome of the lab itself the way Russian *matreshka* dolls do, with the smallest doll hidden deep inside the largest one. Within the tank, glittering bits of silicon and steel swam towards each other, uniting to form progressively larger pieces of circuitry. The electronic components seemed to fit themselves together of their volition; in fact, Iron Man knew, the entire process was being carefully controlled by HOMER by means of thousands of microscopic machines too tiny for the human eye to see. *Nanotechnology at work*, Iron Man thought, impressed as ever by the seemingly miraculous instrumentality. A similar tank existed in the sub-subbasement of an adjacent building; that was where HOMER built each one of Iron Man's new suits of armor. He used this above-ground tank for less confidential experiments.

Iron Man glanced at Christine. Despite her danger, he could see that the captive scientist was awestruck by HOMER's ability to create and manipulate new technology at a submolecular level. *Guess Stark Enterprises measures up to A.I.M.'s exalted standards after all*, he thought with some satisfaction.

Debris littered the floor of the lab. Iron Man saw an open snakeskin pouch, a smattering of moist earth and clay, and one-third of the adamantium sphere. Modok was already assembling the ingredients for the energy chip. *I'm too late.*

But where was the adaptoid's master? At first, Iron Man could not spot A.I.M.'s latest cyborg monstrosity, then he heard a high-pitched cackle coming from the other side of the tank. Peering through the murky turquoise fluid, he could make out a bulky, block-shaped mass moving around the base of the tank, coming towards them. A minute later, Iron Man got a good look at the freakish entity responsible for the adaptoids' rampage of theft and murder.

He was grotesque. Modok 1.5 closely resembled his late, unlamented predecessor, except that his sunken eyes were blue and his massive head was topped by a thatch of flaxen hair. Like the first Modok, this version was nearly all head. His skull, housing his artificially enlarged brain, was the size of a Cray supercomputer. By contrast, the rest of his body was atrophied and withered. His torso was no larger than a ten-year-old's, and his arms and legs were both stunted and anorexically thin. Because his stunted limbs could not possibly support his oversized cranium, Modok traveled by means of a levitating hoverchair. An invisible column of force lifted the chair about three feet off the floor; Iron Man suspected some form of magnetic repulsion was involved. The bronzed, metallic chair blended seamlessly with the sophisticated exoskeleton encasing his body and supporting his Brobdingnagian head. Only Modok's face was uncovered; his pale skin was dry and flaky. A bronze-colored headband stretched across Modok's enormous brow. A ruby gemstone was embedded in the center of the headband, above and between his malevolent eyes. The gem, Iron Man knew, served to focus Modok's considerable psionic powers. Modok's mutated brain was capable of deadly telekinetic attacks, just as his chair and exoskeleton surely held numerous concealed weapons.

Though this Modok seemed to prefer playing mastermind, sending out his adaptoid followers to perform his dirty work, Iron Man had no doubt that, when push came to shove, the renegade cyborg would prove a formidable antagonist in his own right. He silently cursed Christine's deceased colleagues in A.I.M. for inflicting another Modok upon the world.

Iron Man found the sight of Modok deeply disturbing. Probably because, he conceded reluctantly, this inhuman mixture of man and machine was a perverse reflection of himself. Like Modok, Tony Stark had compensated for the limitations of his

fragile human body by developing increasingly sophisticated suits of prosthetic armor. Like Modok,
Tony had also relied on the power of his mind to
overcome paralysis, heart disease, alcoholism, and
other weaknesses of the flesh. Modok had merely
taken the idea of Iron Man to its most horrific ex-
treme, merging with his exoskeleton until it had become impossible to tell where humanity ended and
technology began. By asserting the supreme domi-
nance of his powerful mind, Modok had reduced his
body to a useless appendage, incapable of functioning without the aid of complex mechanical apparatus. Securely lodged inside his own iron exoskeleton,
Tony Stark repressed a shudder. *There but for the
grace of God go I.* He prayed that he would never
become so dependent on mind and machinery that
Iron Man became a creature like Modok.

"Welcome home, hero," Modok said. His voice
was shrill and squeaky. His stunted arms flapped
spasmodically. "You must thank your employer for
the use of his fine facilities, assuming that you ever
see him again. A prospect which, alas, seems extremely unlikely."

The adaptoid version of Captain America lowered
his shield, releasing Christine, who hurried to join
Iron Man. He held on to her arm reassuringly while
"Cap" and the "Black Panther" took up defensive
positions in front of Modok. The imitation War Machine remained behind Iron Man and Christine, cutting off their retreat. Iron Man clenched his fists.
"What have you done with Bethany and the others?" He knew now that Modok had to be respon-

sible for the ominous silence from his friends. He looked up at the domed ceiling and addressed the empty air. "HOMER, are you here? Talk to me."

The sentient computer intelligence that he knew must be inhabiting the lab did not respond. In the assembly tank, however, bits and pieces of interlocking circuitry continued to come together under the direction of an unseen mechanical maestro.

"Go ahead, HOMER," Modok said. His cerulean eyes had no visible pupils, being both blue and blank. "You may reply."

"Hello, Iron Man," HOMER said. The familiar voice emerged from concealed speakers situated throughout the laboratory. The voice was clear, distinct, and seemed to come from everywhere at once; Tony had equipped HOMER with complete Dolby sound. "Everything is satisfactory. There are no unusual circumstances to report."

Blast. HOMER sounded like he'd been lobotomized. Or brainwashed. "HOMER," he demanded. "Activate emergency security protocols. Terminate and destroy whatever you're growing in the tank."

"I'm afraid I can't do that, Iron Man," HOMER stated calmly. "Everything is satisfactory. There are no unusual circumstances to report."

Aside from the unauthorized presence of Modok and three hostile adaptoids, Iron Man thought, but HOMER was apparently no longer capable of recognizing the direness of the situation.

"I am a master of machines and men," Modok explained. "It was child's play to override the programming that granted Stark's pet AI the illusion of autonomy, especially with the inside information transmitted to me by my obedient Spymaster adaptoid.''

''And what about Bethany Cabe and the rest? Felix Alvarez? Mrs. Arbogast?'' Iron Man asked. He saw Christine scowl when he mentioned Bethany's name. No surprise there; he suspected that Bethany would likewise object to his consorting with Christine—for both personal and professional reasons. But now was not the time to deal with jealous females. ''Tell me what you've done to them.'' He remembered the massacres at both the undersea base and the orbital laboratory, and feared the worst.

A smirk appeared on Modok's overinflated face. The ruby affixed to his forehead reflected the turquoise glow coming from the assembly tank. ''Stark's human servants proved no challenge. A wide-range psionic blast shut down their minds. If you had the opportunity to explore the adjacent buildings, I suspect you would find Ms. Cabe and the others slumped over their desks and fax machines, struck down in the middle of their mundane and trivial labors.'' Modok's maglev chair rotated a half-turn, so that he faced the transparent wall of the assembly tank. ''They will recover in a matter of hours,'' he continued, ''but by then it will too late— for them and for the entire human race.''

I don't like the sound of that. He stared into the depths of the tank. Floating in the turquoise fluids, an intricate silver lattice had formed, like a futuristic spiderweb, around a tiny crystalline chip about the size of a pea. The crystal grew before his eyes, like a pearl forming around a speck of sand. Soon it was about the size of a postage stamp and distressingly familiar-looking. The chip was identical to the one that War Machine had stolen from A.I.M., the chip whose unleashed energy had reduced a centuries-old medieval castle to rubble. The turquoise liquid began to recede, draining away through vents in the floor of the assembly tank. The chip remained aloft, held up by the web of silver filaments.

"What sort of game are you playing?" Iron Man challenged Modok. "Are you after a Cosmic Cube? Is that it?"

Modok did not look at Iron Man. He kept his gaze upon the chip. "No, not yet," he said in his smug falsetto. "The Cube will be mine someday. Even as we speak, teams of brilliant adaptoid minds are addressing the problem. A breakthrough is inevitable. The Cube will come, but you and your pathetic, outmoded species will not be around to see that day."

Iron Man felt a surge of relief to hear that Modok and the adaptoids had not yet learned how to recreate the Cosmic Cube. "I don't get it then," he said. "What do you want that chip for?"

"For the extermination of humanity," Modok squeaked. A stubby finger pointed at the jewel on his forehead. "At present, the range of my psionic blasts is limited to a radius of approximately five miles. Enough to render the personnel of Stark Enterprises temporarily comatose, but no more than that. With the full power of the chip at my command, suffusing my being with the unfathomable energies of another dimension, the power of my mind will increase proportionally. Once I have mastered the secret of controlling the power, I intend to unleash a psionic assault wave that will terminate the existence of every man, woman, and child on the planet. I will render your entire species extinct overnight, leaving me the unquestioned ruler of a world populated only by adaptoids under my command."

Iron Man caught his breath, stunned by the full implications of Modok's genocidal scheme. Could Modok be serious? Was such an apocalyptic catastrophe even possible? Iron Man looked at Christine, concerned about her reaction to Modok's insane ambition to eradicate all human life. She appeared to be holding up well, at least under the circumstances. He gave her as much of a comforting glance as his iron helmet allowed, then looked back at Modok.

"Destroy humanity?" he asked. "Why in heaven's name would you want to do that? What possible purpose could it serve?" *Keep him talking.* Every moment he kept Modok occupied gave Cap, Jim, and T'Challa a better shot at getting here in time to nip Modok's ghastly endeavor in the bud. In a pinch, he'd take on Modok and the adaptoids on his own, but it couldn't hurt to wait for the reinforcements he knew were coming.

"I am the Mental Organism Designed Only for Killing," the hideous cyborg declared. "That is my purpose. That is my destiny. I am the Angel of Death, created by humans to eliminate humanity, to end forever their misbegotten reign over this planet. The human race is primitive, atavistic, obsolete. Your inferior species must give way to a new and better society of artificial lifeforms. The time of the adaptoid is at hand, and I shall rule over the adaptoids, wielding the power of life and death over your evolutionary successors until it is time to eliminate them as well. Then I shall cleanse the planet of all biological and technological life before moving on to spread my killing crusade throughout the cosmos. The Skrulls, the Kree, the Shi'ar—all extraterrestrial civilizations will fall before the unstoppable doomsday machine that is Modok. This is my vision. This is the future.''

"This is garbage," Iron Man said loudly. "You don't sound like a superior intelligence to me. You sound like just another crazed megalomaniac with delusions of grandeur, no better than Dr. Doom or the Red Skull." He pointed at the crystal chip, suspended in its silver lattice. The bulk of the fluid had drained away, leaving only a few drops and tiny puddles behind. Evidently concerned that Iron Man might blast the chip with the weapons in his fingertip, the War Machine adaptoid grabbed Iron Man by the wrist and yanked his arm down.

Iron Man ignored the adaptoid. "I know that chip," he said to Modok. "You're fooling yourself if you think you can control that kind of energy. At best, you'll turn this place into a smoking crater and send you and your plastic buddies straight to robot hell."

The transparent dome containing the chip ascended toward the ceiling, pulled upward by HOMER's invisible tractor beams. Modok contemplated the finished chip. The multifaceted surface of his mind-focussing ruby began to glow. "Do not ascribe to me your own petty organic liabilities. Small wonder you could not control the power of the first chip; despite your vaunted armor, you are merely human after all. The full capacity of my mind surpasses yours by several orders of magnitude. The alien energies of the chip will bend to my will, just as the adaptoids have done."

Iron Man could see Modok's telekinesis at work. The translucent crystal chip vibrated at the center of the silver web. Clinging filaments clung to the chip, but it gradually detached itself from its nanotech umbilicus. The chip floated across the lab to drop into Modok's waiting palm. Aided and abetted by his exoskeleton, Modok wrapped his dwarfish fingers around the chip. "You see?" he said shrilly. "No mechanism, no technology can resist me. I am the master of all artificial creations." His hoverchair rotated again, so that he faced both Iron Man and Christine. "Isn't that so, Adaptoid #4CWB?"

Christine stepped forward. Her gorgeously expressive face suddenly turned cold and unemotional. *Dear God, no*, Iron Man thought, realizing the terrible truth at last. His heart sank, because he knew what she was going to say before she opened her mouth.

"Yes, Modok," she said.

CHAPTER 10

Christine was an adaptoid.

It made sense, in a heartbreaking sort of way. Hadn't she herself said that Modok would surely have been shrewd enough to leave some kind of monitoring device behind at the undersea lab to alert him to any unusual comings and goings at the ruined lab? Well, Christine had certainly been right about that; what she hadn't mentioned was that *she* was the device. Iron Man wondered momentarily if there had ever been a real Dr. Christine Bright and, if so, what had happened to her? *Probably an inconspicuous pile of ashes somewhere at the bottom of the Atlantic Ocean*, he decided. He mourned her, even though they had never really met.

His face rigid, Iron Man swept his gaze over Modok, the three phony super heroes, and Christine. It gave him a chill to realize that he was the only truly human person in the laboratory. *And even I have an artificial heart and nervous system*, he thought wryly.

"Join us," Christine said, with what sounded like genuine emotion in her voice. "Look at you. You want to be a machine, I know you do. Why waste all that magnificent strength and power on beings of mere flesh and blood? Yes, I am an adaptoid. What difference does that make? Except I am stronger and more durable than any fragile human woman. I can be just as beautiful, just as loving." Her brown eyes wept synthetic tears. "I will never age. We can be together forever. The real Christine could never love you the way I can. I can see past your metal shell to the true machine inside you. You are not human, you're Iron Man, and you belong with a superior woman. An adaptoid woman."

She held out her arms invitingly. Modok looked on, seemingly bemused by Christine's unexpected declaration of love. Surprise, and something like fascination, were painted across the oversized canvas of his colossal face. "How intriguing," he commented. "I fear that #4CWB has adapted too well to her role as a tempting damsel in distress. Some serious reprogramming may be in order." He fixed a curious eye on Iron Man. "Unless, of course, you are inclined to take her up on her offer. I can always use a double agent in the Avengers."

"Yes, Iron Man, please," Christine urged him. "Tony Stark does not deserve your loyalty. You are twice the man he is: a man of steel and silicon. Come to me."

Iron Man shook his head. "Sorry, I'm not even tempted." The crushed look on Christine's lovely face seemed achingly real, but he wasn't about to betray the entire human race for a woman, especially not a fake one. Still, he felt an unmistakable sense of loss as he stared into Christine's tear-filled eyes. The intensity of her passion disturbed him; she had seemed so *real*. He tore his gaze away from the female adaptoid and faced Modok defiantly. "Now what, big brain? You know I won't let you leave with that chip.''

Modok dismissed him with a wave of his stunted arm. ''I require a moment or two to examine the chip,'' he told his adaptoids. ''Eliminate Iron Man.''

So much for small talk. His bootjets fired instantly, lifting him off the floor just as the three adaptoids charged at him. The fake War Machine's iron fist almost collided with the false Captain America, but he halted his attack at the last minute. Iron Man fired twin repulsor rays at the adaptoids, hoping to bring the fight to a rapid conclusion. The Cap droid blocked one beam with his shield, while the artificial Panther nimbly jumped out of the way of the other ray. The real Panther could not have reacted more swiftly than the black-clad adaptoid, Iron Man noted. The counterfeit Cap's shield seemed just as indestructible as the real thing. *This could be rough.*

The imitation War Machine took to the air after him. Iron Man kept his eyes on the armored adaptoid, identifying him as the primary threat, at least until Modok figured out how to interface with the newborn energy chip. The fake War Machine came at him with weapons blazing, apparently unconcerned about the damage he was inflicting on the domed laboratory. *Thank heavens I have insurance*, Iron Man thought as a barrage of bullets shattered the plastic interior dome and blew off the porcelain tiles covering the ceiling. The chain gun on War Machine's shoulder, a sort of high-tech gatling gun, fired round after round of ammo at Iron Man. The minicannon in the adaptoid's gauntlet peppered him with explosive cartridges. The sound of gunfire filled the lab. Iron Man reversed the polarity of the magnetic field surrounding his armor, which sent the bullets ricocheting back at the phony War Machine. The ammo detonated against the adaptoid's armor.

Iron Man knew full well the volley was not enough to penetrate the War Machine armor, but he took advantage of the cascade of explosions to go on the offensive. He targeted the missile launcher on the adaptoid's other shoulder with a concentrated laser blast from his chest beam projector. The matte-black metal of the positioning rail glowed red where the intense heat of the laser beam struck it. *Good.* In theory, that should have fused the connection between the missile launcher and the armor's main targeting computer. *Surgical strikes, that's the ticket.* One on one, the Iron Man and War Machine armors were pretty evenly matched; there was no way he could overpower the adaptoid through sheer force alone. He needed to make every shot count.

''I built that armor,'' he muttered, ''and I can take it apart.''

He aimed for the chain gun next. *Let's take that out of the equation*, he thought, directing his laser at the gun's aiming guidance system. Then, unexpectedly, Cap's shield came from out of nowhere, turning the beam projector in Iron Man's chest into a bull's-eye. The shield smashed into Iron Man, its hard edge cracking the lens of his tri-beam projector before bouncing back to the waiting hand of the Captain America adaptoid. *What in the periodic table is that shield made of?* His chestplate could withstand artillery fire without a taking a scratch, but now his chest-beam had been rendered out of commission until he could replace the broken lens. *Serves me right for underestimating Captain America. Even an artificial one.*

He tried to anticipate which weapon the duplicate War Machine would employ next. He had provided that armor with an unusually generous assortment of armaments; now he could only guess what the adaptoid would throw at him. The saber? The flame thrower?

Glancing down quickly at the floor below, he saw Christine taking shelter from the flying bullets and debris by crouching beneath one of the worktables running along the interior of the dome. Modok did not look up at the ongoing battle between Iron Man and the counterfeit War Machine; the cyborg appeared engrossed in his analysis of the small crystal chip. The Captain America adaptoid stood poised to fling his shield again the moment a good opportunity presented itself; the sight of the murderous imposter clad in Cap's legendary red, white, and blue costume seemed like a desecration. But where was the Black Panther droid? Although he swept the lab with his gaze, he could not locate the ebony-clad adaptoid.

All of his proximity alarms went into overdrive as the fake War Machine came rocketing at him like a black-and-silver missile. The adaptoid surprised Iron Man by resorting to his fists instead of his firepower. An iron-plated fist, backed up by the full force of the accelerating War Machine, slammed into his chin, ramming his head back. Several layers of protective shielding kept his neck from breaking, but Tony Stark felt his jaw hit so hard his teeth rattled.

Iron Man felt like the losing side of a Rock'Em-Sock'Em Robots match, where the object was to knock the other robot's head off. Dazed, he shook his head, hoping to regain his concentration before the adaptoid delivered the final, fatal punch.

The false War Machine veered away from Iron Man after delivering his blow. He performed a loop beneath the roof of the dome, then came zooming at Iron Man once more. Putting on an extra burst of speed, Iron Man darted out of the way a millisecond before the adaptoid's fists could collide with him again. The wind whistled past his helmet as Iron Man zipped between the dome and the floor. The adaptoid pursued Iron Man through the air. The enclosed dome made maneuvering difficult; at these speeds, it was only a matter of time before one of the flying armored figures smashed through the wall of the dome.

Iron Man executed a partial barrel roll and fired back at the adaptoid with both palm repulsors. Zigzagging high above the floor, the ersatz War Machine dodged Iron Man's dual beams. He directed his own repulsors at the empty air in front of Iron Man, hoping to intercept his adversary's flight path. Iron Man almost flew straight into the beams, but his armor's computer had tracked the trajectory of the enemy beams, giving him just enough warning to change course and dive beneath the repulsor blasts.

This is turning into an old-fashioned dogfight. He took advantage of the moment to strafe the floor of the dome with a series of pulse bolts from his gauntlets. Discrete bursts of ionically-charged plasma tore into the cement foundation of the lab, shooting the floor out from beneath the bogus Captain America's boots. The Avenger-induced earthquake barely affected Modok, however; gyroscopic controls in the cyborg's hoverchair kept him levitating evenly over the shaking floor. He gave Iron Man a look of mere annoyance, as if slightly surprised that the outnumbered hero had not yet been disposed of.

"Don't go away, Modok," Iron Man called out. "I'll deal with you in a minute."

A stream of bullets tore up the air in front of Iron Man. "Watch your mouth, ShellHead," the false War Machine boomed at maximum volume. He dived at Iron Man like a kamikaze. "Don't go making promises you can't keep."

"Watch yourself." Iron Man brought himself to a dead halt in the air. Momentum carried the adaptoid past Iron Man. He hit the adaptoid with both repulsors as the speeding War Machine whizzed past him. The ion beams knocked the adaptoid off course, sending him into a spin. The imitation War Machine fell straight toward Modok. Hovering fifty feet above the floor, Iron Man paused to watch the other armored figure plummet at incredible speed. *With any luck*, he hoped, *I'll take out two bad guys with one blow, including the big brain himself.*

But before he could view the outcome of the imminent crash, a heavy weight suddenly landed on his back. A thick black sheet was wrapped around his helmet, blindfolding him. A pair of powerful legs locked onto his waist. Strong hands tugged at the collar of his armor, trying to pry his helmet loose.

T'Challa, Iron Man realized. Or rather, the adaptoid who was impersonating T'Challa. He must have climbed to the top of the ceiling, then dropped onto Iron Man as silently as his feline namesake. The dense black shroud engulfing his head had to be the copycat Panther's cape, which the adaptoid had turned into a weapon. He activated his radar only to discover that unexpected levels of interference had reduced his sonic guidance system to nothing but static. The adaptoid War Machine had to be jamming Iron Man's radar with the transmitters in his own armor. "Blast," Iron Man muttered. The duplicate War Machine must have averted his fall before he connected with either Modok or the floor. Some War Machines had all the luck.

Flying blind, he tried to shake the false Panther off him, but the adaptoid held on with both legs. His fingers continued to search the exterior of Iron Man's armor, looking for a chink, socket, or accessible system. An alarming thought occurred to Iron Man: Had the adaptoid Panther also duplicated T'Challa's mechanical genius? If so, he might well find a way into the internal communications layer of his armor.

Eager to discourage the Panther droid, Iron Man channeled the excess heat from his boot rockets into the wafer-thin heat exchange piping that ran through his armor. Almost immediately, the outer temperature of his armor rose from a little above room temperature to almost one hundred degrees centigrade.

Iron Man smelled the odor of burning fabric, then grinned wolfishly beneath his helmet as he felt the false Panther loosen his grip on Iron Man and spring away in a hurry, no doubt to land on both feet like the jungle cats emulated by the man whose form and abilities the adaptoid had assumed.

"A little too warm and toasty for you?" Iron Man asked. The heavy cloth covering his helmet muffled his words. "You know what they say: If you can't stand the heat, get off of the armor."

The sable cloak covering his eyes burst into flames. Photosensitive lenses protected him from the sudden glare. Ventilation filters in his mouthpiece kept him from inhaling smoke and flame. He let the cape burn; it seemed quicker than trying to unknot it. As the charred fabric fell away from his faceplate, he found himself staring directly into the silver-plated scowl of War Machine's evil twin.

"Peekaboo," the adaptoid said, slamming his fist into Iron Man's face so hard that his knuckles left dents in the hero's golden visage. The fake War Machine held onto Iron Man with one hand while his other fist used Iron Man's helmet as a punching bag.

Overcoming his initial surprise, Iron Man struggled to break free from the adaptoid's grip, pounding the creature's armor-covered ribs with both fists, determined to make the adaptoid let go.

They grappled in the air, sixty feet above the cracked and broken floor of the lab. They spun wildly as they fought hand to hand, their jets leaving twin trails of exhaust to mark their path across the lab. Defying gravity, they brawled and belted each other far above the watchful eyes of Modok, Christine, and the other adaptoids.

Iron Man couldn't take much more of this pounding. Despite the shockproof insulation in his helmet, his face felt like it was being struck repeatedly by a sledgehammer. His lower lip was cracked and bleeding. One eye was swollen shut. His nose felt like it was broken. *I almost wish I was back in the space armor; it could withstand this sort of punishment.*

Could adaptoids feel pain? Iron Man kept pummeling the adaptoid with short, sharp jabs to his midsection, but so far the imitation War Machine had shown no sign of distress or discomfort. He could only hope that if he hit the same spots over and over something would give—before the adaptoid's fist turned his face into so much hamburger. Iron Man's armor had not yet cooled down, but the adaptoid kept holding on to the scorching metal as if it were as cool as the bottom of a riverbed. *It's all my fault. I built all that heat shielding into the War Machine armor.* Now his own ingenuity and craftsmanship was beating the stuffing out of him. *Pretty damn ironic.*

A resounding crash echoed in his ears. At first, Iron Man thought the ringing sound came from his own battered armor, giving up the ghost at last. Then he caught a glimpse of the moon peeking out from behind a cloud, and he realized that the fight had carried them outdoors. The crash had been the sound of the dome shattering as they blasted through it. He winced at the thought of the damage done to his laboratory. That was one more thing he owed Modok, if and when he survived this tussle with the duplicate War Machine.

Fleeting glimpses of lawns and rooftops and clouds and sky and lawns whirled past Iron Man as the armored warriors rolled over and over in the smoggy night air. Vertigo threatened, along with nausea, but Iron Man resisted the dizzy feeling; he had never thrown up in his helmet before and wasn't about to start now. The adaptoid seemed oblivious to the kaleidoscope of images rushing past them; he remained intent on smashing his armored knuckles through Iron Man's faceplate. Powerful blows rained down on Iron Man's face, flattening his injured nose, and once again he cursed his own part in developing War Machine's motorized muscles.

Wait a sec. Maybe there was a way to turn his acute familiarity with the War Machine armor to his advantage. *The Security Override,* he recalled. The real War Machine had personalized the armor's securicode months ago, so that not even Iron Man knew how to shut the suit down, but maybe this duplicate armor was still set to the original default code? It was worth a try. The phased array communications antenna in Iron Man's armor broadcast a message to its counterpart in the counterfeit War Machine suit. With luck, the adaptoid would not notice the transmission until it was too late.

Interface protocols established, Iron Man's armor reported, setting up the link. *Remote access confirmed.* He transmitted the default security code and hoped for the best.

It worked. The adaptoid's iron fist froze in mid-blow. His bootjets shorted out immediately, turning the bogus War Machine into four hundred-plus pounds of dead weight. "Hey!" the adaptoid protested, still conscious inside his frozen armor. "What sort of dirty trick is this?" His other hand remained locked in place around Iron Man's upper arm.

"The best kind," Iron Man answered. "A sneaky, human trick." No longer caught up in the heat of battle, Iron Man took control of their spinning, headlong flight. Righting himself so that the paralyzed adaptoid hung beneath him, he headed back for the domed laboratory. He wasn't looking forward to taking on Modok and the remaining adaptoids, but he had no choice. He could not allow Modok to tap into the boundless power of the newly-created energy chip. He'd seen what that chip could do.

His and the false War Machine's unplanned exit from the lab had left a gaping hole in the roof of the geodesic dome. Jagged shards of steel surrounded the gap, looking like fangs ringing the open maw of some voracious beast. He flew between the razor-sharp tines, relatively unconcerned about whether any of the prongs came into contact with the immobile form of the adaptoid. He heard the sound of jagged metal scraping against iron armor and permitted himself a thin smile of satisfaction.

A tremendous blast of concussive force wiped the smirk from his face. The blast hit him like a tidal wave, stunning Iron Man and shaking loose the phony War Machine. The adaptoid crashed to the laboratory floor, throwing up clouds of dust and gravel from the devastated concrete floor. Seconds later, Iron Man smacked into the ground only a few feet away from the fallen adaptoid. He landed flat on his face, bellyflopping into the ravaged tile and cement. Inside his helmet, blood trickled from his broken nose and lips. On his forehead, a bump the size of a doughnut pressed against the padded interior of his golden mask. He felt like hell.

Ambushed. Shot out of the air like a clay pigeon. But where had that thunderbolt come from? Neither Captain America nor the Black Panther had the power to produce that sort of blast, and neither should their adaptoid copies. Must have been Modok, he guessed. The original Modok had been able to focus beams of telekinetic force through the gem in his headband. Apparently the new model came with all the standard trimmings.

There was no time to rest and recover from the crash. He rolled quickly onto his back and started to sit up, only to have a brightly colored figure ram into his chest. The adaptoid Captain America sat down hard on top of Iron Man. He pressed the edge of his indestructible shield against the front of Iron Man's neck assembly. "Don't move," he rumbled, filling Cap's deep voice with jarring tones of hate and malice. "Don't try anything or I'll take off your head!"

The shield remained poised above Iron Man's throat like the blade of a guillotine. Dazed, fighting a concussion, he felt disoriented. Even though he knew the costumed figure sitting astride him was really an adaptoid, it still disturbed him to see such murderous hostility displayed on Captain America's face. Anger flared within his soul, burning away the fog in his mind. How dare this . . . inhuman thing . . . sully the image of a national hero? It was sacrilege.

His eyes darted from side to side, taking in the scene. The Cap droid glared at him, his face less than a yard away from Iron Man's. A black-clad figure walked past Iron Man. A moment later, he felt the fake Panther holding down his arms. Despite the adaptoid's borrowed strength, Iron Man suspected that he could easily shake off the pseudo-Panther's restraining grip, but could he do so before the false Cap could decapitate him? Iron Man didn't know for sure if the adaptoid's shield could really slice through the armor's reinforced neck assembly, especially after the pounding the armor had taken, and he didn't want to find out. He'd been on the receiving end of the real Cap's shield during numerous training exercises at Avengers Mansion and he'd learned never to underestimate what that shield could do. Like Thor's Uru hammer or the Silver Surfer's cosmic surfboard, Captain America's shield was the very definition of an irresistible force. If the adaptoid's duplicate shield was even half as formidable as the real thing, Iron Man didn't want to test his armor against it. After all, the counterfeit shield had already taken out his chest beam.

Several yards past Iron Man's boots, Modok hovered above the heaps of rubble covering the floor. Christine stood beside Modok. She stared at Iron Man's supine form with an anguished expression on her face. Her brown eyes seemed full of sorrow and regret. *Not bad for an adaptoid*, he thought bitterly.

If she was only faking human emotions, then she was doing a darn good job.

Above Christine and her deformed cyborg master, the gap in the ceiling offered a glimpse of the sky beyond the dome. Moonlight brightened the night somewhat, dyeing the sky a deep, dark purple. Iron Man eyed this avenue of escape, considering his options.

"What did you do to War Machine?" the false Cap demanded, pressing his shield even harder against Iron Man's throat. Tony felt the pressure even through his armor.

"If that's War Machine, then I'm Robby the Robot," Iron Man replied. "And you're not fit to polish the real Captain America's shield."

"Arrogant human trash!" the adaptoid snarled. "The future of America belongs to us, and so does the rest of the world! We alone are entitled to life, liberty, and the pursuit of happiness. *E pluribus unum.* In Modok, we trust."

Oh my God. Iron Man had to repress a shudder. The adaptoid's words sounded like a twisted parody of something the genuine Cap might say, and were all the more chilling because of their distinct but distorted resemblance to the real thing.

"This land is our land," the adaptoid continued, "but the price of liberty is eternal vigilance against the weakness and stupidity of mere flesh and blood." He kept his gaze fixed on Iron Man, watching intently for any sign of resistance from the fallen Avenger.

"Enough, Captain," Modok said. "I believe my

psionic examination has discovered the cause of our comrade's infirmity.'' A sparkling golden beam leaped from Modok's brow to strike the prostrate form of the false War Machine. A luminescent glow suffused his armor, briefly turning its burnished silver plating a gleaming gold. Iron Man heard the sound of miniature servo-motors whirring back to life as the vanquished adaptoid climbed back onto his feet.

Blast. He'd hoped to put the War Machine droid out of commission permanently, but now the most powerful of Modok's adaptoids was back in play again, apparently as good as new. *One step forward and five steps backward. This is no way to save the world.*

''Do not fail me again,'' Modok admonished the counterfeit War Machine. ''I may not be so beneficent a second time.'' His hoverchair brought him closer to Iron Man and the other two adaptoids. ''I have examined the chip,'' he said, ''and I am ready to place its awesome power under my direct and exclusive control.'' Iron Man spotted the tiny crystal chip between two of Modok's child-sized fingers. It was hard to accept that so small and inconspicuous an item could contain so much destructive potential, but Iron Man knew from painful experience just how dangerous that chip could be. His own fingers ached to snatch the chip away from Modok, but the pseudo-Panther still had both of his arms pinned to the floor and the fraudulent Captain America looked eager to slice off Iron Man's head, helmet and all.

There was nothing he could to do to stop Modok from claiming the power of the chip.

He looked on in horror as a two-inch slit opened up in Modok's metallic headband. The slit resembled a standard PC disk drive. "Now then, my dear," he said to Christine. "Would you kindly do the honors?"

Modok handed the chip to Christine. Iron Man realized that the cyborg's stunted arms could not reach his own headband; *a rather serious design flaw*, he noted. Christine took the chip, glancing briefly in Iron Man's direction. *What's this?* Was that a trace of guilt he saw upon her face?

"Don't do it, Christine!" he begged her. "If you have any feelings at all, don't let that monster get control of the chip."

The Captain America imposter rammed the edge of his shield into Iron Man's armored throat. "Shut up!" he said as blue sparks jumped from where his shield hit the armor.

Iron Man ignored him, focusing all his attention on the synthetic woman holding the precious chip. *Please, Christine*, he prayed. *Show me you're more than one of Modok's soulless creations.*

"I'm sorry, Iron Man," she said. A single tear streaked her cheek. "I wish I could be the woman you think I am. Adapting this form has stirred strange sensations in me: spontaneous biochemical responses, and recurring thought-linkages, that run counter to my fundamental mission parameters. But I *am* an adaptoid and I must obey my programming. How I wish it were otherwise."

She slid the chip into the slot on Modok's headband. Iron Man saw the crystal chip glitter for a heartbeat before the slit slid shut, sealing the chip in the bronzed headband. "Yes!" Modok exclaimed triumphantly. "At last, the ultimate power is mine!"

There was only one thing left to do. Iron Man activated the self-destruct mechanism in his armor, setting it on a ten-second timer. Excess energy began to accumulate in his solar power cells. Conductive piping circulated the liquid oxygen in his boot joints to key stress points throughout his armor, mixing with solid chemical reagents to produce a massive exothermic reaction. A shrill, piercing whistle escaped his armor as the pulse bolt generators went into overdrive, building towards an explosive release of surplus radiation. Iron Man had installed his self-destruct system, with its multiple levels of redundancy, to keep his armor from falling into the wrong hands. Hopefully, the resulting conflagration would also consume Modok and his adaptoid pawns before they could inflict any more carnage on the world. A digital LED display in his headpiece gave him a countdown to his self-inflicted immolation.

10 . . . 9 . . . 8 . . . 7 . . .

A shadow fell over Iron Man and the others. He heard the sound of a roaring jet engine above the whine of his overheated armor. He looked up to see a black-and-silver mechanical warrior soaring through the hole in the domed ceiling. The flying man-machine held up two more figures, each man dangling from one of War Machine's arms. Iron Man saw a lithe man dressed entirely in black hanging

beside another man clad in the colors of Old Glory.
"Avengers Assemble!" Captain America shouted as
they leaped from War Machine's grip to the floor
below.

6 . . . 5 . . . 4 . . . 3 . . . .

The countdown to destruction continued unabated.
Iron Man hastily countermanded the self-destruct
command. His armor requested confirmation of the
rescinding order and Iron Man had to cybernetically
input his own securicode before the computer would
acknowledge the command. Tony Stark didn't
breathe once before the countdown ran out.

*2 . . . 1 . . . SELF-DESTRUCT   PROCEDURE
ABORTED.*

Iron Man exhaled slowly, making a mental note
to streamline the abort sequence the next time he
upgraded his suit's programming. The phony Captain America gave Iron Man a suspicious look,
blithely unaware of how close they had both come
to instant incineration.

Then two red-gloved hands grabbed the adaptoid
by the symbolic wings on his temples and yanked
him off of Iron Man. "I believe that face belongs to
me," the real Captain America declared. He delivered a solid right hook to the adaptoid's square chin.
He threw a friendly glance at Iron Man. "Good to
see you, ShellHead. Looks like you could use some
backup."

"The more the merrier," Iron Man agreed. He
stood up quickly, brushing the dust and gravel from
his armor. It would take his suit only a second or
two to power down from its near detonation; already

neutralizing agents had dampened the volatile chemical reactions initiated by the self-destruct process. Liquid oxygen flowed back into his bootjets. The pulse generators's harsh whine faded to a thin whistle before going silent completely. *That was a close call, but nothing I can't walk away from.* He wondered how the real heroes had gotten to California so quickly.

That question would have to be addressed later, though. They still faced Modok, now imbued with the power of A.I.M.'s energy chip, as well as adaptoid duplicates of Iron Man's three allies. *And don't forget Christine*, Iron Man reminded himself. She had proven where her true loyalties lay. He spotted the female adaptoid's shapely legs through the gap between Modok's hoverchair and the floor. Christine hid behind Modok's immense, swollen cranium, as if ashamed to show her face in front of Iron Man. *Is she for real, or was this all just part of her programming?* Could an adaptoid truly feel regret—or was she only mimicking a familiar human response? *Either way*, he decided, *she was on the wrong side of this fight.*

Iron Man inspected the battle as his armor restored itself to full battle strength. With dual versions of several combatants taking arms against each other, the potential for confusion—and dreadful mistakes—were enormous. He was glad to see that Cap, War Machine, and the Panther had each chosen to confront their own doubles. *Good.* That should cut down on the danger of any of his allies succumbing to friendly fire from one of their fellow Avengers;

Cap and the others knew who they really were, even if he couldn't tell the duplicates apart. Even as he looked on, two Captain Americas clanged their shields together, locked in mortal combat. Two Black Panthers grappled hand to hand, evenly matched in strength and skill, while overhead, beneath the ruptured dome, twin War Machines fought an aerial dogfight, expending countless rounds of deadly ammunition. Laser-powered sabers extended from both War Machines's gauntlets. They slashed and parried with blades of concentrated laser light. Crimson sparks blazed whenever blade met blade. The lab was full of the sounds of battle: roaring engines, heartfelt threats, and the constant *rattattattat* of gunfire. The air smelled of sweat and blood and cordite.

Modok himself kept apart from the fray, hovering at the sidelines, his sunken eyes clamped shut as he tried to assimilate the unearthly energies of the chip. Sheer mental exertion drained the blood from his hugely out-of-proportion face. Beads of sweat glistened upon his immense forehead. Iron Man knew he would never have a better moment to take the fight to the mastermind behind all the violence and destruction of the last few days. "Keep up the fight," he hollered to his fellow heroes. "Modok is mine!"

The cyborg's eyes snapped open at the sound of his name. The gem on his headband was glowing like a searchlight. His once-blue eyes were now streaked with pulsating veins of red. A thin stream of saliva trickled from the corner of a mouth that was bigger than most people's bodies. Teeth the size of bricks were clenched together tightly.

"What's the matter?" Iron Man taunted him. "Bite off more than you can chew?" He permitted himself a surge of hope. Was the extradimensional power of the energy chip more than Modok could handle? It would be poetic justice if Modok 1.5 fried his voluminous brain with the very energy he had killed to obtain.

"Nonsense," Modok asserted. "I know how you destroyed the castle of Baron Wolfgang Von Strucker with the original prototype of the chip— and destroyed the chip in the process. My network of adaptoid spies and informants have provided me with all the details concerning the fate of the first chip, but I shall not make your mistake. I shall not release the entire fury of the chip in one all-consuming torrent of unbridled power. I shall harness the chip's power in stages, level by level, erg by erg, until I can master the full capacity of the chip without danger to myself."

That sounds like good news in the short term, Iron Man thought, unsure if he could withstand the full power of the chip a second time, *but bad news for humanity in the end.* "No way, Modok," he said. "As far as I'm concerned, you're not even getting a test drive on that chip."

Modok's mammoth mouth twisted into a scowl. His shrill voice dripped with disdain. "Your crude attempts at humor are beneath my notice, Avenger. I do not even need the chip to destroy you." His dwarfish finger drifted toward a button on the bronze armrest of his floating chair.

"No," Christine cried, emerging from behind Modok's capacious skull. "You can't hurt him! I won't let you!" She grabbed onto his arm and wrestled it away from the control panel on the armrest. Modok's spindly arm looked like a toothpick compared to hers; if not for his metallic exoskeleton, she could have broken it easily. "Give me the chip," she said. "Give the chip back or I'll kill you!"

Tony Stark's jaw dropped. He stood by silently, momentarily stunned by this unexpected turn of events. Had Christine really switched sides, he wondered. *Has an adaptoid really fallen in love with me?* It was impossible to tell who was more shocked by Christine's rebellion, Modok or Iron Man.

The cyborg reacted first. "Traitor!" he snarled. "Defective, malfunctioning trollop!" he accused. His ruby gemstone flashed, blinding Iron Man for an instant, and an invisible wave of telekinetic force picked Christine up and threw her against the wall of the dome. She hit a six-foot-high computer screen with a tremendous smacking sound.

Iron Man saw red. He had not realized how much he still cared about Christine until he saw her insensate body slump onto the floor. "No more, Modok!" he shouted. "No more victims. No more casualties." He fired both repulsors at the freakish creature's gargantuan skull.

I have to give Modok credit for one thing: he makes a terrific target. It's hard to miss that head.

The twin beams converged on the ruby centerpiece of Modok's headbands. Iron Man hoped he'd knock the gem halfway through the cyborg's over-sized cerebrum. Instead the beams abruptly came to a halt only inches from Modok's expansive forehead, then turned around and came back at Iron Man.

He ducked just in time to avoid being clobbered by his own repulsor rays. The beams zipped above him, smashing into an elaborate and expensive spec-trophotometry station. *There goes another $325,000*, Tony thought, mentally adding up the repair bills. He decided he liked it better when it was the villain's headquarters that got wrecked.

Modok's force field posed a problem, though. Probably another manifestation, Iron Man guessed, of the same telekinetic energy that had hurled Chris-tine away. Apparently, Modok could even reverse the direction of an ionic beam by using the power of his mind. *Ouch.* He was afraid to guess what else this new and improved Mental Organism might be capable of.

"What a disgusting display of primitive primate chivalry," Modok said. His fingers toyed with the controls on his armrest. Bronze metal slid away from the ends of both armrests, revealing the open maws of twin cannons. Iron Man spotted the tips of two missiles within the previously concealed muzzles. He was not too surprised; Modok's hoverchair was typically equipped with all manner of concealed weapons. "Rest assured, Iron Man," Modok said, "I will have that treacherous adaptoid dismantled—after I have disposed of you."

He launched his missiles at Iron Man. A pair of

rocket-powered projectiles shot out of Modok's chair and converged on Iron Man, who attempted to evade them by taking to the air. The missiles passed harmlessly beneath him, then reversed course and climbed toward him.

Heat-seekers, he guessed, not unlike the missiles that formed part of War Machine's arsenal. In theory, there would be forward-looking heat sensors mounted into the tip of each missile and a gimbaled steering nozzle at the rear of the projectile, directing the thrust of a solid fuel rocket. Snapout fins, located along the sides of the missile, gave it additional aerodynamic stability. Iron Man ran through the missiles' probable design, looking for a weak spot, while he flew higher with Modok's rockets in hot pursuit. Several yards above, the dual War Machines continued their high-flying duel. Iron Man was careful to stay clear of the other armored warriors; the last thing he wanted to do was get caught in a crossfire between them.

The guided missiles accelerated, narrowing the distance between them and Iron Man. *Have to change my thermal signature.* He increased the amount of coolant in his exhaust and lowered the surface temperature of his armor. *That should confuse them.* He swerved to the right, hoping to lose the rockets, but the missiles altered their course to turn with him. "Blast!" he swore under his breath. He had been wrong about their guidance systems; they weren't heat-seekers at all. *Perhaps,* he speculated, *Modok is directing them by remote control?*

His antenna scanned through the broadcast spectrum, searching for the missiles' frequency. If he could just figure out how Modok was controlling the missiles, he might be able to jam the transmission. No such luck, though. Iron Man suspected some form of telepathic communication. Unfortunately, nothing in his armor was capable of picking up psychic emanations. He resolved to look into adding telepathic monitors to his suit's sensors, provided he got out of this adventure alive and in one piece.

All of his failed efforts ate up time. Modok's missiles were closing fast. He put on another burst of speed, seeking to widen the gap between him and the guided rockets, but they matched his velocity, gaining on him relentlessly until they were literally at his heels. The exhaust from his bootjets didn't stop them. He fired back at them with his palm repulsors, but the ionic beams bounced impotently off the missiles' armored plating. The engineer in Tony Stark was jealous; he would have loved to see the design specs on these seemingly unstoppable hunter missiles. A.I.M. deserved its reputation for technical excellence where weapons of destruction were concerned.

He couldn't escape them, he realized. Contact was only seconds away. *Okay*, he thought grimly. *Let's share the experience. Why should I have all the fun?* Fists outstretched, he dived at Modok. The cyborg's hoverchair tilted backwards so that Modok could watch Iron Man's rapid descent. An alarmed expression appeared on Modok's gargantuan face. Iron Man savored the cyborg's look of distress. *Let's see just how tough your force field is.* He plummeted toward Modok, the twin missiles trailing in his wake.

The nearest of the missiles connected with Iron Man's boots. The resulting explosion rocked his bones—and sent him hurling with even more force at his freakish foe. Iron Man couldn't have changed direction now if he had wanted to. The shock wave carried him along. He slammed into Modok's psychic force field just as the second missile detonated against his back. His own armor smashed into Tony Stark's spine and he had to bite down on his lower lip to keep from screaming. The combined impact of the two explosions plus Iron Man's own acceleration was more than Modok's hoverchair could handle. The chair tipped over backwards, hammering the top of Modok's enormous skull into the cracked concrete floor. The blow broke Modok's concentration, causing his telekinetic force field to evaporate. Iron Man's falling body struck Modok squarely in the face, then tumbled away and onto the floor.

Sprawled amidst the dust and debris, Iron Man fought to remain conscious. His entire body felt like one enormous bruise. He gasped for breath, shaken by the explosive force of the missiles. His armor automatically ran an all-systems diagnostic program. Damage reports appeared on the LED monitor inside his helmet. He assessed the situation as he tried to summon the strength to stand up.

Could be worse. Despite some minor cracks and scratches, the armor had maintained its structural integrity. *It takes a lickin' and keeps on tickin'*, he thought proudly. A magnetic field continued to hold the armor together, while power levels remained at about seventy-five percent of their full capacity. Various internal monitoring and communications systems had gone offline, but, in most cases, emergency backup systems had kicked in to pick up the slack. According to the readouts, he still had working repulsor units in both gauntlets. *Thank heaven for small favors, and I must remember to give HOMER a commendation for his improvements to my weapon systems.*

On the other hand, his propulsion system seemed basically trashed. His boots had taken the brunt of the explosions and their built-in microturbines appeared fused and unresponsive. He could probably still walk in the damaged boots, but flying was out of the question. He was grounded.

Although his body ached with every small movement, Iron Man sat up and looked around. About five yards away, Modok still lay flat on his back upon the overturned chair, his tiny arms and legs flailing uselessly in the air like the limbs of an capsized tortoise. A small puddle of blood spread from back of the chair. *Probably a head wound.* No other part of Modok was big enough to bleed that much. He prayed that Modok was down for the count.

All around the lab, fighting raged on between his allies and their adaptoid duplicates. Iron Man tried to get a sense of which way the tide of battle was turning, but found it impossible to tell the contenders apart.

Someone was winning, though. As he watched from below, one of the twin War Machines skewered his double on the point of his saber. The laser blade burned through the loser's chestplate and emerged between his shoulders. The impaled War Machine stiffened, his gloved fingers splayed out in shock, then went limp. The chin of his helmet sagged against the perforated armor of his chest. The surviving War Machine withdrew the blade and the loser went into a spin, spiralling down towards the waiting floor, gusts of fire and smoke still trailing from his boots. "Ha!" the victor crowed, soaring through the air holding his saber aloft. "I guess the Force is with me!"

He sure sounded like Jim, Iron Man thought. Did adaptoids watch old science fiction movies? He watched the defeated War Machine crash to the ground, narrowly missing both Captain Americas, who dove out of the way with identical speed and agility.

Iron Man stared at the patriotic-looking pair of combatants, trying to distinguish the real Cap from the imposter. Both men sprang to their feet within seconds of hitting the floor; one of them ended up standing only a few inches away from the fallen War Machine. Like mirror images locked in synchronous motion, they flung their flag-colored shields at each other. The metal disks collided in midair, bouncing back to their respective owners. Iron Man wondered if even the brawling twin Caps could tell which shield was whose.

Then one of the Caps did something unexpected. Dropping his shield, he reached down and, in a tremendous show of strength, wrenched the automatic chain gun from the shoulder of the downed War Machine. Tearing steel screeched in protest as the gun came away from the armor. Sparks flew from severed electrical wires. Bedecked in stars and stripes, the costumed figure aimed the gun at his counterpart, then grabbed up a fistful of sparking wires and pressed them against the gun's firing mechanism. A hail of bullets flew at the other Captain America as the man with the borrowed gun emptied round after round at his opponent. His lips were moving, too, but Iron Man could not make out the man's words over the steady blare of the gunfire. *If he's the real Cap, then he's probably delivering an inspiring speech about the essential courage and fortitude of the American people. Cap's the only person I know who can outdo the Gettysburg Address while fighting off a horde of super-villains and defusing a bomb at the same time.*

The other Captain America responded with actions, not words. He blocked the rain of bullets with his shield. The ammo ricocheted off the shield in all directions. Iron Man felt glad to be safe inside a metal suit. Not a shot got past the red, white, and blue barrier. The barrage of bullets did not even scuff the shining surface of the shield. *Could this be the real Cap?* Iron Man wondered. He'd never known Steve Rogers to rely on a gun.

The first Cap kept on firing at his double, but that wasn't all he did. With both hands occupied with the chain gun, he flipped his own shield up onto its side with the toe of one foot. A quick kick got the shield rolling across the floor, picking up speed as it raced across the lab at the other Cap. That man saw it coming, but was too busy defending himself against the rapid-fire assault of the chaingun to do anything to stop it. The shield rammed into the man's legs, knocking him off balance. The minute his back hit the floor, the first Cap tossed his gun aside and leaped at his foe, moving faster than sky-rockets on the Fourth of July. His fist clobbered the other Cap's chin before his boots even touched the ground. "There's one thing that no machine can fake," he said, "and that's the one-two punch of Yankee ingenuity coupled with good old American gumption!"

He pummelled the other Cap until his opponent's eyelids drooped and his head sagged groggily. The unconscious Cap dropped like a dead weight onto the floor. Iron Man didn't know whether to cheer or mourn; which Captain America had triumphed in the end, the actual living legend of World War II or his adaptoid clone? The winning Cap rubbed his knuckles absently as he contemplated his fallen double. Then he retrieved both shields and looked for the Black Panther. Iron Man followed his gaze to where two ebon-clad athletes fought like leopards.

They rolled back and forth across the floor, wrestling furiously. Looking on, Iron Man could barely tell where one Panther ended and the other began. They were a tangle of straining limbs and shifting black shadows. Two identical masks concealed their faces, but Iron Man heard the muffled grunts and groans of men in violent conflict. He saw Captain America, a shield in each hand, hesitate at the periphery of the fight, evidently uncertain as to how to proceed. No doubt the victorious Cap could not, like Iron Man, tell Avenger from adaptoid. *And which side is this Cap on?* he wondered.

The surviving War Machine looked similarly confused. He hovered above the fray, keeping one repulsor focused on the last Cap left standing and the other repulsor aimed at the battling Panthers. *Nobody knows who is who*, Iron Man realized, glad that he wasn't the only one still in the dark. It was a volatile situation, however, and one that could blow up in everyone's faces unless he could sort out the heroes from the impostors. *I need to settle this fast. Every second we spend fighting each other gives Modok more time to recover*

"T'Challa!" Iron Man hollered. He clambered awkwardly to his feet, feeling every battered muscle ache from the exertion. "Let us know who you are!" It was the best idea he could come up with; ultimately, only the real T'Challa knew who the fake was.

One of the Panthers threw the other one over his shoulders. The thrown Panther landed nimbly on his feet about a yard away from his double. Separate but apparently equal, the two Black Panthers faced each other, only to discover themselves surrounded by unidentified versions of Iron Man, Captain America, and War Machine. "ShellHead?" one of the Panthers said to Iron Man. Tony realized that he was only hero here who didn't have an adaptoid clone to contend with. "I'm assuming you're you," the Panther said.

"That's a safe bet," Iron Man answered. He

glanced anxiously at the surviving incarnations of War Machine and Captain America, either of whom could be an enemy adaptoid. *What I really want to know is am I outnumbered here or not?* "How do I know you're the real T'Challa?"

"You don't," the other Panther said. Like his double, this Panther's English was impeccable. "Don't listen to him, Iron Man. Only I am the Black Panther, Avenger, King of the Wakandas, and your friend."

"Can you prove that, mister?" Captain America asked, ready with his shields. *Was he the real Steve Rogers or another of Modok's convincing facsimiles?*

"Yeah," a War Machine added. "I want some reliable I.D. from all of you, except for Iron Man, I guess." *Another fake?* Iron Man wondered. He tried to run through all the possible permutations and combinations of heroes and adaptoids possible at the present moment, but thinking about it just made his head hurt. He scoured his brain, searching for a sure-fire way to distinguish friend from foe. In the movies, he recalled, whenever this situation arose (which it did with alarming frequency), the hero always came up with an ingeniously personal question that only the real individual could answer. Iron Man's mind went blank, however. *I only see T'Challa once or twice a year these days. What I don't know about his personal life could fill the entire Library of Wakanda.*

Besides, he reminded himself, there was no way to tell how closely the adaptoids resembled their originals. How much of T'Challa's mind and memories did the adaptoid share? Ditto for Cap and War Machine. It was an insoluble problem, which left him with only one alternative solution.

"Everybody surrender," he announced. "If I have to, I'll take you all down and sort out the good guys from the bad apples later." *Preferably, with the help of a well-armed Stark security team.* "The way I see it, that's the only way out of this mess."

There was a moment of tense silence, then War Machine raised both hands above his head and slowly lowered himself to the ground. "That's fine with me," he said. "I've got nothing to hide."

Captain America nodded and dropped both shields onto the floor. "Good idea," he agreed. "You do what you have to do, ShellHead, even if it means putting all of us under until the situation is under control. There's too much at stake to take any unnecessary chances."

Iron Man was encouraged and relieved by the two heroes' apparent compliance with his plan. For the first time, he felt confident that these were the real McCoys, that both Cap and Jim had defeated their adaptoid duplicates. He kept his repulsors ready, though, just in case he was wrong.

All eyes turned toward the pair of identical Black Panthers. One of them, Iron Man knew, had to be a villainous adaptoid, but which one? Both looked exactly like the T'Challa he remembered, the African hero he had fought beside in so many adventures. The familiar black costume covered both men from head to toe. Amber eyes stared out from behind the mask of the Panther. Both men stood as poised and silent as the feline predator they emulated.

"Stun me," said the Panther on the right. "Stun us both, then stop Modok for all our sakes."

"Very well," Iron Man said. He raised his repulsors.

"No, wait!" the other Panther protested. "It's a trick. You need my help to win. Don't let him fool you into shooting your own ally!"

"Blast us both," the righthand Panther insisted. "It is the only way to be sure."

Iron Man looked at both Panthers. "No," he said finally. "That's not necessary." He fired his repulsor at the Panther on the left. Only the real Panther would be so willing to sacrifice himself for the good of others.

The false Panther, his reflexes as razor-sharp as the real Panther's, dived out of the way of the repulsor ray. "You are clever for a human," he snarled through his mask, "but not clever enough!" His costume began to change before their eyes, the tight black fabric transforming into loose folds of emerald silk, his panther mask condensing into a glittering purple domino that left the lower half of his face exposed, revealing a cruel mouth that definitely did not belong to T'Challa's real face. The Panther's dark skin grew lighter. Talon-like fingernails extended from the adaptoid's gloves. Iron Man saw the embryonic shapes of ten golden rings forming on the adaptoid's fingers.

The false Panther was the same adaptoid that he

had fought several hours ago in A.I.M.'s zero-g laboratory in space.

"He's turning back into the Mandarin!" he shouted. "Stop him before he finishes the transformation!" A phony Panther was bad enough; an imitation Mandarin could take them all on.

War Machine fired a barrage of machine-gun fire at the elusive adaptoid. Captain America hurled his shield. The adaptoid, still retaining some of the Black Panther's agility, snatched the shield out of the air and used it to block War Machine's deadly onslaught. The Mandarin's rings of power grew larger and more fully formed with each passing moment. Iron Man fired his repulsors again, but the adaptoid's shield moved as if it were possessed of an intelligence all its own, defending the adaptoid from the Iron Man's desperate offensive.

But Captain America still had another shield. Putting his entire body into the throw, he sent it flying at the adaptoid, who deftly evaded the shield by stepping to one side at the last minute. The shield whizzed by the adaptoid's head—and right into the waiting hands of the one true Black Panther. The Panther raised the shield high and brought it down hard on the back of the adaptoid's head. The evolving creature, half Panther and half Mandarin, collapsed like a marionette whose strings had been cut. The Panther looked down at the insensate adaptoid with a look of disgust in his eyes. "I have seldom delivered a more satisfying blow," he said.

"And just in time," Iron Man said. "A few more seconds and we would have had a fully functional replica of the Mandarin on our hands, complete with working rings of power.''

''I can live without that,'' War Machine said. The last time the real Mandarin reared his ugly head, it had taken the combined efforts of Iron Man, War Machine, and the super hero team known as Force Works to stop the villain from taking over the entire world.

''So much for the adaptoids,'' Cap retrieved his shield from the fallen droid. Iron Man wondered again how he knew which one was his real shield. *Then again, after fifty years he probably knows that shield better than I've known any suit of armor I've ever built.*

''You know,'' he said to Cap, ''for awhile there I was sure you were the adaptoid, especially after you went after your dopplegänger with that machine gun. I mean, Captain America actually *shooting* somebody?''

The real Cap shrugged. ''The adaptoid knew all my usual moves. I had to do something he couldn't possibly expect, something completely unlike myself.''

Of course. It was obvious in retrospect. The adaptoids were perfect mimics; the only surefire way to prove you were real was to act like you were someone else. The paradox was enough to make his head swim. *Could this get anymore complicated?* he wondered.

A high-pitched groan interrupted his ruminations. He hoped that it was Christine, but knew that it wasn't. The soles of his boots were charred and battered; even still, Iron Man spun around quickly to see Modok's maglev chair lifting off the floor. *Blast! We spent too much time on his minions.* Now A.I.M.'s custom-made mastermind was back in the game.

The bronze hoverchair righted itself, and Iron Man found himself face to monstrous face with the Mental Organism Designed Only for Killing. His violent encounter with Iron Man had left the grotesque cyborg considerably worse for wear. A watery stream of blood still leaked from a gruesome gash in the creature's gigantic scalp. His ample nose was bent and bleeding. Several of his front teeth were cracked and chipped. A bloody froth dripped from down-turned corners of his enormous mouth. Only the gem upon his forehead remained intact; if anything, it seemed to be glowing ever brighter than before.

His injuries had not improved Modok's mood. "I underestimated you, Iron Man," he squeaked. "I see I shall have no peace until I have squashed you utterly." His dwarfish hands were clenched in rage. His tiny feet kicked the air. He would have looked ridiculous, Iron Man thought, if not for the awesome mental power contained in his abnormally hypertrophic brain.

"Iron Man's not alone in this, Modok," Captain America declared. He strode over to stand beside Iron Man. War Machine and the Black Panther joined him. United, they stood assembled against the inhuman monstrosity that was Modok 1.5. "Listen to me, Modok," Cap said. "You have no more chance of conquering humanity than your predecessor did. The first Modok came to a violent end; don't make the mistake of following in his footsteps. If you turn yourself over to the authorities now, I promise I will do everything in my power to see that you have your humanity restored to you."

Iron Man was impressed by the power of Captain America's words. *Leave it to Cap to remember the individual human soul trapped inside that mutated body.*

Modok laughed, a chilling sound. "Typical human arrogance. Why do you assume that I would want to be restored to my former self? I was nothing before I volunteered for the great experiment, merely another faceless technician toiling in the ranks of Advanced Idea Mechanics. Now I am Modok, the messiah of the age of the adaptoid. I shall be the unquestioned ruler of a brave new world of artificial beings. None shall ever defy me again!"

Iron Man couldn't believe what he was hearing. "My God, man. You actually *volunteered* to become . . . this thing." He couldn't imagine anything more sick.

"It doesn't matter what your motives are, Modok," Captain America stated. "Humanity will never bow to your tyranny. Even if we fall, free men and women will always oppose you."

"You misunderstand me, Captain," Modok said. "I do not intend to dominate humanity. I mean to *exterminate* them, every pathetic specimen of *homo sapiens*."

Cap remained unimpressed. "You're not the first madman to conceive of that sort of Final Solution.

I've stopped your kind before, and I can do it again.''

"What he said,'' War Machine added. His targeting laser fixed a tiny red dot directly between Modok's eyes, echoing the ruby glow of the cyborg's chip-amplified psionic headband.

"So say we all,'' the Black Panther confirmed.

Iron Man wished he shared his comrades' bravado. He alone understood the cosmic power of A.I.M.'s miraculous energy chip. Once Modok fully mastered the chip's energy output, he might be strong enough to overpower the collective heroism of the Avengers, S.H.I.E.L.D., SAFE, Force Works, the New Warriors, Alpha Flight, the X-Men, X-Factor, and the Fantastic Four all put together. Even now, the glow upon Modok's forehead was so bright that Iron Man could not look at it directly. His sensors reported that the energy buildup in Modok's headband was increasing at a geometric rate. Soon it would be literally off the scale.

"No more talk,'' he instructed his allies. "We've got to stop him *now*.''

"Not now, not ever!'' Modok squealed. "I was a fool to toy with guided missiles and other technological toys. I have transcended my instrumentality. All I need now is the augmented power of my mind.''

The crimson radiance of his psionic gem flickered momentarily. Modok's huge, bloodshot eyes grew as wide as the screen on a desktop PC. Iron Man felt a curious tingling run up and down his spine, followed by a wave of nausea, then watched in horror as Cap and the other heroes went into convulsions. Their limbs twitched spasmodically. Their eyes stared blankly inward, the pupils contracted to mere pin-pricks. Cap's shield slipped from his fingers; it landed upside down on the ground, rocking slightly. All three Avengers dropped gracelessly to the floor, the Panther landing partially on top of Captain America. War Machine, partially supported by his armored exoskeleton was the last to fall; his massive iron suit just missed crushing the Black Panther's skull. He clanged noisily against the broken concrete floor. All three heroes twitched for a moment more, than ceased to move at all.

Fearing the worst, Iron Man extended one hand over the inert bodies of his friends. A unidirectional microphone built into his gauntlet picked up the faint sounds of heartbeats and shallow breathing. He breathed a sigh of relief inside his own armor. The others were comatose, but still alive for now. But what unseen force had struck them down so effec-tively? "Answer me, Modok," he demanded. "What have you done to them?"

The crazed cyborg looked puzzled as well. Irrita-tion warred with curiosity upon his immense face as he stared at Iron Man. "A psychic blast of magnif-icent power," he explained, "delivering a massive neurological shock to their fragile human bodies. But I don't understand—why do you still stand? My mental thunderbolt was enough to render a dozen would-be heroes helpless. How can you resist its power?"

Because I don't have a normal nervous system,

Iron Man realized. A couple years ago, after a long string of accidents and disasters had effectively destroyed the neurology he was born with, Tony Stark had replaced his damaged human tissues with an artificial nervous system of his own design. Its inorganic nature must have insulated him from the full effect of Modok's psychic attack, giving him a small but much-needed edge. He would have to make the most of it.

This is it, Iron Man realized. After days of violence and conflict, of valiant heroes contending against inhuman foes, only he and Modok remained to carry on the battle to its conclusion. *It's him or me. Let's get down to it.*

Repulsor rays burst from his gauntlets, followed by a volley of high-intensity pulse bolts. Neither weapon had any effect on Modok. His psychically generated force field was back in place, more impervious than before. Iron Man had to hastily erect an ionic force shield of his own to protect himself from the beams and pulse bolts as they rebounded at him. A net of coruscating sapphire energy formed between his gauntlets, shielding him from the brunt of the rebound. Nevertheless, the cumulative force of his redirected attack staggered him. The beams assaulted him on several levels: concussive, thermal, and electrical. He was shocked and burned and battered. He stumbled backward in the scorched and broken remains of his boots. *I can't even fly away, not that I would ever leave the others behind.*

Not even Christine, he added silently. Iron Man

glanced at her unconscious body, still lying where Modok had tossed her during his telekinetic tantrum. Dust and pieces of broken lab equipment, strewn about during the heroes' ferocious struggles with their duplicates, littered her deceptively human form. Iron Man saw the rubble slide off her as she began to stir; even though he knew she was only an adaptoid, he was relieved to see her recovering. If nothing else, he recalled, she had suffered her injuries on his behalf.

But none of them would be safe unless he somehow derailed Modok's genocidal ambitions. He turned his attention back to the cyborg's shocking visage. Modok's dessicated flesh quivered beneath the strain of harnessing the energy chip's vast potential. Inside the fiend's psionic headband, Iron Man knew, a storm was growing, an extradimensional tempest that might soon sweep the entire human race off the planet unless he could deprive Modok of its unchecked fury. *To think, this all began with that artificial Spymaster snooping around this very installation and zapping me with his electromagnetic pulse.*

Wait a minute! Maybe another EMP burst was just what the doctor ordered. It was a desperate, last-ditch ploy that would shut down his own suit for exactly 5.3553 minutes, the minimum time it took his armor to reboot, but it might prove even harder on Modok. Despite his boasts, the cyborg had not really transcended his instrumentality; he still depended on his hoverchair and exoskeleton to compensate for the weakness of his withered body. Even his formidable psionic abilities required the cybernetic circuitry in his headband to focus and amplify them. Without his technology, Modok was nothing but a big head with a stunted body.

And what am I without my armor? Tony Stark asked himself. Just a man, he realized, but more of a man than what Modok had become. The so-called "mental organism" had sacrificed his humanity in pursuit of power. *Maybe I can give him cause to regret that choice.*

For the sake of all humanity, he had to try. Iron Man initiated an EMP buildup procedure, cybernetically commanding the electromagnetic spectrum conversion system running beneath the surface of his iron-mesh armor to override its standard safety protocols. The same solar-powered, photovoltaic substratum that ordinarily generated the magnetic field binding his armor together now accelerated toward an unstoppable cascade effect that would produce an intense electromagnetic pulse capable of scrambling the circuits of all electronic equipment within a five-hundred-foot radius. Iron Man tracked the EMP program's implementation on his helmet's visual display. *Only 4.2 seconds until the moment of truth.*

Modok might not let him live that long, though. Not content to fling Iron Man's own attacks back at him, Modok unleashed every destructive force at his command. Red-hot lasers erupted from the fingertips of the bronzed gauntlets covering Modok's dwarfish hands. Iron Man's armor sizzled where the beams hit him; melting iron dripped like teardrops from his chestplate; his tender flesh felt like it was trapped inside an oven. A sonic disruptor fired from the base of the hoverchair, rattling both the armor and the man within. His eardrums throbbed in agony. His head felt like it was going to explode.

Modok's psionic ruby flared brighter than ever and a wave of telekinetic force hit Iron Man like a gale force wind. A hurricane of concentrated thought tore at him. He tried to dig his heels into the defaced surface of the floor, but the psi-wind was too powerful to resist. It lifted him off the floor and sent him spinning through the air. Modok's weapons pursued him, the lasers still burning away his protective armor, the sonic assault still torturing his flesh and bones. Tears leaked from his eyes. He choked back a scream. *Have to hold on. Only another second more. . . .*

The digital display before his eyes counted down to zero, then blinked off entirely, a victim of the same electromagnetic pulse whose creation it had dutifully monitored. Silence fell over Tony Stark's world in a single instant; for a moment he feared that Modok's sonic barrage had rendered him deaf. Then he heard the sound of his own breathing and realized that the ear-splitting vibration had been cut off abruptly, as had all the routine hums, beeps, and clicking noises he associated with the normal operation of his suit. His armor had gone dead; not a single electron coursed through its multiplicity of circuits and transistors.

The telekinetic hurricane had subsided as well. Gravity seized Iron Man and sent him slamming into the floor. The impact knocked the breath out of Tony

Stark, who was grateful that his armor's interior padding was not dependent on any electrical systems. He found himself stuck inside a heavy, inert suit of metal, much like some medieval knight in full plate armor. He couldn't believe how much the armor weighed, now that he had only his own human muscle power to make his ironclad body move. *What I wouldn't give for a couple of working servo-motors.*

Despite the cumbersome suit, he struggled to stand up. No heat rays or sonic vibrations assailed him. *A good sign. I hope that the EMP incapacitated Modok as well.* Tony's skin was raw and sore where the laser had scorched him; his flesh chafed against the padded interior of his chestplate. A killer headache still throbbed behind his watery eyes, and there was a stubborn ringing in his ears.

He climbed clumsily onto his feet, feeling every pound of his lifeless armor, and searched the lab for any evidence of his foe. His neck muscles were not strong enough to make the helmet pivot on their own, so he had to turn his entire body to look one way or another.

Where's Modok? he wondered frantically. His own armor required another four minutes to recover from the effects of the EMP and to restart all its systems. Who knew how long he had before Modok was fully functional again? He had to stop Modok now, while he still could, but where was Modok? *Where?*

A string of shrill, vile obscenities attracted his attention. Rotating his entire body a few degrees to the right, Iron Man spotted the murderous cyborg resting on the floor about fifty yards away, the bottom of his hoverchair partially embedded in the broken concrete. "Miserable human filth!" Modok shrieked furiously. "How dare you subject a superior being to such an inexcusable indignity?"

The EMP had obviously done a number on Modok's technological infrastructure. The magnetic propulsion beam holding his chair aloft must have conked out immediately, stranding the wrathful cyborg on the ground. His diminutive arms hung lifelessly at his side; Iron Man suspected that Modok lacked the muscular strength to lift them without mechanical assistance. Only his tiny fingers, now deprived of their searing laser weaponry, trembled with rage inside their segmented metal casings.

"I shall make you pay for this treachery!" he screamed. His giant teeth gnashed together. "Because of you, I shall make all humanity suffer before I annihilate them forever!"

Iron Man ignored Modok's ravings. He contemplated the distance separating him from his adversary. The force of Modok's telekinetic gale had carried Iron Man even farther than he had realized from his attacker. An empty stretch of cracked and broken tile lay between the Golden Avenger and A.I.M.'s berserk man-machine. Straining to move inside his unresponsive armor, Tony thought every foot of devastated flooring looked like a mile. *I have to make it*, he told himself. Even now, for all he knew, Modok's high-tech support system could be warming up again.

"Beware my vengeance," Modok said. The ruby

in his headband still glowed ominously. Iron Man guessed that the extradimensional forces tapped into by the energy chip must be immune to the damping effect of the EMP. The alien energy probably flowed from a source completely different from ordinary electromagnetism, maybe even beyond gravity and the subatomic forces that held the universe together. Fortunately, Modok's operating systems were still based on earthly science. All the power of this world or the next could not save Modok as long as his chair was shut down. "I have the memory of a computer," he warned. "I never forget who my enemies are."

"Good for you," Iron Man said, unimpressed. He lifted one heavy boot and brought it down hard on the floor in front of him. The lab echoed with the sound of his iron tread. He teetered awkwardly upon armor-clad legs; he hadn't felt this clumsy and uncertain since he took his first steps in his crude, original armor so many years ago.

One step after another, he crossed the laboratory floor. He could feel the fatigue poisons building up in his aching leg muscles. His mouth was dry and he would have killed for a glass of cold water. Sweat poured down his back, soaking the padding of his armor. Not even his osmotic moisture control system was working, let alone the air conditioning. He wondered if this was what marathon runners felt like at the end of a long and grueling race. It was tempting to rest for a bit, to give both his body and his armor a few moments to recover, but he knew he couldn't spare a second. Christine, Cap, and all the others were depending on him. *This is why I pay myself the big bucks.*

Intent on reaching his hideous target, Iron Man didn't see a broken segment of the ruptured ceiling lying in his path. He tripped over the twisted metal sheet and started to fall forward. He would have waved his arms, fighting to keep his balance, but his arms were too heavy to lift. He toppled over, his face smacking hard against the floor. His vision dimmed, the world going black for a second, but he refused to slip into unconsciousness. Placing both palms firmly against the floor, he pushed himself up onto his knees, then stood up once more. Breathing hard, his lungs sucking in air, he stumbled toward the insidious abomination responsible for the hardships of the last few days.

"Don't go away," he called out to Modok. His voice, unamplified for once, was hoarse and raspy. "We have some unfinished business."

Finally, after what seemed like hours, he came within spitting range of the grounded cyborg. *Too bad I haven't got any spit left*, he thought wryly. Modok glared at him, his once-blue eyes suffused with red. The base of his chair was wedged deeply into the surrounding rubble, tilted slightly to one side. The huge, horrible face filled Tony's vision. "Get back!" he squawked. His breath smelled like chemical disinfectant. "Stay away from me."

Stripped of his technology, Modok 1.5 had been reduced to a defenseless, malformed humanoid. Iron Man almost pitied him. Then he remembered the murdered victims of the massacres that Modok had orchestrated and his resolve hardened into the icy conviction that this Mental Organism Designed Only for Killing must never kill again.

Iron Man raised his arm, pining nostalgically for the weight-free, zero-g environment of the space lab. Several pounds of armor dragged down his arm, but he slowly overcame both exhaustion and gravity until his iron fist was clenched and ready, only inches away from Modok's gargantuan face. The psychotic cyborg was helpless before him.

Or was he? To his alarm, Iron Man suddenly heard the unmistakable hum of a computer coming back online. Miniature lights flickered on the control panels built into the arms of the chair. "Hah!" Modok laughed triumphantly, his colossal face alight with malevolent glee. The blood-red gem on his forehead cast an eerie scarlet glow over his distorted features. "You are too late! I am restored! Now all who live will satisfy my hunger for revenge!"

"Eat this," Iron Man said. A fistful of iron smashed into Modok's nose. Mutated flesh and cartilage crumpled into a bloody ruin. Modok's sunken eyes rolled in their cavernous sockets. His face went slack, the massive jaw dropping into his own lap. The beached hoverchair jerked upward, wobbled back and forth, then tottered over, landing on its back amidst the rubble. Modok's face stared blankly at the domed ceiling overhead. The cyborg's breathing was shallow yet steady. A.I.M.'s inhuman creation was down for the count.

And just in time. That was closer than I like to call it. As if on cue, he heard his own armor begin to power up. A reassuring hum filled the interior of Iron Man's suit as a visual display lighted up inside his helmet. He watched the main computer run through its setup procedure, ticking off each operating system as it came back on. His bootjets were still trashed, he remembered, and his chest beam had a cracked lens that needed repair, but otherwise Iron Man was back in business. It was a good feeling.

All I need now is some serious R&R. His tongue probed his broken front teeth. *Well, and maybe a trip to the dentist,* he added silently.

"I don't believe it," said a shaky female voice. Iron Man turned around to see Christine Bright stagger toward him. The female adaptoid held one hand to her head. Her blue vinyl bodysuit, borrowed from Bethany Cabe's wardrobe, was torn and covered with dust. "You really did it," she said. "You defeated Modok."

"It wasn't as easy as it looked," Iron Man said. He wondered if the Vault, a special federal facility designed to hold super-criminals in custody, had a cell that could contain Modok. Disconnected from his chair and psychic amplifier, the cyborg would no longer pose a threat to the world at large. *Until the next time that A.I.M. decides to create another of its Frankensteinian monstrosities.*

And speaking of artificial creations, what in the world was he supposed to do with Christine now? She paused a few steps away from him, evidently nervous about approaching him too closely. She looked as human as any woman he had ever known. *What is it about her that really bothers me,* he wondered, *that she's an adaptoid or that she worked for Modok?* Unable to meet her eyes, he glanced at the fallen forms of Cap, the Panther, and War Machine. The other heroes remained unconscious, but he suspected they would recover shortly from Modok's psychic blast.

He headed over toward Cap, amazed at how easy walking was now that his armor was transistorized again. A diagnostic scan of the hero indicated a steady heartbeat and no permanent damage to Cap's brain or body. *I shouldn't be surprised. It will take more than Modok to stop Captain America for good.* He commenced a similar scan of T'Challa, not expecting any traumatic surprises. At the same time, he brooded over how to handle Christine. She was an enemy agent—and an adaptoid—but she had also risked her artificial existence to defy Modok.

And she thinks she loves me.

That was the really tricky part. How did he really feel about her? Tony wasn't sure. *I had barely gotten used to her as a brilliant-but-misguided scientist before finding out that she was a double agent and an adaptoid to boot!* Then again, he recalled, one of his fellow Avengers was the super-powered synthezoid known as the Vision. *I've always treated the Vision exactly as I would another human being. I even attended his wedding when he married the Scarlet Witch. Why should things be any different between Christine and me?* Was Christine essentially a woman—or only a dangerous product of advanced technology?

"Iron Man!" she cried out. "There's something wrong. Look at the gem!"

The gem? Iron Man looked anxiously at Modok, fearing that the cyborg had somehow roused himself from the debilitating effect of Iron Man's knockout punch. But, no, the immense face remained blank and unaware. Modok 1.5 was still dead to the world.

His psionic ruby, on the other hand, looked more alive than ever. It glowed so brightly that it was like staring into the sun. A ghastly realization came over him as the full implications of that crimson incandescence sunk home.

It's the chip. Once activated, the dreaded energy chip could not be turned off. Modok's hyper-developed brain may have been able to exert some control over the unearthly power of the chip, at least for a time, but now even that restraint had been shoved violently aside. The ultimate expression of the chip's true potential was upon them. Just as the original energy chip had destroyed every last stone of a ancient British fortress, the chip inserted into Modok's headband was building toward a catastrophic overload/meltdown that would turn all of Stark Enterprises into a huge crater.

A chill ran down his spine as he remembered Bethany, Felix, Mrs. Arbogast, and the others, still out cold in their offices, sleeping off the residue of Modok's telepathic assault. There was no way he could evacuate them all in time. With his bootjets out of order, he could not even rescue himself. From the way the gem was glowing, Iron Man guessed that the final conflagration was only minutes away.

"What is it, Iron Man?" Christine asked. "What's happening?" Fear overcame her inhibitions. She ran to Iron Man's side, throwing her arms around him. Iron Man returned her embrace, unable to deny her the comfort she needed as they faced total obliteration. *Maybe mortality*, he mused, *is all a human and an adaptoid really need to have in common.* Confronted with the knowledge of their own imminent extinction, all the differences between them seemed petty and meaningless. *We are united by our vulnerability.*

"The chip," he explained gently. "It's burning out of control. There's no way to stop it before it consumes us all."

He could feel the raw energy pouring out of the gem, electrifying his nerve endings even from several feet away. He felt like he was in hell already, albeit in the arms of a synthetic angel.

"I'm sorry I lied to you," she said. "Please forgive me."

"Of course," he replied. He hugged her tightly against his armored chest. "Despite everything, I'm glad to have known you." Now that the end was in sight, he found himself surprisingly at peace. *In a sense, I've been living on borrowed time ever since I first put on an iron suit to keep my heart beating.* He felt guilty, though, for dragging Cap, Jim, and T'Challa into this mess. The world didn't deserve to lose so many heroes at once.

Christine pulled away from him, slipping out from between his arms. "What is it?" he asked, wondering if perhaps his armor had grown too hot to touch.

She gazed back at him sadly. A tear dripped from an artificial eye. "Good-bye, my Iron Man," she said. "Remember me as I was when we were together."

Before his eyes, her beauty melted away, running like liquid mercury down her face and figure. Her hair and skin dissolved into a uniform dull green substance that reminded Iron Man unpleasantly of the viscous slime the false Mandarin had immersed him in back on the space station. Her brilliant brown eyes disappeared beneath the flowing sheets of green protoplasm. The vinyl bodysuit slid off her body to land in a heap at her feet. An adaptoid stepped away from the fabric, its face flat and featureless, its body generically sexless. An olive-green plastic sheen covered the adaptoid from head to foot. It looked like a mannequin, and a not very convincing one at that.

"Christine?" he asked, unable to recognize the woman he had known in the humanoid simulacrum she had become. He experienced a heartbreaking sense of loss.

The adaptoid had no mouth with which to reply, nor any eyes with which to see him; still, the thing that had called herself Christine Bright seemed to give Iron Man one last, lingering glance before turning its back on him. The adaptoid approached the supine form of Modok 1.5. Its generic body was silhouetted against the fearsome crimson glow escaping the vanquished cyborg's headband, eclipsing Iron Man's view of the gem itself. He didn't understand. What was it—she—trying to do?

The plastic sheen coating her body rippled and flowed. In the inescapable red light, the greenish pseudoflesh looked brown. Iridescent flashes of darkness and light, like the swirling reflection of sunlight on an oil slick, sparkled over her frame as the very substance of her body spread out to engulf both Modok and the glow. The malleable, infinitely adaptable protoplasm covered Modok completely, until not a single photon of crimson light escaped the shell she had formed around the cyborg.

Iron Man realized at last what the adaptoid was attempting. "Wait!" he cried out. "You don't have to do this!"

The shell solidified visibly, growing denser and harder by the second. Soon only a large black sphere could be seen where the adaptoid had enveloped Modok, the gemstone, and the chip. Iron Man held his breath. Whatever happened, it was about to happen now.

A thunderous explosion went off inside the thick black shell, almost deafening Iron Man, who fully expected to be incinerated within a nanosecond. The all-consuming blast never came, though. Instead, the sphere swelled up instantly, expanding outward like the universe after the Big Bang. It grew to twice, four times, ten times its original size; Iron Man scrambled backwards as the sphere (Christine?) threatened to fill up the entire dome.

Is it possible? Has the adaptoid actually contained and absorbed all the power unleashed by the chip? Then, just as quickly as it had expanded, the sphere suddenly collapsed in on itself. The wall of the sphere caved inward, liquefying at the same time, so that the entire mass of what had been the sphere fell with a splash onto the floor of the lab. Rushing towards the site, Iron Man found himself, still alive and intact despite all his expectations, standing at the edge of an oily black puddle. Not a trace of Modok or his burning gem could be seen; Iron Man guessed that the explosion within the sphere had consumed both cyborg and chip entirely. He found it hard to mourn either.

But what about Christine? Iron Man stared at the pool of inanimate liquid, torn between hope and dread. Was there any way the adaptoid could have survived the incredible outpouring of destructive energy that had destroyed Modok?

He looked on in silence, praying without much hope of success that the greasy black fluid would congeal and reform back into the alluring shape of Christine Bright. He waited for several long minutes, even as he heard Captain America and the other heroes waking up behind him. Nothing stirred in the puddle except his own reflection. Whatever artificial lifeforce had once animated this substance seemed to have been extinguished forever.

Iron Man knelt beside the glistening pool. He cupped his metal gloves together and lifted up a handful of the dark fluid. It ran like water through his fingers.

"Good-bye, Christine," he said.

"I am so sorry, Anthony," HOMER said. His disembodied voice came over the intercom in Tony

Stark's office. "I can't believe I actually cooperated with that defective Modok creature."

"You didn't have any choice," Tony emphasized. "Modok overrode your programming. No harm done."

"I appreciate your understanding," HOMER said. "I'll supervise the repairs to the assembly dome personally."

Iron Man's helmet rested on the top of Tony's desk. He still wore the armor he had fought Modok in, less than three hours ago. Things were gradually returning to normal at Stark Enterprises. Bethany and his other friends and employees had been checked out by paramedics and given a clean bill of health; aside from some headaches and bad dreams, none of his staff had been seriously injured by Modok or his adaptoids. No doubt the deranged cyborg had intended to finish them off at the same time that he exterminated the rest of humanity. Tony was relieved that Modok's insane overconfidence had apparently worked to his friends' advantage, although Bethany was howling mad at the ease with which Modok had conquered Stark HQ. He knew his Head of Security would not rest until she had developed an effective defense against telepathic intruders. *Hmmm. That might be something Stark's experimental neurology division could look into.* He scribbled himself a memo to talk to Dr. Erica Sondheim about it on Monday, then returned his attention to his comrades.

Behind the closed doors of his office, they had all removed their respective masks. After all they had been through together, they had no need to hide their true faces from each other. "Thank you all for your help," Tony told Steve, Jim, and T'Challa. "Without your well-timed assistance, I could have never defeated Modok *and* his adaptoids."

Jim Rhodes smiled. His War Machine armor looked to be in better shape than Tony's Iron Man suit. "I'm just glad you were able to win the game in the final inning."

"Indeed," T'Challa said. He had picked up one black eye in his fight with his adaptoid dopplegänger; the swelling around his eye matched the color of the Panther's costume. "I feel vaguely embarrassed for having slept through the closing act of this singular drama."

"Maybe next time you'll be the one to pull everyone's fat out of the fire," Steve Rogers told T'Challa. "That's what teamwork's all about." Even though his face looked like several miles of bad road, Tony couldn't help grinning. Mask or no mask, Steve always sounded like Captain America.

"There's still one thing I don't understand," Tony said. "How in the world did you all you guys get to California so fast? You were in Africa and Eastern Europe the last I heard."

Jim shrugged his armor-clad shoulders. "I used that parabolic orbital reentry stunt you taught me. I just went into space and hung over the Earth until California was beneath me." He grimaced slightly. "God, I hate that trick."

Tony couldn't blame Jim for having bad associations with suborbital drops. One of Jim's tenures as

Iron Man had ended when he nearly burned up in reentry, resulting in a weeks-long hospital stay. "I see," he said. He fixed his gaze on Steve and T'Challa. "What about you two?"

Cap and the Panther exchanged conspiratorial looks. "Experimental Wakandan technology," T'Challa said eventually. Tony waited for him to elaborate, but the Panther merely winked at Cap. "Don't forget," T'Challa reminded Steve. "You're sworn to secrecy until the device has been patented." He grinned at Tony. "No offense, Tony, but there are some scientific secrets that the King of Wakanda should not share with a leading American competitor, even when the CEO of that company is a friend and fellow Avenger. Strictly business, you understand."

"Listen, T'Challa," Tony said, intrigued. "I keep up to date on the latest applications of vibranium-based technology and I know damn well that there's no way, no matter how brilliant you are, to make that quinjet go any faster than I designed it to go."

The Panther gave him a cryptic smile. "Who says we used the quinjet?"

Later, after the other heroes had returned to their own lives and adventures, Tony Stark sat alone in his office, thinking. The sun was beginning to rise outside, heralding the beginning of a new day, one free from the heartless machinations of Modok. Tony pulled open a drawer in his polished mahogany desk and removed a sealed glass flask. Inside the container, a translucent black oil contained all that

was left of the adaptoid who had called herself
Christine Bright.

Tony had not wanted the last residue of Christine
to be washed away by the cleaning crew. She deserved better than that, no matter what she had done.
Tony tilted the flask, watching the fluid flow slowly
south. It was about the same color as her hair, he
realized, and almost as lustrous. He let his mind
wander through the events and dilemmas of this
strange adventure.

Where, ultimately, did technology end and humanity begin? Had Christine truly sacrificed herself
out of her love for Iron Man, or was she only mimicking those emotions as she had been programmed
to do? Tony stared into the murky depths of the flask
as if it might hold the answers to the questions that
plagued him. For a man whose very nervous system
was intrinsically linked to the same cutting-edge
technology that Iron Man embodied to the world at
large, these were hardly irrelevant concerns. Where
was the evil in Modok born, in his original human
heart, filled with hate and resentment, or in the ob-
scene experimentation that had stripped him of his
humanity?

In the end, Tony mused, putting the flask down
with care and reverence, *perhaps humanity is not
defined by how organic or artificial we are, but by
the depth of our relationships to our fellow beings,
whether or not they're human, android, mutant, cyborg, or some exotic combination thereof. As long
as we define humanity as being* humane, *regardless
of biology, then the Age of Humanity can never truly*

be snuffed out, no matter how much technology changes our future.

Tony Stark tapped one finger of a metal glove against his iron chestplate. It rang clear and pure like the chime of a bell. *Yeah*, he thought. *I can live with that.*

Greg Cox is the author of the previous Iron Man novel *The Armor Trap*, as well as the co-author of two *Star Trek* novels (the *Deep Space Nine* novel *Devil in the Sky* with John Gregory Betancourt and the *Next Generation* novel *Dragon's Honor* with Kij Johnson), and is presently hard at work on a pair of solo *Trek* novels. Greg served as co-editor of two science fiction/horror anthologies (*Tomorrow Sucks* and *Tomorrow Bites* with T.K.F. Weisskopf), and he has also published many short stories, in anthologies ranging from *Alien Pregnant by Elvis* to *100 Vicious Little Vampire Stories* to *The Ultimate Super-Villains* to *OtherWere*. By day, he serves as an Editor for Tor Books.

* * *

Tom Morgan has worked in comics as an artist for several years now, having drawn pretty much every major character in both Marvel and DC's pantheon of characters, including a lengthy stint on the monthly *Iron Man* comic from Marvel. He recently broke into book illustration with work in *The Ultimate Silver Surfer*, and *The Ultimate Super-Villains*.

THE SPECTACULAR NEW NOVEL!

SPIDER-MAN ®

THE OCTOPUS AGENDA

A NOVEL BY *NEW YORK TIMES* BEST-SELLING AUTHOR

DIANE DUANE

MARVEL COMICS ®

NOW AVAILABLE IN HARDCOVER

BOULEVARD/PUTNAM